Portal Healers

THE COMPLETE DIVINITY HEALERS SERIES

MICHELLE M. PILLOW

MICHELLEPILLOW.COM

Portal Healers: A Divinity Healers Box Set

© Copyright 2009 - 2022, Michelle M. Pillow

ALL RIGHTS RESERVED.

ISBN 978-1-62501-323-1

Published by The Raven Books LLC

Edited by Suz Gower

Cover design by Silvana G. Sánchez / SP Designs

Divinity Series

Divinity Warriors
Lilith Enraptured
Fighting Lady Jayne
Keeping Paige
Taking Karre

Divinity Healers
Ariella's Keeper
Seducing Cecilia
Linnea's Arrangement

Qurilixen Lords
Dragon Prince
Marked Prince
Feral Prince
Fire Prince
Her Lawless Prince
Poisoned Prince
Cursed Dragon

Captured by a Dragon-Shifter Series
Determined Prince
Rebellious Prince
Stranded with the Cajun
Hunted by the Dragon
Mischievous Prince
Headstrong Prince

Space Lords Series
His Frost Maiden
His Fire Maiden
His Metal Maiden
His Earth Maiden
His Woodland Maiden

Dynasty Lords Series
Seduction of the Phoenix
Temptation of the Butterfly

Ariella's Keeper

BOOK ONE BY MICHELLE M. PILLOW

Ariella's Keeper (Divinity Healers) © Copyright 2009 - 2017, Michelle M. Pillow

Second Electronic Printing May 2013, The Raven Books

First Electronic Printing December 2009

ISBN 9781625010452

Edited by Suz Gower

The Raven Books
Published by The Raven Books

About Ariella's Keeper

DIVINITY HEALERS BOOK ONE

Alternate Reality Romance, Part of the Divinity Universe

When his father threatens to take away his research facility's funding if he doesn't come home, Dr. Sebastjan Walter has no choice but to do so. This isn't just a family reunion. It seems his father has arranged a marriage—Sebastjan's. Seeing his chance to make one last final deal to get his father out of his life, he agrees to marry the off-plane woman. After seeing her, he can't help but think he's made the better bargain.

Ariella has been held prisoner by the Medical Supreme since he cured her of a childhood illness. Forced to stay in his home as his ward, she has no choice but to do whatever he wants. When he demands she marry his son, Ariella finds this is one order she might not mind obeying.

To my editor, Suz.

Chapter One

CITY OF ASCLEPIUS, COUNTRY OF CHIRON,
DIMENSIONAL PLANE 187

There was little worse than being stuck in a medical dimension as the undeserving prisoner of an overbearing doctor. And, since that doctor happened to be the Medical Supreme, by all rights the most powerful man on dimensional plane 187, Ariella was even more out of luck. For who would go up against such a powerful man in order to save an off-plane woman from an alternate reality? A woman with nothing and no one to make her rescue worthwhile?

Supreme Walter didn't trap her in with chains or lock her away with iron bars. No, his plan was much simpler and much more diabolical. He had injected her with a virus, specifically engineered by him to keep her within his home and forever under his control. Her body became her jailer, the boundaries of her flesh her prison walls. She couldn't run, couldn't escape. If she wasn't so tormented by what was done to her, she might actually admire the sick perfection in which the Medical Supreme kept her.

Then again, probably not.

Only the chemical antidote he pumped into the mansion's air vents kept her alive. Sure, she had an inhaler so she could walk the grounds or for when he wished to take her out and show her off as his

7

ward. But if she were out for longer than six hours, she'd die a horrifically painful death.

If Ariella disobeyed him, he took away her cure. If she vexed him or refused his orders, he took away her cure. If she didn't make certain the servants had his evening sustenance on the table on time, he took away her cure. If she didn't log in at least an hour of exercise a day and keep her food intake down, he took away her cure.

Yep, a definite pattern.

"And when he tires of me or demands more than I can give, he'll take away my cure," Ariella whispered, staring at her reflection in the mirror. Sometimes she barely recognized herself. It wasn't just the toning of her daily exercise, though that did take away the softness from the figure prized in her youth. Her clothes were the height of Chiron fashion consisting of a pair of loose black slacks and a long gray shirt with a stripe of green down the front to match her eyes. She'd been forced to grow out her blonde hair, letting the waves fall down over back. Running her finger over her lips, she watched the color stain smear only to regroup exactly where it belonged.

One of the benefits of living on one of the most medically advanced planes of existence was the constant monitoring of health. She'd never felt better in her life—unless her cure was taken away, of course. Every meal, though bland, was perfectly balanced with her body's dietary needs for the day. If she became overly stressed, one of the maids appeared to give her a shot in the neck to take the symptoms away. Her heartbeat was monitored by the mansion's central computer, as was her location.

Captive. Prisoner. No escape.

The words filtered through her mind in a constant stream, repeating over and over throughout her day. She wondered if she were to run and never come back if she'd even be allowed to die. It was possible Supreme Walter would save her and force her back, after a sufficient amount of punishment of course.

Ironically, she'd come to this dimension for a cure, but while she was getting treatment there was a rebellion on her home dimension and her family was killed. Without her father's political position, Divinity Corporation had little use in demanding the Medical

Supreme send her back to her home reality. Besides, there was nothing on her home dimension to go back to but certain death. She'd be murdered the moment she appeared through the portal.

Though the viability of alternate realities was well known and accepted on her home dimensional plane, Divinity Corporation had the only known source of inter-dimensional travel technology. They were her only hope, for no one in the Chiron capitol city of Asclepius would take her word over the Medical Supreme, and Divinity was not coming to save her.

Out of the four hundred thirty-six known dimensions, Ariella had only been to three alternate realities—home, a Divinity base and this one. Each foreign dimension was like looking at a copy of her home world, if history had evolved in a different way. To a point there were many similarities. Languages were relatively similar. Some people appeared the same, but were not the same people. Certain events, like natural disasters, were shared, and the planet was still basically the same planet.

"But this is not home." She looked at the ceiling of her bedroom. The longer she stared, the smaller the great room felt. Like all places on this plane, the room was overly sterile, each surface hard and unwelcoming but for a few engraved curls and wisps decorating the edges. Marble and metal blended together with great square columns to form self-sterilizing walls. The gray and green chairs and bedding matched her clothing. By Chiron standards, it was the most lavish of places.

Swallowing nervously, she again turned her attention to the long mirror. Supreme Walter had been acting strange, becoming more possessive of her time and ordering a full array of checkups—tests that centered a little too intimately on her private regions, as if confirming she was a virgin yet again. The man was obsessed ever since he'd discovered her maidenly status at her first medical appointment. Where she came from, it wasn't such a rare thing. People were expected to wait, though she knew not everyone did.

Ariella was no fool. She knew what men wanted with their leering eyes and lustful bodies. She had seen the educational films, read the forbidden manuals, whispered girlish secrets to her now-passed sisters.

9

She had seen the way Supreme Walter stared at her stomach and hips, as if calculating the children she would have. It left her feeling cold and empty.

"Tonight wear the new clothes I bought for you and wash your body well," he had said as she stood from the dining table. "I have put scented lotion on your dressing table. Use it. Everywhere."

Lifting her fingers, she smelled the herbal concoction on her hands. It was pleasantly sweet and a horrible omen of what was to come. If she thought it would do any good, she would jump from her second-story window. Though, the last time she tried to end her life, the mansion's security devices activated and caught her in an invisible net. Walter had not been pleased.

"If I must do this, I beg the goddesses that he should find his release quickly." Her thighs tightened, clamping together. The very idea of him coming over her naked body made her stomach ache. "Or perhaps his heart will seize before the time comes and I will be free."

Who was she kidding? The other doctors would only save him.

Chapter Two

"Father." Dr. Sebastjan Walter didn't appreciate being summoned to the family mansion—even if the summons had come a month earlier to give him plenty of time to make arrangements. He had no use for the cold marble and hollow feelings that filled his childhood home. The moment he was of age with his medical degree in hand, he'd left for his first and only post—a research facility on the far side of the planet, about as far away as he could get from the societal life of Asclepius and the mansion home of his Medical Supreme father.

"Sebastjan," his father acknowledged with a self-satisfied grin. The smooth, almost youthful appearance of his skin belied his years, but the calculating light in his blue eyes made up for it. He'd allowed some of his black hair to gray along the temples. People often said Sebastjan looked like the man, but for his nose that came from his late mother's side. Sebastjan didn't necessarily like hearing that. "How happy I am that you have arrived safely, son." The man looked at the screen on the wall. "If not on time."

Sebastjan followed his father's gaze to the time on the wall. He was over an hour late. "I didn't have much choice." He took a seat in front of Walter's desk, trying to force himself to relax in the wide-cushioned chair. He hated the oversized furniture. It made him feel like a kid again, dwarfed by his father's all-consuming presence. He turned his attention back to the blank medical interface screen on the wall, wishing it were time for him to go. "Apparently, it was be here or my laboratory was going to be permanently sealed. I could have fought your shutdown order if you were to make it. My team has just come into possession of a new, very promising substance. However, I thought making an appearance would be easier."

His father's smile faded at the comment. "I had hoped you would have gotten over your childish impulses and lack of verbal control. You are a director of a research facility now, Sebastjan. Not some schoolboy running about in knickers, searching for ways to vex his father."

Impulses? Sebastjan frowned. His father considered anything contrary to what he wanted a childish impulse whether it was words or deeds.

"I asked you not to call in that favor," Sebastjan answered, irritated and growing more so by the second. "I could have made director on my own. I *preferred* to make director on my own."

"In another five years or so," the Medical Supreme quipped. "My son does not work for anyone. You are above the others of this planet. You were meant for more. Someday, you will be meant for my position. There are expectations that—"

"I don't work for anyone? So you're saying I don't have to listen to you?" Sebastjan smiled at the very idea. If only.

"What substance?" his father asked, not deigning to answer his son's rude interruption or insolent questions. "That blue mineral water we took off a visiting Divinity Corporation analyst? Your lab took point on that?"

"Yes. It's from an underground spring on a plane called Staria. I've put in a request with someone named Sans Lady Lilith for trade. Apparently, she is a Divinity liaison living amongst a race of barbarians. I hope to obtain more." Sebastjan relaxed. Medical advancements seemed to be the only subject in which he and his father could have a decent conversation. "It stays eternally warm, even without a heat source. If we can synthesize the mineral, just think of the possibilities.

Deaths by freezing will be drastically decreased. All of our mountain and deep sea expedition teams can go longer and farther."

"So you are waiting to hear from this Sans Lady Lilith?"

"Yes." Sebastjan nodded. "The Starians are making a list of what they would like in return. I should be able to get it for a few medical lasers and a handheld unit. Though she appears civilized enough, I can't imagine the barbarians knowing what to ask for beyond a few toys."

"Ah, so there is no need for you to get back to your lab right away. Wonderful. You can stay here for a couple weeks."

A couple weeks with my father? Ah, no. Make that no poppicockin way. "I can't. There is much preparation to—"

"I insist." His father stood. "I have a surprise planned, but first you must meet my ward. We call her Sans Ariella for she is without a surname. She came to us through the inter-dimensional portals. Her father was murdered on her home plane and she has nowhere else to go."

"Another *ward*?" Sebastjan grimaced. Since his mother's death when he was a boy, his father had taken in many "wards". "I have no interest in meeting your newest lover. I am sure she's as vapid as the last twenty."

"Oh, you will want to meet Ariella. She is special." His father picked up a news reader and handed it over to him. "Very special. Her mind is unspoiled by the logic of our society. She does not think like a doctor." Walter hummed thoughtfully. "She is...innocent."

Sebastjan took the small, square, electronic unit. The front of the social pages stared back at him. He stiffened. This had to be a joke. "You're planning a wedding?"

"I believe the correct phrase would be, I *have* planned a wedding." His father grinned. "And it takes place tonight."

"I want no part in this," Sebastjan said, standing. His father placed his hand on a scanner and he heard the exterior shields lowering around the house. The lights dimmed as the orange glow from the early evening sun was blocked out. Small panels opened up on the walls and candleholders slid out. Fake candles lit, giving a soft orange glow as the shields fell into place.

"You don't have a choice. If I could do it without you, I would, but unfortunately the law requires that you be here as a willing participant when you take a wife." His father smiled and Sebastjan fell back into his chair at the look. "One call and everything you hold dear will fall down around you, or you can do this one simple thing I ask of you."

"You want me to get married to your lover?" Sebastjan had the vague impression that the ceiling would come crashing down at any moment. Out of all the orders he had been given in his life, this was the most insane. If not for the mandated medical checkups that said the Medical Supreme was fit to serve, Sebastjan would have thought his father was losing his mind. Instead, he knew the man was just calculating and manipulative. Walter would stop at nothing to force people to his will.

"She is not my lover and I command you to marry her. She is everything you need in a wife—a paragon of social values and morals, the very picture of decorum and etiquette. I have groomed her for you. She is meek and pleasant to look at..."

His father kept talking but Sebastjan barely heard a word he said. The kind of woman Walter described hardly sounded like someone he'd choose to marry. But then, he wasn't choosing. Somehow, Sebastjan had always known that his marriage would be something of a political, if not genetically based, alliance. Though, he never expected his father would outright choose for him.

Sebastjan had dated the kind of women his father wanted for him —vapid, shallow, mindless future doctors' wives. In Chiron if you weren't a doctor, you did everything to make sure you were married to one and lived your life to serve. He didn't want to be served. If he ever did marry, which wasn't the plan, it wouldn't be to someone his father would like. He wanted a woman who thought for herself, had her own work obsession and, quite frankly, left him alone so he could do his research.

Apparently, Walter didn't think his son answered fast enough, because he warned, "Consider carefully. Think of your job, your friends, your life, your inheritance, your position as a doctor. I may be your father, but I am also Medical Supreme. I can take everything away from you."

Sebastjan drew his finger over the screen, sliding the article up so he could see the announcement pictures. No surprise that the "bride" was pretty. The picture of her showed her turning toward the camera, green eyes lifting for the briefest of seconds as if to meet with his. His stomach tightened slightly at the recorded look, but he kept all emotion out of his voice and expression. "If I do this, you will promise never to meddle in my life or career again." Sebastjan threw the news reader on the desk. It landed with a hard thud. "And I want it in writing. This is the last time. After this, my life is my own."

Chapter Three

Ariella took a deep breath, stopping on her way down the stairs to look around the quiet house. An array of items from other dimensional planes decorated Walter's home, her prison. A loud cranking sound echoed as the lights grew dim. Something slid over the windows, blocking out the light. This had never happened before. Slowly she continued down, cautiously watching the darkening stone floor below. False firelight replaced sunlight. The romantic implications were not lost. Her breathing became shaky. She was always trapped, but seeing the outside light fade as the home became encased made the tomblike feelings all the more real.

"I can't," she whispered, stopping on the bottom step. "I can't do this. Don't make me."

"Ariella. Join us." Supreme Walter appeared around the corner. He smiled, but that was nothing new. He always smiled at her, like a great benefactor bestowing his grace upon those beneath him.

Beneath him.

She grimaced, pushing the thought from her brain. "I'm a little tired. Perhaps I should rest? I need to rest. I'll just go—"

Supreme Walter reached into his pocket, the action cutting off her hasty words. He took out a remote. Pressing a button once, he turned on the room's medical interface screen. Instantly, Ariella's statistics appeared, giving him every intimate detail of her body's inner workings. She refused to read the details. There was something all the more violating about being physically read. "Your lidic levels are elevated." He pushed another button, ordering medication. "I'll have the maids bring you a correcting shot. Though, you have no reason to be stressed, my dear. You should be happy. This is a great day."

Ariella gave a pained laugh. A great day? Happy? No reason to be stressed? Her entire life had become a reason to be stressed.

Supreme Walter frowned and his eyes narrowed in obvious displeasure. "I should not have to explain myself, but I will. You owe your life to me. Without me you would be on the streets, homeless, dimensionless, starved and dying if not dead already. I cured your diseased bones. I took you in. I gave you social status and grace. I did not have to do any of this, but I did out of mere generosity of spirit."

Ariella knew better than to comment.

Walter took in her silence. "Now, you owe me for that generosity. You will walk into that room and do what I tell you. You will not speak of our arrangement to anyone, under any circumstances. Tonight you will do exactly what I require." He grabbed her arm, hauling her across the front hall toward his office. There was a frenzied rush to his steps as if he were beginning to lose his patience. She'd never seen him out of sorts. He paused by his office door. "If my son suspects anything, I will not be pleased. You know what happens when I am not pleased. Now put a smile on that pretty face of yours. Good. There it is."

Ariella held her expression. She had no idea what she was walking into. Her feet dragged as she forced herself to follow him. The doors to his office slid open without him touching them. Inside, the room was cast in shadows. One of Supreme Walter's friends, Dr. Grace, waited in front of his desk holding an electronic reader. Next to him was a man she didn't recognize. The stranger's back was to her, but he was dressed in loose black pants and a long gray shirt to match hers.

"What is this?" Ariella whispered. At her words, the man in gray turned. She squinted, unable to see his face in the shadows. She studied his silhouette, seeing the stiff way he carried himself. Broad shoulders led to a trim waist. Firelight danced on black hair cut a little long for Asclepius' style. It curled slightly at his ears. She narrowed her eyes, stepping closer, trying to see his face.

"Sans Ariella," Dr. Grace said. He was a short man whose body was withered with age and yet he moved with ease.

"Doctor?" Ariella continued forward, remembering the Supreme's order to smile. If the expression looked strained, none of the men let on or perhaps they didn't care.

"Please offer your hand to Dr. Walter as a sign of your intent to join with him," Grace said.

Ariella inhaled sharply. She looked at the Medical Supreme. The man eyed her coolly, expectantly.

Grace continued, "Dr. Sebastjan Walter. Take Sans Ariella's hand as a sign of your acceptance of her intention before the witness of myself and your father."

Sebastjan? Supreme Walter motioned Ariella to obey. She turned to the stranger, to Sebastjan, to her keeper's son. Her hand shook as she lifted it, confused. Intention? The man hesitated briefly before lifting his hand to clasp hers. He held her firmly in his large, warm palm and seemed so steady against her uncertainty.

"Do they have your blessing, Medical Supreme?" Grace leaned to look around the hand-holding couple.

"They do," Supreme Walter said.

"Congratulations, Dr. and Sans Sebastjan Walter." Grace held up his reader and pressed a button. Light flashed as he took the new couple's picture. Sebastjan's face lit for the briefest second. It was enough for her to see the fullness of his lips and the hard set of his eyes.

"I'm sorry," Ariella said. "Did he call me...?"

"Wife," Sebastjan said. His voice was low and dispassionate. His hand tightened on hers. That one word caused chills to work over her body.

"Wife?" she repeated.

"Congratulations," Supreme Walter said. "Go on upstairs. Sebastjan, your room is ready. I expect you both down tomorrow morning to confirm the union and to receive your guests." To Dr. Grace, he added, "Once you have finished your report to the statistical office, why don't you join me for a drink?"

"I'm sending them the photographic evidence and confirmation now," Grace answered, tapping on his reader as he followed behind the Medical Supreme. "All I need is your signature and it's done."

The candle lights flickered as the scraping sounded once more. Light was slowly let in from outside as the thick shutters lifted. It had gotten darker out during her wedding. Wedding. The word reverberated in her head as if whispered from far away. Ariella didn't move as she watched the light shine on her husband's face. Husband. Out of all the ways she expected this day to end, married to the Supreme's son wasn't one of them.

"What does this mean now?" she wondered, only realizing afterwards that the words were said out loud.

Blue eyes met hers, their depths stormy and discontented. He searched her face, not smiling as he did so. Was he displeased with her? With the marriage? Then why did he agree? Is that why Supreme Walter turned down the lights so his son wouldn't see? Or so his son wouldn't try to jump out of the window? He didn't let go of her, even when she lightly tugged her hand.

He was handsome, even by a medical plane's standards where everyone had surgical help if they so needed. Full lips and a proud nose and those tormented eyes. He blinked and his expression blanked. "Come on then."

He finally let go of her and she flexed her aching hand, realizing how tightly he'd been holding on to her. Sebastjan didn't look at her as he walked from the room. A moment's relief flooded her as she realized she'd been wrong. She wasn't going to have to give herself to Supreme Walter. The relief was short-lived. She might not have to give herself to her keeper, but it appeared as if she would be expected to give herself to his son.

Chapter Four

Sebastjan flexed his hand, not bothering to turn and look at the woman behind him. He knew she would follow. She had agreed to marry him, hadn't she? Him, a stranger to her. Undoubtedly the lure of his position in Chiron society was enough for her. She, the rich doctor's wife.

It didn't matter now. He had his agreement. One wife in exchange for freedom in all other matters. It was a small price to pay. She was pretty and her body would satisfy his lusts as well as any other. And if it didn't, he'd keep a mistress as a lover and this woman in some home as a wife. Perhaps he'd get his father to buy the mansion next door. Let Ariella and Walter enjoy each other's society while he continued on as he pleased without their interference.

Despite himself, he felt his body stir as he took the stairs to his room. How long had it been? Weeks? No, more than a month since he'd been with a woman—Dr. Candra Sunn when he visited her arctic facility to arrange an ice mineral transport six weeks ago. She'd been more than eager to have an out-of-facility man in her bed. Merely hours after meeting her, she'd been on her knees with his cock in her mouth. By her skill, it was a service she provided men often. No wonder so many of the male underlings at the arctic facility walked around with smiles on their face.

Sebastjan coughed lightly at the erotic notion as he pictured this woman doing the same. Well, not to the whole male population of an arctic facility, but definitely to him. Actually, he found the idea of her serving him drinks more probable than her serving his carnal appetites. It didn't matter. Even if the sex was bad, it would happen.

Keeping his head held high and his shoulders back, he turned as he reached the top of the stairs, going down the long hallway that would lead him to his old rooms. Medical screens switched on as he passed, automatically monitoring the beat of his heart. He felt lasers trying to scan him, but he kept walking.

"What now?" Ariella asked. Her soft voice sounded so uncertain. He supposed he could speak to her, placate her somehow, but out of the two of them she was the willing spouse.

"I think you know. We finish what was started." He opened his bedroom door and stepped aside, letting her enter first. She moved inside, standing close to the wall. Sebastjan closed the door and automatically punched the keys on the panel next to it. The lights dimmed and the fireplace lit. Shades slid into place to block the evening light. He reached for the button on his shoulder, unfastening it.

Sebastjan pulled his long shirt over his head. Her breathing became labored and he glanced at her. She hadn't moved. He stopped short of unbuttoning his pants. "There is no reason to be nervous."

"Are we really...?" She glanced around the room, swayed but didn't move.

Sebastjan again reached for his waistband, but something in her expression made him hesitate. Instead he sat down on the bed. At first the mattress was stiff but soon it began to mold around his ass, conforming to his body. Unbuttoning his boots, he kicked them aside. "We both understand what this match is. You know what reasons you have and I get what I need."

Chapter Five

Ariella tried not to stare at Sebastjan's chest. She knew what he expected but suddenly all the knowledge she had of carnal activities left her and she couldn't think. Warmth curled inside her, creeping over her belly and throughout her limbs. She found herself breathing deeply. Her hands shook. As he rolled onto his back, she took a step forward. It would be so easy to reach out and touch him, glide her fingers over the ridges of muscles.

You know what reasons you have and I get what I need.

This is what Supreme Walter had been grooming her for. She glanced at the ceiling, thinking of her cure floating in the air. There was nowhere to run. Should she beg Sebastjan to let her go? Was he different than his father? Would he give her freedom? Would he give her a cure? Or would he keep her like some living doll, trapped in his home to smile for his guests and pass out drinks at parties?

The goddesses taught her people that, once married, what happened between a man and woman was all right. She found herself walking toward him. "Your father hasn't said much regarding you."

"I'm surprised," Sebastjan answered, giving her a slight frown. He rolled up on the bed. The action brought him to sit before her. She stiffened as he reached to touch a strand of her blonde hair. "Since I am the reason he's brought you here. Didn't you care who you were going to marry?"

"I..." Ariella closed her mouth and glanced around the room. She couldn't speak ill of the Medical Supreme. "I was sick. I was sent here to the Medical Supreme so that I could be cured."

"Ah." His hand dropped. "So that is how he found you."

"I'm healthy now," Ariella quickly asserted, wondering why she felt disappointment at his withdraw.

Healthy for the most part.

"So I see." He motioned to the monitor on the wall. Ariella didn't realize it had come on, showing both of their vitals. "Shall we begin? Had I known a wedding was required of me, I wouldn't have stayed up working all of last night."

Ariella wasn't sure how to begin, so merely stood before him. He lifted his hand, again, picking up the strand of hair. He rubbed it between his fingers, as if the task was the most important in the world.

An animalistic vitality radiated off him, so much so that she had to wonder at his restraint. There was no hesitation in him, not like inside her. He didn't fear her, or this, wasn't uncertain about what to do. He dropped the lock of hair and he let his fingers brush over the top of her breast. An instant heat stung her flesh at the light touch. Her nipple tightened and her breathing deepened.

The orange fake firelight cast his features in hard contrast. He watched his fingers, taking his time as he brushed the back of his hand over her breasts. Even through the clothing, she could feel the small caress. Heat seemed to radiate from him, surrounding her, drawing her closer.

His blue eyes rose to meet hers and she held her breath. He lifted his hand to her shoulder, unbuttoning her tunic. Following the stripe, he deftly unfastened the hidden buttons until he made just enough room to reach inside. Fingers swept beneath the material, meeting flesh. This time, when he rubbed over her chest she felt the full press of his touch.

Ariella's lips parted and she inhaled a shaky breath. His opposite hand lifted to her hip, rubbing it as he worked her tunic up. He massaged her breast and hip at the same time. Fingers slid around to her back, drawing her closer.

Sebastjan unfastened a few more buttons. The front panel of the shirt fell open, exposing her breast to his eyes. He pressed his thumb to the hard nipple.

"You're trembling," he whispered. "I won't hurt you. There is no reason to be nervous."

Both hands found the flesh at the small of her back. They slid beneath her loose pants, curving along her ass cheeks. He pulled her to him and opened his mouth. A light moan escaped him as he kissed her ripe nipple.

Ariella couldn't move. She stared at his lips on her, his bronzed skin close to her paler body. His lips parted, surrounding the sensitive bud. His moan deepened as did his kiss. Soon he was sucking on her breast, pulling it deep into his mouth. Teeth bit lightly, forcing a hard jerk of surprise from her body. She swayed on her feet, feeling lightheaded.

"Mm, your breast is so soft." His tongue boldly flicked the wet nipple. "I wonder what else is soft." He grinned, a predatory look if she'd ever seen one. "And wet."

He edged closer still, bracing his feet on the floor as he parted his legs. She glanced down, seeing the hard protrusion straining between his thighs. The dim light cast shadows so it was impossible to see the size, only the strain.

Instantly all her focus went from her breast to her thighs. A deep ache radiated from her pussy and she did feel damp there. His hands massaged her ass, rubbing deeply, pulling her cheeks apart little by little as they moved lower and around. He groaned, jerking her forward so her thighs hit the side of the bed. This time, she pressed her breast into him and he sucked it deep. His hips rocked forward, bumping lightly against her. The teasing brush of his hidden cock caught her by surprise and she jerked back. Her breast left the suction of his mouth with a loud *swack*!

"I didn't think I'd be so eager," he admitted. "It's been awhile for me."

She merely nodded, not knowing how to respond.

31

"I'm being greedy and doing all the exploring," he continued. "It's your turn. Go ahead. Touch me."

Despite his words, he didn't let go of her ass. Ariella looked down at her breast and wondered if she should cover up first.

Before she could decide, he insisted, "Go ahead. Touch me."

She did. Ariella placed her hand on his strong shoulders. Heat radiated from beneath her fingers, curling through her like a liquid fire to drug her senses. She breathed deeply, detecting his masculine scent. Smooth, hard muscles formed delectable chest and arms.

"Let's get this off you." Sebastjan let go of her ass and reached for her shirtfront. He pulled at the front panels, forcing it open. Buttons fell on the floor as he pushed the material off her shoulders. "Much better." He urged the sleeves off her arms and then tossed the shirt aside.

As his mouth began exploring the newly exposed breast, she ran her fingers into his silky hair. The dark strands pulled between her fingers. Groaning, he jerked her pants down her hips. They slithered to her feet.

"I said, touch me," he commanded, more forceful now as his breath came in heavy pants. He grabbed her by the wrist and brought her hand down to his stomach. Not letting go, he pulled the waist-band forward, away from his cock, and shoved her hand down onto him. Swearing, he uttered, "Ah, *apolloa!*"

Ariella kept her hand against him. The firm, smooth shaft was like nothing she'd ever felt before.

"I didn't think I'd be so..." His eyes roamed freely over her naked body. "You're very beautiful." He pushed up from the bed and slid his pants from his hips. Kicking lightly, he worked them off his legs.

He wrapped his hand around hers, urging it to move. His fingers tightened, forcing hers to as well. When she learned the rhythm he liked, he let go. Sebastjan groaned, a low, completely sexual sound. He palmed her breasts, appearing fascinated with them as she leaned over.

Fingers skimmed up the side of her neck and dipped into her hair. He pulled lightly at the back of her head. Ariella's eyes widened as he tried to guide her head down.

"Mm, let's see what you can do," he murmured, pushing harder, insistently.

The low words washed over her and a scene from the forbidden manuals flashed through her thoughts. He wanted her to do *that*?

He put his hand on his cock, guiding it toward her lips. She gasped, placing her hands on his thighs for support as she leaned over his lap. The tip of his shaft slid past her lips.

Sebastjan groaned. "Suck me. That's it. That's what I like."

No man had ever dared to say such a thing. Maybe it was the sound of his voice, both pleading and insistent. Maybe it was the taste of him, or the smell, or the way his hand pressed downward. Ariella found herself obeying, letting her knees bend so she could find a better position.

He fell back on the bed, holding her head with both hands. Ariella felt powerful. She clutched his thighs, digging her nails into them as she tentatively took him deeper between her lips. Closing her eyes, she refused to think of the ramifications of her actions.

Sebastjan pressed his hips up as he pushed down, trying to force himself deeper. The warm, salty essence of him filled her mouth. She licked along the shaft, exploring the length. Her fingers slid to his cock, touching everywhere—his balls, his hips, the secret place at the base of his shaft.

"Ah, that's what I like," he moaned. His movements became jagged and frantic. Suddenly, he tensed, finding release. The taste of him filled her mouth and she swallowed. His hands fell to the side, letting her go. She pushed up, curious to see his face. He was breathing hard. Narrowed eyes stared at her. "You will make a very fine wife."

Heat warmed her cheeks as she tried, unsuccessfully, not to blush. He grabbed hold of her hips and flipped her around on the bed. She gasped, hitting the mattress. Her hands landed over her head.

His hands and knees anchored her down, trapping her to the bed. He licked his lips, his eyes roaming over her chest. Sebastjan worked his knees between hers, parting her bare thighs.

Ariella stiffened, unable to catch her breath. There was no question as to who was in control now. He ran his hand over her leg, openly exploring her with his eyes.

She wiggled beneath him, drawing her arms down to her sides. Ariella felt exposed, unsure. Sebastjan began at her neck, caressing her throat, her shoulder, each breast and nipple. Lips followed behind, continuing lower as he discovered her ribs, stomach and hips. Each time she tried to move her hands to stop him, he brushed them aside, continuing on.

As he kissed along her hip, she clamped her legs tight against his head. He didn't seem to notice. His lips moved against her thigh, closer, achingly closer to her sex. With a moan, he pressed his open mouth against her pussy. He licked hard, moaning while he did so. She pushed up on the bed, only to find his hand pressing her back down.

Heat exploded between her thighs, sending shivers of pleasure over her. He twirled his tongue, testing her, tasting her, tormenting her. As her whole body jerked, he glided over her. His hips instantly found their place between her thighs. The thick head of his cock brushed her sex. With a groan, he angled himself to her.

Ariella opened her mouth to speak, unsure what she wanted to say. She squirmed as he thrust. The tip of his cock slid inside, stretching her with its insistent push. Sebastjan groaned, his hips jerking.

Pleasure-pain erupted at the intimate contact. She gripped the bedding at her sides. He worked his hips, moving forward, pressing deeper and deeper until he'd conquered her with every inch of his arousal.

Almost breathless, he asked, "Mm, you're so tight—did you have a procedure done?"

"I..." she mumbled, "no."

Sebastjan moved in tiny circles, staying deep as he stretched her to fit him. "You must have. I don't mind. I find I quite enjoy the experience. It makes me want to..." He groaned, pulling out and thrusting forward. "Mm, I want to pound into you." He withdrew and thrust, hard and sure. She clamped her legs against his hips. His claiming hurt, but there was a curious pleasure there too. "Ah, you're so wet and hot and tight. Relax your legs. I want to fuck you hard. I have to..."

"I..." she managed weakly. She touched his arms. The fullness of him rubbed her in a way she'd never imagined possible.

Sebastjan's cock slid in and out. He pushed back on his hands. "That's it. So good. So, uh, good. I don't want to stop. I can't stop."

With each tattered confession he began to quicken his pace until she found her body being bounced on the bed with the driving force. She began to move in rhythm with him. A light sigh escaped her and wondrous sensations filled her, building toward something she couldn't quite reach.

Sebastjan jerked violently with release before collapsing against her. Eyes wide, Ariella stared at the ceiling. He rolled next to her, his hand resting on her thigh. The light brush of his fingers caused her leg to jerk.

"You are very quiet." He rolled onto his side next to her and she saw him squinting in the dim light. "Did you not...?"

"I, ah..."

His hand moved between her legs and he leaned close to her ear. The heat of his breath fanned over her cheek. He drew his fingers to her sex. "Let it never be said I am a greedy man."

Fingers stroked her sex, continuing where his body had left off. His thumb encircled her clit, rubbing lightly as he thrust a finger into her. He worked his hand against her, rebuilding her pleasure.

Teeth grazed the lobe of her ear. "Mm, there it is. You like when I do this, don't you?" He pressed his finger inside her, causing her body to tense and release. His words were a low whisper, as if telling her a secret even though they were alone in the room. "I can hear it in the way your breath catches." He did it again, pressing and releasing his finger inside her.

Ariella bit her lip and moaned. The sensations burst through her, spilling over her entire body. She trembled, sighed, tensed. Her mouth opened and she turned toward him. He still spoke, but she couldn't understand what he was saying. Blood rushed in her ears. His lips moved against hers and she realized he'd stopped speaking and was instead kissing her. The slow passion in the light brush of his lips made her feel weak. Or perhaps it was the aftermath of tremors dying and calming inside her.

"I suppose if we have nothing else in our marriage, there is that," he said against her mouth. He rolled onto his back, closing his eyes.

Ariella tugged at the blankets to cover herself. She watched Sebastjan's face. A small smile curled the corner of his mouth, but he didn't look at her again. Even as her heart slowed and her breathing regulated, she could barely gather a thought in her head beyond, "Oh."

Chapter Six

Sebastjan left his new "wife" asleep as he left his room to face his father. Despite his desire to dislike the choice his father had forced upon him, he found his step lighter than it had been in weeks. Though a little quiet, and with what he could only assume was shyness due to the newness of their situation, Ariella was quite sweet. She tasted like decadence and looked like the model of medical perfection. He'd seen the way her eyes took in everything around her, the depths of them filled with an astuteness not said with words. It made him wonder what secrets she held, what mysteries.

"Where is she?" Supreme Walter asked his son as soon as Sebastjan sat down at the long, narrow, metal table for his morning sustenance.

"Sleeping," Sebastjan answered drolly. "Would you like me to wake her for your inquisition?"

"Why? Is there a reason I should need to question her?" His father began to stand up, his brow knitting just as it did before a long lecture.

"Not that I would know," Sebastjan said. Had he been in the mood, he would have tormented the man, stringing him along with his worry. But somehow, discussing the completion of his marriage with his overbearing father didn't seem like a topic for...well, for *ever*.

"Ah, good!" His father clapped his hands. "I see I did very well grooming her for you. You will not be disappointed. She's a perfect societal gem—meek, controllable, not like your willful mother before she died. Ariella will be perfect for this family, and with the unique genetics from her plane, she will give you magnificent children—beautiful, physically perfect, strong, smart." Then grinning, he said knowingly, "And there is nothing like untouched, trainable fruit, eh?"

Sebastjan frowned, eyeing the bowl of cream-colored gruel set before him by a maid. "Untouched fruit?"

"If you insist on being indelicate," his father scolded, "then I suppose you'd say there is nothing like a pure woman untouched by man."

Sebastjan's frown deepened and he refused to eat. Out of the two men in the room, he was hardly the indelicate one. Standing, he said, "Excuse me."

"I expect you to greet your guests!" the Medical Supreme yelled behind him as Sebastjan hurried to go back upstairs. "This match will be made official!"

Coming to his chambers, he went inside. Ariella stood in the middle of the room, concentrating on her buttons. At his entrance, she glanced up. Sebastjan didn't go to her, instead choosing to stare. Hair tumbled around her shoulders, messy from the night's sleep. Wide eyes watched him, seeming to grow wider with each passing second of silence.

"Is it true?" Sebastjan managed, well aware that his voice sounded faint.

She furrowed her brow and carefully asked, "You mean to ask if we are truly married?"

Sebastjan took a step forward, noticing how she took an involuntary step back. "Why didn't you stop me? Why didn't you say anything?"

She paled. "Your father warned me never to speak of it. I wasn't sure how you would react if you discovered the truth or if you already knew. I couldn't trust that you would do the right thing. I still don't know if..."

"Of all the meddling," he muttered. Then, going to her, he

touched her cheek and forced her eyes to meet his. "You should have told me you were untouched. I would not have acted... Women on this plane are not...I didn't even think that you would be."

"Untouched? Oh, you mean..." She laughed nervously and began picking at her buttons. "I, um, it is fine. The goddesses say that with a husband is when a woman must—"

"Goddesses?" Sebastjan tried to keep the superiority out of his tone, but the confession took him by surprise. The woman clearly had primitive beliefs. His people had abandoned such thinking for the logic of science and the tangibility of facts.

"The guiding spirits," she answered. "My family served in their house."

"Ah. I see." He let her go, moving to sit on the bed. She continued to pull at her buttons, her fingers fumbling. He wondered if he made her nervous. "How did you come to be on this plane?"

"Divinity Corporation's inter-dimensional portal."

"I assumed that much since they have control of all of the portals. I meant why did they bring you?"

"I was sick and needed medical attention. My father was a political official, a very important man. Divinity Corporation wished to please him. They brought me here for a cure. When my family was murdered, they left me here for my safety. You father took me in as his ward."

"How altruistic of him," Sebastjan mumbled sarcastically. "Undoubtedly he found something in your genetics that would make you highly compatible to mine. Medical Supreme Walter only thinks of himself and the continuation of his legacy."

The overhead air-filtering sterilizer turned on, misting the room with its light fragrance. Ariella looked up and breathed deeply several times. After a few seconds, she turned back to her task, fastening her clothes with steadier hands. Finishing, she turned her full attention to him. "I need to get back to my chambers. I can't greet your guests looking like this."

Sebastjan let her leave, despite his urge to draw her back to his bed. He couldn't touch her, not after what he'd learned. Women on his plane were not shy when it came to sex, and often by the time they were well into adulthood, they had experience. Adult virgins were practically a myth. He'd never even considered meeting one, let alone marrying one. When he'd come back up and looked at her face, remembered the hesitance he'd taken for shyness, he wanted to kick himself. He should have seen it. He should have known. She should have told him.

Chapter Seven

Ariella raced toward her chambers, feeling physically stronger now that she had her medicine. She'd almost made a big mistake. She'd almost told Sebastjan about her "forced illness". By the stricken look on his face when he walked into the room, she'd just assumed he'd been told about her entrapment. Instead, he was worried about her lost virginity.

The door slid up automatically as she neared. Once inside her chambers, she took a deep breath. She barely had time to process what had happened—the wedding, the wedding night, a husband—when a maid walked in holding a syringe.

"Sans Ariella," the maid said, "your lidic levels are high and your plytomikin and homytobin levels are low. I've been instructed to—"

"I know," Ariella grumbled, pulling her hair aside and tilting her head. The maid injected medicine into her in the neck. She didn't need the long explanation that came with her shots—half of which she didn't have the background to understand. If she didn't take them willingly, they'd be forced on her by Chiron's medical laws.

"There is a little extra in there to help you smile for your guests," the maid added, "and to take away any pain."

"Pain?" Ariella repeated before noticing the soreness between her thighs lessened. After a lifetime of chronic pain from her bones, she didn't even think twice of a little sexual discomfort. "Oh, never mind. Thank you for the shot."

Chapter Eight

The finest of Asclepius society filtered past the newlyweds' receiving line. Ariella felt herself smiling and nodding politely at each individual doctor. After some time in Asclepius, she recognized many of them. Women in fine-cut cotton and linen clothing intermingled with the dignified men. The soft sound of laughter and muted amusements created a constant background to the "thank you for coming" and "it is so kind of you to say" phrases she was forced to repeat like a trained animal.

Many of the guests looked at her with vacant eyes, seeing past her as if she were unimportant. The only exception was a few of the men. She didn't need a lifetime of sexual experience to know what they were thinking about. In fact, she overheard one of them offer to buy her from the Medical Supreme. The exact words were "I would be most honored to give the darling woman a place in my home, if you would be so good as to part with her" to which Walter answered, "Not this one. Not this time. She is not like the others."

"Congratulations, Dr. and Sans Sebastjan Walter," a woman said, looking down her hooked nose at the new bride. Ariella couldn't remember her name, but she'd talked to her often. The woman's disapproving demeanor never changed. Taking the offered gift, Ariella handed it over to the waiting maid to be set on the mountainous pile behind her.

"It is so kind of you to say," Ariella said politely.

"Thankfully it is almost over. I abhor these events," Sebastjan whispered in her ear. She glanced at him, surprised. It was the first thing he'd said to her in nearly three hours of standing in the front hall.

"Congratulations, Dr. and Sans Sebastjan Walter."

Ariella glanced away from her husband, about to answer when Sebastjan laughed and said, "Dr. Fauchet, how good of you to come."

"How could I not?" Dr. Fauchet answered. He had an easy smile with lively brown eyes that seemed to laugh at some sort of private joke.

"Couldn't miss my reception?" Sebastjan asked.

"I couldn't miss the Medical Supreme's summons," Fauchet corrected. "You didn't think everyone was here to see you, did you?"

Ariella gave a short burst of laughter in surprise at the insolent joke.

Fauchet winked at her but continued talking to Sebastjan. "Apparently, I am to host two off-plane dignitaries coming here to learn our secrets. However," he turned his full attention to Ariella, "while I am here..."

"Sans Ariella," Sebastjan introduced, "my childhood playmate and local lawbreaker—"

"That is distinguished gentleman and dignitary host," Fauchet corrected.

"Dr. Gerard Fauchet," Sebastjan finished.

"A great pleasure," Gerard said, his playful eyes studying her face. "And it was only one tiny law fourteen years ago. There was a medication mishap, it was hot and it was only the male chairmen who complained about my nakedness. I swear I am a reformed man." Ariella laughed again before catching herself. She couldn't help it. The man was just too likeable. Sebastjan cleared his throat. Gerard chuckled, not showing a single second of remorse at having been caught flirting with the new bride. Leaning in to Ariella, he whispered, "An even greater pleasure to see you've managed to make Sebastjan jealous over you."

Ariella blushed. Sebastjan frowned at them. Gerard bowed his head and moved on.

"What? No present?" Sebastjan mumbled after him. Gerard laughed, but didn't turn back around. "What did he say to you?"

Ariella didn't answer as another guest came to offer her congratulations.

When the woman passed by, he repeated, "What did Fauchet say?"

"He said he was trying to make you jealous," Ariella answered, hiding the first genuine smile that day.

"He always did have a strange sense of humor." Sebastjan stiffly turned back to their guests.

Chapter Nine

Five hours. That's how long it took the procession of his father's guests to pass through the hall. Thousands of presents stacked behind them, each one demanding to be opened, each one demanding a thank-you message to be delivered.

Sebastjan grimaced. Ariella hadn't spoken to him since Gerard whispered in her ear. He liked Dr. Fauchet well enough, but didn't appreciate the fact the man made his bride blush, or that he'd winked at her on his way out of the house. "It will take us ten hours just to deliver a personal message to each gift and another thirty days to discreetly throw half of them into the incinerator."

"I'll have the maids go through them and make us a list. Perhaps a few generic messages will suffice for the bulk of them." Ariella lifted her hand, suppressing a yawn.

The Medical Supreme said farewell to the last guest. Before he could turn to them, Ariella had turned to the stairs and was walking toward the bedrooms.

"Ariella, won't you join us?" his father asked.

"I should begin organizing the gifts," she answered, stiffly turning. Sebastjan watched her carefully, noting how her eyes didn't look directly at the Medical Supreme. He had a feeling it was more than respect that kept her from the man's company. "I wouldn't want to be remiss in my duties and you have so very many friends."

"Of course," Supreme Walter agreed. "Very well."

Ariella glanced at Sebastjan, briefly meeting his eyes before turning to rush away. He wasn't sure whether to be frightened or amused by her quick handling of his father. As he'd suspected before, the woman appeared to be much smarter than the pleasant expression on her face would have people believe.

"I told you, societal perfection," his father said. "She knows her duty."

Or perhaps her reaction was merely societal training.

Sebastjan watched his father walk away. There was more going on here than he'd been told. He'd bet his medical license on it.

Ariella waited for her husband to come to her and rescue her from the endless opening of packages. She was obliged to watch, even if she didn't do the unwrapping herself. Over a dozen maids worked, several opening, others carting out the garbage to be picked up for incineration, another keeping record. Fine cotton scarves, marble figurines, linen robes, money—all of it beautiful and elegant and rich. But Ariella knew it to be more of a testament to her father-by-marriage and her husband than to herself.

Looking at the door, she willed Sebastjan to come for her. He didn't and she was not saved from her duty.

"From Dr. Darcin, an urn," one of the maids announced.

Ariella sighed, turning her attention from the door. She folded her hands in her lap and nodded her head in acknowledgment.

Chapter Ten

I t took two and a half days to go through the gifts, another to record the messages necessary, two seconds to send them all out, and still another day to have them packaged and sent to Sebastjan's home at a faraway research facility. Just the idea of that facility gave Ariella cause for excitement. Finally, she would be free of her mansion prison.

Only one thing worried her. Sebastjan had not come to her as he had their wedding night. He was polite when they spoke, let her walk through doorways first and even made her laugh a few times. But she always felt as if he was watching her, waiting, searching, wondering. Several times she wanted to ask him what he was thinking, but refrained. Her favorite part of the day came when they were alone outside in the garden for her afternoon walk. Though glass containers covered all of the greenery, the air was fresh and the company handsome.

"This was my mother's favorite plant," he said, pointing at a small leafy bush. "She used to say it was the sturdiest of plants, the quiet ones, that truly made the garden. They were the ones you could depend on."

"She sounds like a wise woman," Ariella had answered.

57

"She used to sneak me into the garden boxes to touch the trees. My father found out and that is why all the doors now have locks. My mother hated my father and he hated her because he could not control her."

"But I am sure she loved you if she wished for you to see nature," Ariella assured him.

He didn't look comforted. "She was committed to five weeks in a mental care facility for having tried to kill me with plant allergens. She was not the same when she returned."

Ariella had no answers for that.

Each night, as she lay in bed, Ariella thought of what had happened between them on the wedding night. When he touched her, her skin had been on fire. She wanted to feel the flames again, the tense rise and trembling fall.

It was with that thought she slipped from her chambers into the dimness of the hall. Her feet whispered over the stone. The wall monitors detected her, turning on to light her way as they let her know her heart was racing a little too fast and her breathing had become hitched.

Coming to Sebastjan's door, she tried to hesitate and catch her breath, but the sensors didn't give her a chance. The door opened automatically, like a veil passing over her vision to reveal his bed. Her eyes found him easily in the dim light. He lay on his side, his back to her, bare, strong. The long line of his spine led from the shock of black hair to the tight curve of his ass.

"Sebastjan?" she whispered to see if he would awaken. He stirred, slowly coming around to look at her with sleepy blue eyes. Ariella tugged at the string holding her new robe closed. The wedding gift slithered off her shoulders. Sebastjan instantly pushed up, his gaze going to her naked breasts. Light caressed his naked flesh, contrasting the hard lines of his muscles. The limp member between his thighs stirred, straightening with interest.

Ariella had thought of this moment a lot, of what she would do and say. Words failed her and she found it hard to move when he looked at her with those smoldering eyes. She slowly stepped toward the bed. Her knee hit the mattress. Sebastjan didn't move.

"Sans Ariella," he said, the tone like an acknowledgement, but his look made it feel more like a game.

"Doctor," she answered, her voice not as strong as she would have liked. She lifted her knee, placing it on the bed to slowly climb on.

"How may I be of service?" he inquired.

Ariella leaned forward and lifted her second leg onto the bed. "I thought I might be of service to you." She felt heat rising over her features but didn't back away. She sat back on her legs. Ariella's flesh tingled and she felt the gathering moisture between her thighs. "You have not been to see me and I thought perhaps..." Her voice failed.

His breathing visibly deepened and his member lifted and firmed. He lay back on the bed. "After..." he paused, studying her, "after our wedding night I thought it best to give you space."

"Space?"

"To wait for you to come to me. I know that I did not behave, that I did not take care of you as I should have. Had I known you were a maiden, I would have been...better."

"Better? You mean the pleasure we felt could be better?" She arched a brow in surprise. His lips parted, but no sound came out. Ariella blushed. "That did not come out right. It was too forward. That is not how I meant to say..."

"Oh? What did you have in mind?"

She opened her mouth, but couldn't think of anything clever to say.

"An examination, perhaps?" he prompted, rolling slowly onto his stomach. "With your consent, of course."

It took her a moment to realize he meant for her to play the doctor and he her patient. She smiled, nodded and reached to touch him. Shaking fingers met warm, hard flesh. She followed the length of his back, pressing along his spine. Mesmerized, she cupped his ass, massaging the cheeks. He groaned, his hips flexing into the bed. Ariella explored his legs before coming back to his hips. Every time she worked her fingers, he groaned and thrust his arousal into the bed.

"Mmm." He turned back around, faster than before, to rest on his back.

She drew her hand over his chest, following the valleys of his muscles. He bit his lip and closed his eyes. She traced her way down the center of his stomach, following the dark trail of hair leading to his cock. Before reaching the imposing shaft, she changed course, moving back up to his neck.

Ariella touched his silky black hair, caressed his cheek and traced his firm lips. He opened his mouth, sucking her fingers against his tongue. He moaned, loud and deep.

"I ache for you," he whispered seconds before he opened his eyes in surprise, as if he hadn't meant to speak.

"Would you like me to relieve that ache?" she asked, wrapping her fingers around his cock.

Sebastjan reached for her breasts, massaging them in his palms. "Very much."

He urged her to come over him. She let go of his shaft, moving to straddle his thighs. He caressed everywhere he could reach, letting her take the lead. Ariella rubbed her sex against him, getting used to the feel. When she didn't move to take him inside her, he lifted her up by the hips and flipped her onto her back. He threaded his legs between hers, parting her thighs.

Then his lips met hers, sweet and easy. Gentleness poured into her from that kiss. It took her by surprise. Against her mouth, he whispered, "You set the pace. I will do it however you wish. I don't want to hurt you."

His cock brushed against her pussy. He took her slowly, groaning as he rocked into her. Sebastjan continued to kiss her, tracing her lips with his tongue, distracting her senses. Her eyes drifted closed. She held onto his neck, kneading the muscles she found there. He took her in shallow thrusts, his hips working in small circles. Despite his offer, Ariella simply enjoyed the pace he set, letting him slide in and out. It was unlike anything she'd ever experienced.

Tension built and she eagerly awaited the finale. The excitement made her pant into his mouth. When he thrust, she pushed up harder than before and was rewarded with a jolt of sensations. And then it happened, a complete explosion of the senses. Her body shook as tremors racked over her. His release joined hers. For a long moment, he stayed frozen above her, breath held.

Sebastjan rolled next to her, his arm touching hers. "I'm glad you came to me. I've been waiting for you every night."

"I think you put too much guilt on yourself for the wedding night," Ariella said. "The pain was really nothing to the bone pain I grew up with. I know people here like to treat me like I'm a delicate piece of silk, but I'm not."

"Mmm," Sebastjan moaned, reaching for her. He palmed a breast. "Are you sure? Your skin feels like silk."

She reached for his hand, touching it briefly before touching her shoulder. "It wasn't always. I used to have these scars everywhere. There was a long one across my shoulder. One of my sisters hit me with a ritual candlestick."

"I'm sorry you lost them."

"I was told it was quick." Even though she'd started the subject, she didn't want to talk about that. Not right now.

As if sensing her desire to change the topic, he said, "I know we are supposed to leave in a week, but I'd rather go sooner. I find it hard to breathe here. Would you mind?"

Ariella couldn't stop the grin from coming over her features. "I would really like that."

"If you don't mind my asking, why are you here? What happened to your family?"

Ariella stiffened, her smile fading. Perhaps he hadn't read her mind in that regard. "I told you. They were murdered on my plane. I was here, so I survived."

"We don't have murder," Sebastjan said. "What reason would someone have to do that?"

"There was a rebellion between the two ruling houses. My father represented the House of the Goddesses. The House of Gods attacked and killed him and my older sisters."

"Why?"

"It was discovered that my sisters were not pure. Vessels of the goddesses are meant to be pure. And the most ironic part of it all was that it was the sons of the gods who took their maidenhoods." She sighed, dropping her hand from where his fingers lightly rubbed her breast. "It all feels so far away. I was only supposed to be here for a few weeks. My bones were fragile. They broke all the time despite the precautions everyone took. That is how I got most of my scars. When Divinity Corporation came seeking to copy our sacred texts for inter-dimensional analysis and comparison, they offered to bring me here in return. I never saw my family again. Divinity brought pictures of the aftermath as well as a faithful servant to tell me the news. I couldn't go back. I don't know any other planes and had nothing to trade with Divinity to take me anyway."

"And we fixed you." Sebastjan drew his fingertip down her arm. He sounded so certain of the fact. They all did on this plane, as if they could cure everything—even death by old age. But the truth was, they had only managed to prolong life, not find the cure for the ultimate death.

"The Medical Supreme fixed my bones and took away my physical scars," she corrected. "He instituted my health regimen."

Suddenly, Sebastjan sat up on the bed. He turned to study her. For a long moment, he didn't say anything. Then, touching the side of her face, he asked, "Is that why you agreed to this? Gratitude?"

Gratitude? Ariella suppressed the urge to laugh, though she felt no humor in the idea. It wasn't gratitude. She hadn't even agreed. Not really. Still, as she looked at him, for all his newness to her, she couldn't help but think there could be more between them. He had a brooding quality to him. It shone in his eyes, as if he was trapped in the same cage she was in. Still, after less than a week, she didn't know him well enough to trust him.

Closing her eyes, she said the only truth she could, "I am grateful to no longer carry the sickness I had when coming here."

Chapter Eleven

"If you know what is best for you, you will make him stay another week," Supreme Walter said without preamble as Ariella walked through the door.

"How do you propose I do that?" She stopped just inside the room, not approaching the desk.

"Tell him you wish to stay," Supreme Walter answered, as if it was the simplest thing in the world.

"But I don't," she said. Her warden raised a brow at her tone. "I never did."

"Such gratitude," he muttered.

"I'm really beginning to hate that word, gratitude. What should I feel gratitude for? My family being killed? Being held prisoner? Being on an alternate reality that is nothing like my real home? Saved only to be poisoned? Forced to marry? Forced to smile? Forced to...?" Ariella didn't know why, now, out of all the time she'd had these thoughts, that she allowed them to spill out of her mouth. She shrugged helplessly. "Sure. I'm grateful."

"I see my son is having an effect on you. I had rather hoped you would have had an effect on him." Supreme Walter stood. "Regardless. If you leave before the week is up, I won't give you the cure. If you tell my son, I won't give you the cure. I will have this my way. Do you really want to give up the rest of your life to deny me one week."

"One week? What's to stop you from—"

"If you don't stop talking and leave my office this instant, I won't give you the cure." His words were low, hard, and she saw the arrogance in every nuance of his expression.

"Don't make promises you don't intend to keep," she answered. So what if he didn't give her the cure. Sometimes she thought it might be better if he didn't.

"What was that?" he demanded.

"I said, I'll talk to him." Her words were faint as she backed away from the hateful man.

"See that you do."

Sebastjan frowned at his wife, wondering at the sudden change in her demeanor. The night before, he'd felt as if they'd connected. They'd stayed up all night, talking, laughing, whispering, kissing. They even came together in the morning, finding sleepy release.

"You wish to stay?" Sebastjan sighed heavily. "I thought we discussed this."

"Your father insists," Ariella answered, as if that should have made a difference to him. "It is only for a week."

"Then it will be two weeks, then three. I know how the man works." Sebastjan frowned. "No. I'm leaving. We're leaving."

She refused to look at him, instead turning to stare at the hallway monitor. "I can't."

"Why?"

"I can't tell you."

"What does my father have on you?" Sebastjan reached for her face, but she pulled away from him.

"I can't tell you."

"What can you tell me?" He reached for her again, this time forcing her to meet his eyes.

Still she looked past his shoulder. "Nothing that pertains to this."

"You're my wife, but your loyalty belongs to him." Sebastjan let her go. "I should have known there was more to this arrangement than what I was seeing." He sighed heavily, correcting himself, "I did know. I just didn't want to think about it."

"Sebastjan." The plea in her voice managed to stop him from walking away. "I want...I'm sorry I can't tell you."

When he looked in her eyes, something inside of him wanted to believe her, to trust her and help her. But all he really knew about her was that she came from tragedy to his home plane and married him because his father wanted it. "Fine. If you wish it, we will stay one more week. No more."

"One week. That is all," Sebastjan informed his father sternly. "Any more than that and I will be shirking my duties."

Ariella hated the pleased look on Walter's face as Sebastjan told him of their plans to stay. She took a quick bite of her food, hurrying to finish it so she could be excused.

Medical Supreme Walter didn't comment on his son's statement. "Have you finished your communications, Ariella?"

"Almost."

"Father," Sebastjan said, standing. "Excuse us."

Walter nodded. "Check your monitor. I've posted a schedule for this week for you."

Ariella pushed up from her seat and followed Sebastjan from the room. When they were alone, he said, "You looked like you wanted out of there as fast as I."

"I want out of this house," she admitted. "But if we go out the side door to the gardens he'll see the door alarm and will most likely join us."

"Not so. Come, I'll show you a way to escape undetected. I discovered it as a boy." He led the way to the side door and reached to the small computer next to the door. Touching the screen, he set the unit to do a detailed maintenance check. "If you enter my father's code, six-six-nine, the system will run a diagnostic that takes seventy three minutes. This door will remain undetectable for that time. It's a glitch in the security system. I know, because I programmed it in. Since my father doesn't trust anyone to touch the system, no one has ever bothered to fix it."

"You're not worried someone will break into this place?"

He pulled her with him outside. "Into the home of the Medical Supreme?" Sebastjan shook his head. "Not likely. The only crime on this plane is stolen research and that is rare. Everything is documented."

Ariella felt the tension roll off her shoulders as the cool breeze caressed her skin. The glass walls holding in the trees surrounded the path, keeping the true smell of nature trapped. She breathed deeply. "I sometimes think about lighting a torch to melt through the glass walls, just so I can crawl in and lie on the grass."

"I wish I had a secret way into the gardens so I could take you." Sebastjan reached for her hand.

"You're not afraid of the pollen?"

"No. It was my grandfather who had an aversion to pollen. He boxed in all the plants. There are places, outside of Asclepius, where nature is not put away in boxes."

Ariella pulled him closer, drawing the hand clasped with his around her back so he was forced to hug her. "There are many things put away in boxes here."

"What do you mean?"

Ariella thought it best not to clarify. The night was beautiful, made even more so by the fact Walter didn't know where she was. It was the first time since she'd met the man that he didn't know her exact location. A giddiness filled her at the tiny taste of freedom. She looked up into Sebastjan's eyes, noticing how well his body fit against hers. Letting go of his hand, she ran her fingers up his arm. He didn't let go as he held her to his chest.

The stir of arousal filled her and was echoed back in the lift of his erection and soft sigh of his breath. She trembled in anticipation, wondering if he'd take her here on the garden pathway. Licking her lips, Ariella offered her mouth to him. He didn't deny her. His kiss was gentle, brushing over her lips until they parted to allow him deeper access.

Breaking free, he grabbed her hand and led her through the garden until the mansion became a blurred obscurity behind glass. Sebastjan pressed her against the glass wall. He cupped her cheek, turning her mouth back to his as he resumed the kiss. Soft noises escaped her and she moaned into him. His hands skimmed over her shirt, running down to lift her longer tunic.

She turned her face to take a deep breath. Sebastjan kissed her throat, biting along the flesh from her jaw to her ear. The combination of hard and soft caresses caused her to shiver. Ariella ran her hands over his chest, liking the feel of him. Her fingers found the hard curves and valleys of his muscles, liking the way he flexed against her touch.

When his hand found the flesh of her hip, baring her legs by pushing down her pants, she closed her eyes. She tugged at his waistband, pulling his pants to free his arousal. Her senses became sharp. Their light pants mingled, backdropped by the sound of wind against the plant boxes. The texture of his palm sweeping along her thigh contrasted the hard glass against her back.

Sebastjan lifted her leg. Ariella pulled at their tunics, trying push the disheveled clothing out of the way. He brought his hips to hers and she jerked with sensation at the intimate contact. Holding onto his neck, she let him pull her other leg up so she straddled his waist. He kept his hands on her ass as he drew his body to hers. He entered her slow and deep. Ariella wanted more. She hooked her ankles behind him, pulling him forward in harder thrusts.

Moonlight caressed his skin, shadowing and lighting his face. The blue tones changed the shade of his flesh, tinting it so it looked almost pale. She held on tighter, feeling free from the bonds of her imprisonment. The end felt so near—the end of threats and disease, the end of the tension building in her stomach. Hope welled inside her. Soon she'd be truly free, away from this awful city with its locks and bars. Perhaps this was why the goddesses sent her here. They were rewarding her for her pious life. They knew the House of Goddesses would be attacked and they saved her. They sent her to not only be cured, but to find Sebastjan.

All these thoughts swirled in her head, flowing through her consciousness like a sudden burst of understanding. In this moment, this perfectly blissful moment, it all made sense. The universe lined up and she understood. She didn't like all elements of the journey, but she felt the symmetry of it. The pleasure pushed her body over the edge. Her muscles tensed. Her nerves tingled. Her entire body jerked in helpless release.

Sebastjan thrust harder, his body pressing tight. He bit at her earlobe. "I want to devour you. I want this to last. I want to take you from here and—" The words were cut off as he came, trembling against her. He gripped her ass tight, as if to keep from dropping her.

Somewhere in the back of her mind, she longed to hear him finish the sentence. Another part of her was frightened of what he would say. He dropped her legs and their bodies pulled apart. Ariella reached to right her clothing and Sebastjan did the same.

"I don't want to go back inside," Sebastjan said, but they both knew that they had to. There was a tenderness in him when he looked at her. Or perhaps she imagined it. The moonlight and passion could have been giving her more hope than was realistically plausible. "Come stay in my room with me tonight. I would have you sleep near."

Ariella nodded and they both silently walked back into her prison.

Chapter Twelve

D ays passed, yet Sebastjan found he didn't hate being at the mansion. Sure, he didn't care to be around his father, but the fact that every second of it was spent next to his new wife made up for the Medical Supreme's presence. Unfortunately, direct conversation with her was limited to stolen seconds between streams of social insipidness. And, for all her protesting to stay, Ariella seemed to enjoy it as little as he. Their only reprieve was the night, when nothing mattered beyond the boundaries of his bed.

He closed his eyes, wishing more than anything to be back there—hands roaming her flesh, lips exploring, bodies joining. Last night, they'd barely made it to his room. Her thigh had brushed his during the evening sustenance and he'd been lost in erotic thoughts of what he would do to her once he had her alone. He'd thrown her over the side of the bed, long shirt tossed up along her back and had his way with her. It had been wickedly wonderful.

"Are you ready?" Sebastjan asked, as Ariella's door slid open. He adjusted his hips, trying to hide the all-too-obvious evidence of his arousal. His breath caught as she turned. Her green eyes practically glowed because of the perfect green shade of her long shirt. The charcoal gray pants matched his shirt, an effect undoubtedly planned by his father's maid when she laid out their clothing the night before.

Ariella smiled, reaching to brush her long hair over her shoulders. She seemed completely unaware of the effect she had on him. "What is it we're doing again?"

"Greeting off-plane doctors," he answered. Sebastjan frowned. Dr. Gerard Fauchet would be there and he couldn't soon forget the man's flirting.

"Ah." She reached for his arm, trying to walk him from the room. "That sounds fascinating. What kind of plane are they from? Do they look like us? I've heard that on some planes the people can't be in the sunlight or they explode into ash. When I was on the Divinity base before coming here, some of the scientists were talking about the different worlds. Did you know that there are people with purple flesh? And a whole plane of people without a single hair on their body?" She looked excited by the prospect. "What if they have extra limbs, or—"

He chuckled, unable to help himself as he said, "Wait. Don't go yet." He pulled her back against his chest. The door lifted halfway and then drew back down as she came out of reach of the sensors.

"What...?" she began, only to stop when she felt the obvious press of his erection to her ass. "Oh. Now? Here?"

"Why not now?" He kissed the back of her ear. "Why not here?"

"We'll be late," she protested feebly. Ariella didn't try too hard to escape his caresses.

"So we'll be late. What can the Medical Supreme do to us? Look stern? Scold us again for not attending to our duties? Let him wait." This time he licked her ear. She shivered, melting into him. "Besides, I cannot greet off-plane doctors in my current state. Imagine the stories that will be told about this plane. They will think us all barbarians on Chiron who think of nothing but sex."

"Is it so far from the truth?" she teased. "Perhaps they would be flattered to be greeted with such interest. I've heard of alternate realities where the people walk about naked and have never heard of clothing. I would have to think they don't have snow where they live. Oh, and there are others who sell sexual favors like food on the street corners and no one thinks it strange. Still other planes are said to have men who are kept inside large, stone homes to be used for the whims of their women."

"Mm, are you saying you'd like to lock me inside a stone house and use me for your whims?" He grinned, part of him liking the idea, however unrealistic.

As if coming to a decision, she glanced at the closed door. "All right, you win, quick, out of those pants. We will have time if we hurry." She pulled up her shirt and began tugging at her waistband.

Sebastjan laughed, not needing to be told twice. He barely had them loosened around his hips when she pushed him toward a chair. The hard surface pressed into his naked ass. A narrow back supported him as he leaned into it, but there were no sides or arms.

Ariella kicked her pants aside and moved to straddle him. Her pussy was wet as she drew it along his shaft, attesting to how desperately she wanted him. She reached between them, enthusiastically angling his body to hers. With a light groan, she sat on his lap, impaling her body.

"Oh," she sighed, lifting up only to fall down. She gripped his shoulders, holding tight as she rode him. He took her by the hips and braced his feet on the floor, balancing their bodies as he let her have her way. "Perhaps this plane could be all about being sex-crazed barbarians. I love the way this feels."

She let her head fall back as she looked toward the ceiling. Her hips moved in hard, fast, desperate thrusts. Sexually engaging sighs left her in soft pants of air. Ariella jerked as she came, pressing down on him. The sight of her pleasure was too much. His release joined hers. Without giving them much time to bask in the aftermath, she stood and began to straighten her clothing. Sebastjan was much slower to follow.

When she finished redressing, she looked at him. Her cheeks were flushed and her eyes appeared to glisten with mischief. "Hurry. I'll meet you by the transport."

If he wasn't so sated he might have been hurt by her quick departure. Instead he grinned. The faster they did their duty the faster they could be done with it.

Chapter Thirteen

The box-shaped vehicle moved soundlessly over the streets, hovering over the ground as it sped along Asclepius' self-navigating streets. Two rows of seats faced inward, making for easy conversation. Once the address was typed into the transport's computer, the occupants were free to enjoy the ride—no driver needed.

Ariella was not enjoying the ride. Medical Supreme Walter stared at her for most of it, clearly disappointed in her tardiness. She tried to ignore the sick feeling she got from the man's unwanted attention, endeavoring to focus her thoughts on Sebastjan. How the two could be related was beyond her understanding. But, the sameness in their physical appearance confirmed that they were indeed father and son.

"I expected lateness from my son," Walter had said when Ariella hurried down the stairs to join him, "but not from you. I expect better from you."

She reached for the buttons next to the window, pushing one so that the outside became more visible. They were slowing near the middle of town in front of the Central Hospital and Optimal Health Centre building. She recognized the giant structure with its thick

Corinthian columns and oversized stone arches. Inside, the metal corridors would look nothing like the fine architectural façade.

As the transport stopped, the doors opened automatically, sliding to the side. Supreme Walter stepped out first, then Sebastjan, who then helped her down. Stone stretched as far as she could see—statues, sidewalks, streets and buildings. Only a little bit of plant life was allowed in the city, and that was blocked by large glass panels.

"Are you all right?" Sebastjan asked, not letting go of her arm.

"Fine," she lied. In truth, Ariella always found it a little hard to breathe in the sterilized environment.

"Is it because this is where the Divinity portal is stored?" he insisted. "Are you thinking of home?"

"Come on," Supreme Walter ordered. "They're waiting on us."

Inside, the metallic gray corridors of the hospital looked like an endless maze, only the orange lettering on the walls gave directions. Unfortunately for Ariella, she wasn't able to understand them. The smell of the hospital's air filtering sterilizer wafted over her. A loud alarm blared overhead, buzzing annoyingly.

"They've arrived," Supreme Walter said, walking faster. "They will be in sterilization right now to check for other dimensional parasites and viruses. We must hurry."

"Why is he so eager to greet these guests?" Ariella asked. "Does he want something from them?"

"He likes the attention," Sebastjan answered with a smirk.

Supreme Walter stopped ahead of them, greeting Dr. Lu. The man wore the standard issue uniform for the facility, a long blue coat with red trim. Like everyone else at the hospital, he kept his hair cropped short.

"Welcome back, Sans Ariella," Dr. Lu said to her before addressing her husband in quiet conversation. He carried an orange electronic clipboard, which he referred to several times. Sebastjan glanced at Ariella with a slight frown, nodding his head. Then, Dr. Lu reached into his pocket and took out a syringe. Like everything else it was electronic. He pressed the tip to the clipboard, waited for a beep and then leaned forward to inject it into Sebastjan's neck.

"We received word from the Starian ambassador, Sans Lady

Lilith," Dr. Lu said as Ariella inched closer so she could listen to the conversation. "It looks like you will be receiving the blue mineral water you requested as soon as the Medical Supreme signs off on a shipment of handheld units."

Supreme Walter actually chuckled, like a kid in possession of a secret weapon. Sebastjan's whole body tightened but he managed to nod in response. "Thank you for making the arrangements, Dr. Lu."

"Yes, thank you, Dr. Lu," the Medical Supreme added.

Ariella shared at look with Sebastjan, wondering what he was thinking as he frowned back at her. She unconsciously touched her hair, smoothing it down. He said nothing as he turned his attention away.

A few minutes later, Ariella found herself standing before two off-plane women. One, a Dr. Cecilia Markos whose serious nature seemed well in tune with the people of Chiron, looked at the flirty Dr. Gerard Fauchet as if he'd grown two heads and had begun snorting fire. She had her brunette locks pulled back from her face, a stern look that suited the disdain on her face.

Dr. Markos' assistant, Sans Linnea Nel, seemed more easygoing. Her shoulder-length black hair had a streak of dark purple down the side. It matched the strange shade of her purplish-gray eyes. She chuckled, hiding her smile in the stack of papers she carried. To Ariella's somewhat disappointment, the visiting women's flesh was of normal color and they didn't have any visible abnormalities. In fact, they were quite ordinary.

"May I present the esteemed Dr. Swift?" The Medical Supreme nodded to the hospital's director. "Director of Central Hospital."

Ariella turned her smile to the director, having met him at a few social outings, but he barely glanced in her direction. The director eyed the newly arrived assistant's hair for a long moment before greeting Dr. Markos. Ariella always got the impression the man found himself too important to talk to the non-medical.

"Come with me."

Ariella stifled a gasp of surprise when Sebastjan whispered into her ear. He pulled her slowly back, leading her away from the others. No one seemed to notice their withdrawal. Well, no one but Linnea who smirked in their direction but said nothing.

Once outside in the corridor, he quickened his pace. Ariella giggled. Her body heated with the idea of getting him alone. She'd heard about the insatiable, those people who couldn't get enough of their lover. She never thought she'd become one of them.

Sebastjan leaned next to a closed door and let the retinal scanner read his eyes. The door slid open and he pulled her in.

"Welcome, Dr. Walter," an animated voice said.

Ariella came up behind him, reached for his ass, squeezing the firm cheek. He took a deep breath. She let her hand slide around his hip. To her surprise, he pulled away from her touch.

"I need you to step into the medical booth for scanning," Sebastjan said. "This is important."

Ariella looked around the private exam room, finally registering where they were. She forced all expression out of her face and all emotion from her voice. "Why?"

"I don't wish to alarm you, but Dr. Lu mentioned he found some anomalies in your scans. They have the most up-to-date equipment here. He has given me permission to use this room to test—"

"No." Ariella shook her head. "This isn't necessary. I'm fine. There's no need to—"

"It's just a scan. There's no reason to be scared," he tried to assure her. "I'll be right here the whole time."

"I'm fine. I swear it." Ariella looked at the booth. "It's being taken care of."

"Ariella," he insisted, stepping to block the door. Worry filled his eyes. "I'm a doctor. You're my wife. Why won't you let me scan you? What are you hiding?"

She took a step for the medical booth. Her hands shook as she touched the side. "It's a small thing. It's being taken care of."

"I insist."

"I—" The lasers turned on before she even stepped inside the scanner. She closed her eyes briefly before doing as he asked. Ariella hoped he'd find whatever it was his father had done to her.

A loud blare sounded overhead. Ariella screamed in surprise at the suddenness of it. Her back hit the wall in alarm.

"Containment," the automated system announced, as a plastic wall slid down from the ceiling, trapping her on one side of the room. "Containment. Exam one. Terminal. Containment. Security level one. Containment."

Ariella stared at Sebastjan's stunned face. The automated message repeated. Sebastjan reached for an electronic clipboard without looking directly at it. Instead, his eyes focused on hers as if he could read the cause of the sudden trouble in her face. His hand hit the wall several times before he found the device. His lips moved, but she couldn't hear him. She shook her head in denial, motioning to her ears.

"Containment. Exam one. Terminal. Containment."

Chapter Fourteen

"Sebastjan! What is the meaning of this? What have you done?" Supreme Walter demanded from the exam room door. It had taken nearly fifteen minutes for it to open after Ariella's containment started. The facility sensors had been testing the exam room air to make sure it and Dr. Sebastjan Walter were safe. "We have equipment at home. You should never have brought her in here."

Sebastjan glared at his father. "Did you know about her condition? Why haven't the home monitors picked up on it?"

"Of course I know," his father quipped. "I know everything that happens in my city. You're first doctor on scene. Clear her so we can go home. I will deal with the two of you in private."

"Then you also know it's not a natural condition," Sebastjan insisted, ignoring the threat. He looked at Ariella, knowing she couldn't hear them. She stood against the plastic shield, hands lifted, palms and fingers pressed so hard they turned white. Her large eyes stared at them. She looked terrified.

"Of course I know." The Medical Supreme frowned. "Clear her. Now."

"What did you do? Program the home monitors so they wouldn't show her abnormality?" Sebastjan refused to hand over the clipboard.

"What's wrong with her? Did you think to trick me into marrying someone who is...sick?"

Sebastjan's stomach tightened. He again looked at his clipboard. The anomaly didn't make sense. It wasn't natural, but he'd never seen anything like it. He began tapping the electronic interface, examining the molecular structure.

"It's not a—" Sebastjan began.

"It's nothing you'd recognize." His father snatched the clipboard away. "Perhaps if you had stayed here and worked with me like I'd asked you to."

"You mean like you ordered me to," Sebastjan corrected as he tried to grab the clipboard back. "What did you do to Ariella?"

"You should thank me. I trained her to be the perfect doctor's wife. She will do as she's told and if she doesn't..." Supreme Walter set the clipboard down decisively. "Clear her now or you can forget about my signing off on those handhelds and any future funding for your research facility."

"That threat is empty and we both know it. Besides, I've already authorized the posting of my preliminary findings to several predominate scientists. I'd like to see you explain your reasoning to them."

"Don't threaten me, son. You're not skilled enough for it."

"It wasn't a threat."

Sebastjan looked at his wife. She stared at his father. Her face was hard, but he saw the fear in her eyes. He tried not to believe his father capable of anything so diabolical. Sure, the man was manipulative and shrewd, but this? Would his father really go so far as to poison a woman just to control her?

"This is how you got her to marry me, isn't it? You made sure she was well and then forced her to marry me by holding the cure hostage from her." He felt sick to his stomach and his heart began to beat a little faster. The wall monitor instantly brought up his stats.

Supreme Walter eyed the wall unit and frowned. "Calm yourself. I did it for you, for the family. You refused to consider any of the women I found for you. Dr. Sanda had too much invested in the marine facility. Sans Franuk was too tall. Sans Gretchen too obnoxious and attention seeking. Sans Angeluv too messy. Ariella is perfect for you. I've made sure of it. The only way I could have found you a more malleable bride is if I built a woman from scratch. If it were possible, I would have done so. But I am merely a man."

Sebastjan frowned. The humble words hardly suited the Medical Supreme. He'd begun to feel something for Ariella, but now, with his father's words, he became worried. What if the woman he knew was merely an act orchestrated by his father? What if her behavior, her attraction toward him, was pretend? What if her affections ended with her illness?

"If you're not pleased with her lack of experience, train her or take a lover. You're married now. That's all I care about. Procedures can be done to ensure she has a legitimate son and the family name will be carried on." Supreme Walter walked to the isolation chamber and tapped on the clear plastic, like examining a specimen in a jar. Ariella pulled away from him, edging to the far side of the chamber. "Let her out of there. You see how scared she is. The longer this continues, the more you risk damaging our reputations."

"Reputations?" Sebastjan demanded, enraged. "You poison a woman and you're worried about how it will look for your reputation? Maybe you should have thought about that before you did what you did. You want her cleared? Fine. Tell me then, how do we reverse whatever it is you've done? Can you even reverse it?"

"Of course I can."

Sebastjan closed his eyes briefly before grabbing the clipboard. He began tapping instructions on the top of it.

"What are you doing?" the Medical Supreme demanded. "Give me that."

Sebastjan jerked away from him. "I'm sending a copy of her medical records to my facility office. If you don't cure her, I'll make what you've done public."

"You wouldn't dare."

Sebastjan cleared his wife, ending her isolation. The plastic shield slid up and a light, sterilizing mist sprinkled over them. Ariella was breathing heavy and shaking. Her eyes flew to Supreme Walter. "They must have scanned me when we walked in. I didn't know this would happen. I didn't say anything. I promise I didn't say anything."

"She's making a scene. Take her, Sebastjan, and meet me at home. I'll take care of Dr. Lu and Dr. Swift." Supreme Walter stormed from the room, mumbling under his breath.

"Come with me, Ariella. All will be well." Sebastjan took her arm and led her toward the door. "Let's get out of here. We can talk in the transport."

Chapter Fifteen

"I wanted to tell you," Ariella said the second the transport door closed and they were alone. "I never meant to keep it from you."

"You should have told me." Sebastjan's brow furrowed in concentration as he studied her from the opposite seat. She wondered what he was thinking. It was impossible to tell.

"He said if I told you he'd take away my cure and I'd die a horrific death." She looked at her hands, studying the lines. "I tried to get away once, to test it. Within six hours I was..." Her hands began to shake at the memory. It started with nausea and built into a blinding headache. She'd been stumbling and incoherent. When Supreme Walter found her, she'd been curled into a ball. He'd only given her relief after she begged for it.

"Tell me," Sebastjan urged crossing over to sit beside her.

Ariella obeyed and told him everything. What did she have to lose now? Besides, his nearness was comforting—his smell, the sound of his voice, the brush of his leg to hers, the gentle tug of his fingers against her hair. When she finished, she added, "I wanted to tell you, but I wasn't sure what he'd do. I'm still not sure. I've seen that look on his face before. He's not happy and he's capable of mean things when he's not happy."

"I see." Sebastjan loosened his hold on her. "That is his game. He thinks to keep you at his house and by extension keep me. I'm sorry you were brought into this. My father was not pleased when I left Asclepius. He wants to groom me to be Medical Supreme, to keep the title in the family."

"You don't want to be Medical Supreme?" Even as she said it, she knew his answer. No. She saw the light in his eyes when he talked about going back to his research facility. He wanted out of the mansion as badly as she did.

"No. I have no use for the politics that consume my father's life. I want to do research and make a real difference in the future of my people. That will be my legacy, not approving funding proposals and hosting evening sustenance parties."

"I think yours will be the nobler legacy." Ariella took a deep breath. Her words soft, she asked, "Do you think you can cure what he did?"

"Given enough time."

"Within six hours?" She gave a wry laugh, not finding humor in her situation.

Sebastjan looked as if he wanted to tell her yes, but he slowly shook his head in denial. "No, not in six hours, not even if I had a fully stocked lab at my disposal. In six months if I was lucky, six weeks if I was very lucky."

Ariella leaned toward the transport window and looked out over the passing city. Light gleamed on the cases surrounding the plants and glistened on the perfect sidewalks, reflecting like tiny jewels. As the mansion came into view, she said, "I don't want to go back to the mansion. Not yet."

Sebastjan reached for the consul, overriding the transport's automatic coordinates. "I'll set it to take us through the arboretum. It won't be too busy this time of day."

She swayed into him as the transport turned a corner. Ariella found comfort in the heat of his body close to hers and didn't pull back. His hand trailed down the side of her arm. "You should leave.

Go back to your research facility. I'm not sure he'll ever give me a cure. Take samples of my blood, or whatever else you need with you. Maybe someday when you find what's wrong with me, you can come back. I can't leave and I can't ask you to stay here. There is no reason why we should both be held prisoner."

Sebastjan didn't answer right away. "I won't leave you with him. I promise. We'll find a way to make you well."

Ariella drew her mouth to his. When they touched, he felt so familiar, as if she'd known him her whole life. She trusted him on a base, primitive level, even if logic told her she hadn't known him long enough.

"There are some things you just know," she whispered against his lips, answering her own thought.

"What?" He pulled away, quizzical.

"Nothing," she quickly amended. She placed her hand on his strong thigh, feeling it flex. "I was merely thinking of the arboretum. You said it wasn't going to be busy this time of day?"

"It—" Sebastjan's breath caught as she slid her hand higher, "shouldn't, ah, be."

"Good." She boldly cupped her hand around his growing member and massaged gently. He opened his thighs as he adjusted his hips on the seat. He sat back, allowing her complete access to his body. She tugged at his clothing, wanting him naked. Ariella jerked the pants from his hips and pushed his shirt aside.

Sebastjan's hands were on her, stripping her of her clothing as she continued to stroke him to full arousal. The transport turned, rocking them to the left. A flash of green passed outside the window as they turned into the arboretum. Ariella loved this place. Though separated from their human visitors, the green landscape stretched before them —trees, flowers and shrubs. Workers in stark white containment suits moved through the gardens, tending the foliage, picking up fallen leaves, plucking dying flowers.

When they were naked, Sebastjan pulled her body over his. She straddled his legs, balancing on the seat. He held on to her, keeping her from falling back. Hungrily, he pulled a nipple deep into his mouth. Moaning, he sucked and licked.

She tried to angle her body to accept his, but he held tight to her hips, gripping her hard. His lips moved to the opposite side, wetting the nipple he found there. Ariella tried again to impale her pussy on his shaft. He gently pushed her back.

"Sit," he urged, pushing her across the transport to the opposite seat.

Her ass pressed against the smooth, comfortable surface. Sebastjan's eyes lit as knelt before her on the transport floor. He nudged the inside of her knee, lifting her calf onto his shoulder. He kissed along the inside of her thigh, making the torturously slow journey up her leg. Lips pressed, tickled, brushed and sucked. His tongue flicked along her flesh, marking his path with delicate sweeps. Ariella tensed as he made his way toward the apex of her thighs. A firm hand on her thigh pressed it open.

"You look very beautiful in daylight," Sebastjan said, jerking her hips forward. He wrapped his arm under her leg, keeping it on his shoulder, as he kept the other one held open. He licked his lips slowly. His eyes flickered with meaning. "I want to watch you find release."

He buried his face in her pussy. Ariella gasped, arching into him. Her eyes lazily moved to the window, watching for anyone who might be looking inside.

Sebastjan moaned, fucking her with his mouth. He nipped at her clit, biting lightly before sucking it between his teeth. She grabbed onto the back of his head, rocking into him. His tongue slid along her sex, dipping inside her before moving up the slit.

Ariella gasped, grabbing her breasts as pleasure rippled over her. It was wicked and wanton and they could be caught at any moment should the transport pass anyone walking along the arboretum path. The hint of danger heightened her excitement. Her heart beat faster. She worked her legs against Sebastjan. He didn't stop, even as his eyes lifted to watch her.

It felt so good that she had to close her eyes. Tremors racked over her, radiating from her pussy, over her stomach and thighs. She came against his mouth, gasping and jerking.

When his lips finally stopped moving and he withdrew from her, she looked at him. He took a seat across from her. She breathed hard. He sat naked. His hand brushed along his leg, slow and steady.

Taking his cock in hand, he stroked himself. His eyes roamed freely over her naked body. He licked his wet lips, moaning softly as if he could still taste her on them. His hand tightened, sliding up and down his thick shaft.

Ariella's body began to tingle with anticipation. His lips had been nice, but she wanted the fullness of him moving inside her, thrusting and filling, pushing and pulling. The needy ache filled her and she touched her sex. Her fingers slid in the moisture left from his mouth.

She glanced around the inside of the transport, wondering how best to position herself so they could come together. As if reading her mind, he said, "Get on your knees and face the window."

Ariella turned to the side, drawing her knees onto the cushioned seat. He came behind her, forcing her to crawl closer to the window so he could fit. Sebastjan braced one foot on the floor and one knee on the seat. He took her by her hips.

The tip of his cock probed her sex as he positioned their bodies. With a groan, he impaled her on his shaft. Ariella saw his passing reflection in the windowpane as a ray of light broke through the trees.

He took her hard and sure, somehow managing to keep their bodies together in the precarious position. Her hands dug into the cushion. They slammed together wildly. Tremors worked over her as she came again. His cry joined hers as he met with release.

Sebastjan fell back. She collapsed next to him, nestling against his chest. He kissed her temple and wrapped his arms around her. For a long moment, they didn't speak. The plant life passed in silence.

"Are you certain every place on this plane doesn't keep its plant life encased?" Ariella asked, more whimsical than searching for an answer she already knew. "I miss the smell of nature. I think I'm going to scream if I'm misted with sterilizer one more time."

"Have you never been out of the city?" he asked, before answering his own question. "Of course you haven't. My father doesn't like to travel out of the city. He thinks everyone outside of high social circles of Asclepius are unworthy of his time."

"Let's not talk about him," she said. An unspoken tension fell over them. They had no choice but to go back to the mansion and face Supreme Walter.

"Agreed." Sebastjan pulled her closer. "Only the larger cities keep their nature locked up thanks to the old Medical Supreme's edict. Where I live we're much more relaxed. We even have a courtyard filled with flowers and vines."

"I wish I could show you my home world. It's nothing like this. Asclepius is so sterile, not only literally, but in its art. Everything is carved in straight lines. We have these beautiful sculptures—bold rounded figures, fanciful expressions, as if the human figure was captured in all its perfections and imperfections before being put into stone."

His hand moved lazily over her breast. "Perhaps someday we'll go there."

"Perhaps." Though Ariella knew she would never go back. Without her family, her home would be a hollow shell of what she remembered. At least this way, her family lived in her memory and she could imagine they were still out there, surviving on a plane of reality she couldn't see. Maybe even now, they stood, outside the transport box, as invisible to this world as air, running and laughing just beyond her range of vision.

"We should get dressed. The scenic trail will end soon and the transport will take us back." He kissed her temple. "I think I have an idea how to deal with my father."

"What will you do?"

"What he's been trying to get me to do for a long time now. I'm going to act like he does."

Chapter Sixteen

"Y ou'll be happy to know that your indiscretion today will not be on record," Supreme Walter said as Ariella and Sebastjan joined him for their evening sustenance.

Sebastjan glanced at his wife, remembering all too well what they'd done in the transport. He hadn't meant for it to happen, but when Ariella looked at him he couldn't resist her. She hesitated, her hand gripping the back of her chair.

"Our indiscretion?" Ariella asked when no one spoke. She moved slowly take a seat.

"I spoke with Dr. Lu and Dr. Swift," Supreme Walter continued, taking a small taste off the plate in front of him. Sebastjan hid his sigh of relief when he realized his father meant the quarantine. He didn't want to talk about his private moments with Ariella. "They will be enjoying their new equipment acquisitions purchased from your laboratory's budget."

"I want you to cure whatever it is you did to Ariella," Sebastjan stated as he took his seat at the long, metal table.

"I will not be dictated to," Supreme Walter stated. He took another bite. Sebastjan knew it was an effort to look calm and controlled. Inside, the man would be raging mad.

"I want you to cure whatever it is you did to Ariella," Sebastjan repeated, keeping his tone even, "or it won't just be my lab's budget that ends up paying people off. I'll take her to every facility in the city and have her scanned. Then, just for fun, I'll spread the rumor that every public building needs to upgrade for viruses because there's something new and nasty that slipped through the Divinity portals. I'll whisper and hint and others will listen because I am your son. Your reign as Medical Supreme will be known as a time of disease and chaos."

"You are bluffing. You wouldn't dare cause a planetary panic just to get even with me." Supreme Walter smiled. "You take your position as a doctor too seriously. Panic and chaos lead to injury and death."

"What I want you to ask yourself," Sebastjan pushed up from the table without touching his food, "is whether my sense of duty as a doctor outweighs my dislike of you and everything you stand for."

His father's smile instantly faded.

"Ariella?" Sebastjan motioned for her to follow him. She stood, not speaking. To his father, he said, "You have three hours to arrange it. We'll be waiting for your answer. Oh, and while we're discussing it, leave my laboratory's budget alone."

Chapter Seventeen

"I can't believe you said all those things to him. When you said you were going to act like him, I thought you meant you were going to do something asinine or worse, like try to take his job as Medical Supreme." Ariella could barely contain her excitement, even as Sebastjan seemed stiff and irritated from dealing with Supreme Walter. "Did you see his face? He was speechless. I've never seen him speechless. His mouth actually opened and he didn't know what to say."

Sebastjan chuckled at her words. He relaxed some as he led her up the mansion stairs toward her room.

"I love you for that," she continued. Then, realizing what she'd said, she stopped walking. "I mean, I love...that...you did that."

His eyes softened. "I knew what you meant."

"I mean, I appreciate what you said to him." Ariella swallowed nervously as he looked at her. Why was she still justifying her statement? The monitor on the wall beeped, capturing her attention. She blushed to see that her heartbeat was elevated and that several of her levels had risen. The screen informed that a shot had been ordered to calm her. When she glanced at Sebastjan's stats, she saw that he also had elevated levels.

"Would you like to find out?" He cupped her cheek, tracing her lips with his thumb.

"Find out?" She looked at him, curious.

"It's a series of chemicals the body produces. We traded medical research with another plane that had done extensive mapping of brain chemicals. They're easy enough to read."

"What is?"

"They call the chemical phenylethylamine—"

"No," Ariella stopped him. "Not what it's called. I won't understand what you're saying anyway. Find out what? What is a series of chemicals?"

"Emotions." His fingers slid along her throat, gently pressing into her hair only to pull out again. "Happiness. Love."

"Oh, I think that someone would know, I mean, the test isn't necessary for the..." She had no clue what she was saying. "Does it matter to you how I feel?"

The question seemed to surprise him. "Of course it matters. You're my wife. I know we didn't meet as couples normally do, but we both chose each other despite the persuasion of my father. There is an easiness between us, even a friendship. I care what you think and how you feel."

Ariella hadn't expected such candor from him. She'd seen his kindness, felt it in his touch, but she'd never expected him to express it in words. She wasn't sure she could be as articulate at the moment. She glanced at the monitor, feeling exposed by the way it told anyone who looked of her fast heartbeat, her quickened breath. But more poignantly, she felt exposed by the fact that he could read what the monitors said better than she could. "I care for you as well."

"I think that is a good start." Sebastjan drew her forward and pressed his mouth to hers. His tongue slid past her lips, hungrily devouring her with his passion. She stiffened for the briefest of moments before melting against him. All thoughts filtered out of her mind until all she could feel was the man before her.

She backed him toward the wall. His head bumped the monitor and he groaned. When she would have pulled back, he kept her from leaving him. He slid along the wall to a more comfortable position.

His hands moved freely over her clothes, fumbling to unbutton her shirt. His hand slipped beneath the material, enveloping her breast in his palm. He pinched her nipple. The sensitive bud peaked at the attention.

Ariella pulled at his clothing, reaching to the front of his pants. She rubbed his arousal, moaning softly to find him ready for her.

Suddenly, he pushed her back. "Ariella, wait."

She blinked, shocked that he stopped her until she saw him looking down the stairwell.

"We should go..." He looked toward his room.

"Come on," Ariella pulled him with her, moving to her room instead. It was closer and she wasn't sure she could wait. She needed him, wanted him. Her skin begged for his touch. Her nerves tingled with anticipation. The door slid open and she hurried through.

"Sans Ariella, I have your—ah!"

Ariella pulled away from Sebastjan at the sound of the maid's shock. She glanced around her husband, quickly adjusting her clothing.

"I have your injection." The maid lifted a shot.

Sebastjan growled under his breath, reaching for the shot. "I'll give it to her. Go."

The maid rushed from the room and the door shut behind her.

Ariella chuckled. She automatically leaned her head to the side. Sebastjan tossed the shot onto the floor, not bothering to inject her.

"But..." Ariella made a move to go after it.

"Leave it," he said. "No more medicine from my father's house. No more food. No more anything."

"No more anything?" Ariella pouted her lower lip. She reached forward to cup his cock. "Anything?"

Sebastjan chuckled. Instead of answering, he tore off his shirt and threw it over the syringe. Ariella tugged at her clothes, eagerly stripping. When they came together, naked flesh pressed against flesh. She reached between them and stroked his arousal. His breathing deepened, catching in his throat.

"I want you," she whispered, nipping at his ear.

Sebastjan spun her around, placing her on the bed. The swift action pulled her hand from his arousal. He ground his hips into her, undulating as she rocked up to join him. His cock rubbed along the wet folds of her pussy, stroking just right. Cream moistened her sex, allowing him to glide against her.

"I want you, too," he said, the word a hoarse growl of emotion as he drew the tip of his shaft to enter her.

Sebastjan pushed up. He grabbed her by the back of her knee, pulling it up to better allow for his claiming. Then, with a hard push, he plunged into her depths, burying himself to the hilt. Her pussy tightened around him.

Ariella met his thrusts with her own. Their hips slammed together. And even though they were bound by the prison walls of her room, she felt free because she had hope. The sensations of ecstasy built.

She came, stiffening beneath him. Sebastjan answered her body's call, releasing into her. He collapsed next to her. His tousled hair and flushed features were more handsome than anything she'd ever seen.

A slow smile curled the side of his mouth. "Pack your things. We're leaving here the second you're cured."

Chapter Eighteen

Ariella peered at the Medical Supreme across the Central Hospital meeting room. She wished she could hear what the doctors were saying. According to Supreme Walter, she'd be cured within the hour—just as soon as he finished a procedure. Dr. Lu stood next to him, looking stern and slightly irritated. Next to them, Sebastjan crossed his arms as he listened to everything his father said. Since she wasn't a doctor with medical clearance, Ariella had not been allowed into the conversation.

When Sebastjan glanced at her, he gave her a small, comforting smile. She returned the look, lifting her hand in acknowledgement. It seemed like an eternity before they motioned her to come over. She did, crossing the distance until she stood across from Sebastjan.

"You have to take a trip through the portal. Arrangements have been made with a plane we have trade agreements with," Sebastjan said.

"I'm being traded?" Ariella gasped.

"No, don't be ridiculous," the Medical Supreme said. "Dr. Lu, leave us." Dr. Lu nodded his head and stepped out of the room. "I designed what you have to dissipate if you were to use Divinity's portal. It's the only way to get rid of what you have."

Ariella stiffened. The way the man said it, so matter-of-fact, so unapologetic. She frowned. "So no one would know what you did if I managed to run away to a plane you don't control."

"I liked you better before I married you to my son," Supreme Walter stated.

"But she's right, isn't she?" Sebastjan frowned. "If she's going, then I'm going though the portal too."

"You can't," Ariella denied. "I don't trust him." She turned to the Medical Supreme. "I don't trust you."

"Like I would abandon my only son on a primitive plane with a bunch of barbarians." Supreme Walter eyed her as if she were a stupid girl.

I really hate you, she thought, but kept quiet.

"Dr. Lu knows we are going. The blue mineral water is too important to this plane to risk ruining a trade agreement with Staria. If we don't come back, Staria will be blamed and our people will demand we take action." Sebastjan took Ariella by the arm. "We're ready. We'll go, make the trade, and be back."

"I'll have them dial the gate," Supreme Walter said.

"No, I'll get the coordinates from Dr. Lu. I'll dial it myself." Sebastjan led Ariella from the meeting room.

Ariella watched as Sebastian turned dials and pressed buttons on the inter-dimensional portal's consul. Behind them, the square arch of the Divinity portal looked innocuous, like some badly chosen piece of decoration thrust against the wall. A blue glow filled the room, directed at the arch. The arch hid a complex configuration of liquid crystals, electrical currents, mirrors and vacuums. When activated, it was held in check by the wavelength of a specific blue light, which kept the portal inactive. Should the light change, a dimensional shift would occur taking whoever stood on the platform to a new parallel universe.

"Are you nervous? You said you've never dimension traveled before." Ariella stroked his arm.

"No. I am fine," he said. Twelve turn dials indicated the color coding, including intensity and saturation.

"I remember the stories people used to tell of the portals. I was so scared the first time I stepped through. Apparently, in the early days, before they made these destination platforms, travel was a haphazard affair and many of the testers died by materializing inside solid objects. Now Divinity sends out microscopic probes to new planes first."

When all the dials were all set, the blue shifted into a brilliant red light. Sebastjan grinned. "Maybe a little nervous. I'm happy you will be cured and excited to see what another world looks like."

"What do you think your father would do if we never come back?" Ariella asked, chuckling. "Have you ever thought about it? Just going to a new dimension and never coming back here?"

Sebastjan didn't answer. He took her hand and walked toward the platform. The closer they got, the more the light lured them in. Suddenly, the strong gravitational field pulled her off her feet, tearing her hand from his and hurling her toward the back of the platform.

Ariella, knowing what was to come, tucked her arms in and closed her eyes tight. The concentrated red light burned her flesh and every cell in her body felt as if it had turned to lead. She couldn't move, even as her body was pulled apart on a molecular level. Seconds later, the sensations stopped and her body was dropped onto a hard surface with a heavy thud.

Coughing, she automatically rolled to the side. Sebastjan nearly landed on top of her. All around them, the blue glow shone. Ariella searched her surroundings. They were in cavelike clearing. The stone walls were etched with the tool marks made to carve them. A domed arch with a back and two side walls covered the platform. Every Divinity portal had a different look to it, but the main construct remained the same.

Sebastjan pushed up. "Ariella? How are you? How do you feel?"

Ariella gave a weak laugh and moaned, "Ow. I hate that part."

"I didn't imagine portal travel would be so painful." He took a deep breath and felt along his limbs as if checking to be sure they were still intact.

"It gets more bearable with time," came a woman's voice, "or perhaps we just get used to it."

Sebastjan helped Ariella to her feet.

"Welcome to Battlewar Castle. I'm Lady Lilith of Firewall. I will be your contact while you are here." Lady Lilith smiled. Her straight blonde hair fell freely about her shoulders and she had kind blue eyes. The tight fit of her white corset outlined her waist and hips, showcasing a generous amount of cleavage. Long skirts billowed around her legs, the dark crimson a stark contrast to the white. Ariella tried not to stare. "You must be new to portal travel. Though, if I recall correctly from my visits to plane 187, not many of your people have stepped through the portal. You usually have people brought to you. I am honored you would come."

Behind the woman, a bodyguard stood, his arms crossed in a protective gesture. He was a burly figure, dressed in a hard leather jerkin and dark breeches. Metal diamonds plated the leather, creating a symmetrical pattern over his thick chest.

"I am Dr. Sebastjan Walter and this is my wife, Ariella," Sebastjan said. "We are honored you would have us for your guests."

"Married?" Lilith looked Ariella over. "That's probably for the best. Single women tend to get claimed rather quickly around here."

"Yes, I'm married," Ariella confirmed, inching closer to her husband.

"Walter, you say?" Lilith arched a brow. "As in Medical Supreme Walter?"

"The same," Sebastjan acknowledged. "He is my father."

"Will there be more of you?" Lilith glanced at the platform. "The Medical Supreme usually travels with at least a dozen armed men when he leaves your capital city—or so I've been informed."

Sebastjan led Ariella forward into the cave. Her legs shook nervously. All she had seen was a cave, a woman and one guard and she could still tell this world was going to be unlike any she'd ever dreamed of seeing. Sebastjan said, "No. We come alone. No guards. Your intentions in negotiation have never been hostile. When we knew you as Divinity Analyst Sans Lilith Grian, you always treated us fairly. I'm sure we'll be able to negotiate for the supplies you need."

Though hardly tense, Lilith seemed to relax at his words. She motioned toward a stairwell. "Please, follow me."

They walked through mazelike corridors of blue-gray stone. Torches burned from their places on the wall. Ariella breathed deeply, loving the smell of stone and fire. The ever so subtle hint of dust tickled her nose.

Lady Lilith brought them to a large dining area. Bright light came from a large fireplace along a far side of the room. Woven tapestries lined the walls in strips of material, showcasing coats of arms and various symbols.

A few warrior men sat at the tables, whispering amongst themselves. Though gruff in appearance, most of them looked recently bathed. Some wore lightweight tunics, others leather jerkins like the guards, others light chainmail and pieces of armor, and still others wore no shirt at all. Big metal goblets had been set before them, next to matching pitchers. She'd thought the guards were scary, but some of these men were practically gigantic. Muscles bulged, littered with puckered scars and tattooed designs.

When Lilith saw Ariella looking around, she said, "Battlewar Castle may look rough, but that is to be expected from a fortress designed by men constantly at war. Hopefully though, that will change now that this plane has found some peace. That is why there aren't too many warriors here now. They've all gone home to their families. As you can see, this plane is fairly rustic when compared to 187, but I assure you, you have nothing to fear."

"Oh, I'm not frightened. It reminds me of home in some ways. More so than 187." Ariella took another deep breath. "Smells like it too."

"You are not from 187?" Lilith asked.

"No, but it's my home now." Ariella refused to say more and Lilith didn't ask. Sebastjan's hand slid across her back in reassurance.

"Please join me at the high table. We can go over the details and, considering everything goes well, there will be a celebration tonight in honor of a successful negotiation." Lilith smiled. "We at Staria love any reason to celebrate."

Chapter Nineteen

"How are you feeling? It's been six hours," Sebastjan touched his wife's arm. He knew he was concerned without reason. She smiled brightly at him, her cheeks flushed, her laugh warm, her eyes bright.

Turning her gaze from where she looked over the hall of Starian people, Ariella leaned over to kiss him. "I'm well. I promise. Now, try your drink. You wouldn't want to be rude."

Sebastjan looked at the goblet before him. He liked to think he was open-minded and didn't live in fear, but having been raised on a sterile planet, with sustenance that was specifically designed for him, he found himself apprehensive to try what the Starians put before them.

At Ariella's playfully challenging gaze, he lifted the goblet to his lips and sipped. The sweet flavor was strange, like nothing he'd ever had before, and though completely different he couldn't help sipping again.

"You look like a child who was just given his first sweet." Ariella laughed.

Sebastjan took another drink. The hall erupted into a crescendo of good-natured laughter and cheering, though he hardly thought the merriment directed at his bravery in tasting the foreign drink. The men who filled the large area were boisterous and loud and covered in primitive black markings and scars. The women danced and laughed and teased. He'd never seen any gathering of people so happy. A raw, potent energy radiated from them—expressed in male posturing, female temptations and an unapologetically open sexuality.

"Mm," Ariella whispered against his ear. "I'm proud of you. That couldn't have been easy for you to try a drink from here."

As the heat from her lips brushed against him, Sebastjan took a deep breath. Lust threaded through his veins, emanating from the drink in his stomach, filtering through his limbs, filling his cock. A few of the couples in the crowd kissed passionately and, though he couldn't be one hundred percent sure, he thought he'd seen a couple of women slip beneath the tables to pleasure their men.

"I see you're not like your father in many ways," Lilith said, joining them. Her cheeks were flushed and her eyes glistened with an inner mischief. Sebastjan stiffened, glad the table hid his arousal. "He never partakes of our foods."

A giant of a man sat next to Lilith. He snorted at her comment but didn't speak. Dark hair framed his face in thick waves, not so long as to touch his shoulders. His eyes were a hard brown, until he looked at Lilith. Then they softened.

Sebastjan relaxed and smiled. Feeling strangely calm, he said, "My father and I agree on very little."

Lady Lilith knew a lot about his homeworld, having been there several times before her present assignment on Staria. The few times he'd met with her, he found her likable and easy to talk to. She had been a great source of information about this new plane and was the whole reason trade had been set up between Staria and Chiron in the first place.

"May I present my husband, Lord Sorin of Firewall," Lilith said, gesturing to the big man next to her.

"Welcome," Sorin said, nodding. Like the other men, his manners and voice were gruff. He exuded an almost violent charm, as if at any moment he'd jump up from his seat and begin to fight. Looking at the man's fists, Sebastjan knew he'd be deadly.

"I've ordered rooms readied for you, should you decide to stay," Lilith said, leaning forward to look at Ariella. "You are most welcome. I'd be happy to show you around the city market tomorrow. You might enjoy it."

"Can we?" Ariella asked him. Sebastjan saw her excitement and nodded. Her hand brushed his leg. At that moment, he'd give her almost anything.

Have you ever thought about it? Just going to a new dimension and never coming back here? Her words echoed through him. In that moment, if she were to ask him to leave everything behind for her, he'd say yes.

"Wonderful!" Lilith announced. She continued to speak, but Sebastjan couldn't think past the hand resting on his thigh.

Ariella grinned, knowing she had to look like a drunken fool but unable to help it. The heady liquor affected her body. Even the meal of warm bread, seasoned meats and delicious cheeses couldn't counteract the effects of the alcohol. She wasn't sure she wanted it to. Staria wasn't exactly home, but it was strong and primal and the exact opposite of Chiron.

Somewhere in the hall a woman screamed playfully. The sound was followed by a sharp rise in male laughter. Lilith paused in her conversation with her husband. It was clear to all she was in love with the man.

Ariella turned her gaze to Sebastjan. "I like being here. It's almost like my visit to Asclepius never happened."

"I'm glad it did," Sebastjan answered. His eyes had a slight glaze to them. Fingers slid onto her thigh, massaging the muscle. "If you never visited my world, we wouldn't be here now." His hand moved to her hip. "We never would have met." He touched her waist, drawing her against his side. "I think to never have met you would have been a sad thing indeed."

Sebastjan turned to Lilith, whispering to the woman. Within moments, a guard was leading them through the passageways toward a private sleeping chamber complete with trunk, large fur-covered bed and a disturbing amount of weaponry hanging on the wall. A fire burned in a fireplace, heating the room and casting it with flickering orange light.

"This place." Sebastjan looked around. "It's like a child's tale from school. I feel like I've stepped into a book."

"I felt like that the first time I went through the portals," Ariella admitted. She pulled on his shirt, drawing him near. "I walked around, feeling as if nothing was real or that I'd stepped into some sort of strange underground society on my world instead being in a Divinity facility."

"Oh, I definitely feel as if this world is real." He grinned, stroking her cheek. "Very real, and soft, and pretty and—"

Ariella laughed, cutting him off. "And perhaps a little drunk?"

"Perhaps a little. I've never felt quite like this from the liquor on our plane." He gave her a lopsided grin. "Though, that could be because at the first sign of any fun, the medical systems alert us to take a shot of correction medication." Before she could again speak, he kissed her. He rocked his hips against her, letting her feel the unmistakable ache of his desire. When he stopped, he held her close. "I've never felt quite like this around any other woman."

He placed his hands on the small of her back, rubbing in circles. Desire wound through her body, unfurling from her stomach. Ariella ran her fingers into his hair. She tasted the sweet tang of liquor on his tongue when they kissed. She wanted him desperately, wanted to feel him inside her. His kisses became aggressive as he nipped at her mouth, drawing her bottom lip between his teeth.

A weight had lifted from her the moment they stepped through the portal and her mood only continued to lighten the longer they stayed in Battlewar Castle. Moaning weakly, she turned her mouth from his and took a deep breath.

"Let's never leave," Ariella whispered. "Let's stay here and make love every night. You can be a lord and I a lady. We'll get a castle. I'll wear tight, corseted dresses. You'll tend to battle wounds and heal scars."

"You have no idea how tempting that is right now." Sebastjan nuzzled her throat, devouring her with deep, passionate kisses. He traced his tongue along her jawline to her ear, where he nipped the lobe. His hard breath resounded in her ear. "You taste sweet."

Her heart beat wildly. Before she realized what was happening, he had her undressed. Sebastjan tossed her clothes aside and began working on his own.

Ariella crawled onto the large bed. The fur tickled in all the right ways. She stretched her arms over her head, lengthening her body. Sebastjan watched with eager eyes. The second his shirt hit the floor, he crawled onto the bed and stretched out next to her.

"Don't move," he said, drawing the back of his hand along the valley of her breasts. His touch whispered over her flesh, sweeping over her stomach and legs, circling her knees, traveling between her parted thighs before making the trip back up her body.

Ariella squirmed restlessly against the bed. Sebastjan moved to settle between her knees. She reached for him, stroking his hair as he placed tiny kisses against her inner thighs.

"So soft and smooth," he said, licking the tender flesh were leg met pussy. Ariella tensed as he blew lightly against the sensitive bud of her sex. He took his time, drawing out the pleasure until she begged him to finish it. He slipped a finger inside her, wiggling and stroking her pussy.

She clutched at his shoulders, pulling him up. He kissed a breast on his way past, before bringing his cock to the slick folds of her sex. A light sheen of sweat covered them, causing the fur to stick to her back. Sebastjan entered her hard and sure. She gasped at the wondrous sensations.

The world seemed to spin around them. Sensations flooded through her, propelled on by the thrusting of their bodies, the soft pants of her voice and the harder grunts of his. Suddenly, she came, tensing as pleasure rippled over her. His release met hers in loud, primitive awareness.

Sebastjan rolled onto the mattress next to her. Ariella watched him close his eyes and take a deep, steadying breath. She placed her hand on his chest to feel the fast beat of his heart and he instantly covered it with his own. She wanted to breathe him in for the rest of her life. She wanted to live in that moment forever, surrounded by the stone of castle walls, lightheaded from a combination of drink and sex.

"I think I love you, Ariella," he whispered.

She smiled, watching to see if he'd open his eyes and say more. He didn't, but that didn't lessen her pleasure at his admission. "I think I love you too, Sebastjan."

Chapter Twenty

Sebastjan's head throbbed, keeping a steady tempo with his heartbeat. Each thump sent a sharp pain from behind his eyes down the back of his head to his neck. He suddenly appreciated the medical monitoring on his home plane. One shot would cure both his drumming head and his blurred vision.

Ariella looked to be in as much pain as he. She kept her movements to a minimum, often rubbing her temples with the tips of her fingers. With the morning, they both realized it would be impossible to stay in Staria, though Lady Lilith did invite them back for a visit whenever they wanted. Ariella readily agreed and promised to return for the tour of the marketplace.

"Good luck with those hangovers." Lilith chuckled as the blue light from the Starian portal washed over them. This time, as the portal activated, taking them back to his home dimension, he was prepared for the sensation of his body being torn apart. Being prepared didn't help his aching head.

Once back in the Central Hospital, a loud alarm sounded. The familiar smell of the hospital's air filtering sterilizer washed over him, cleaning their bodies and clothes.

"Sterilization commencing," the automated male voice commanded. "Please move away from the platform."

They obeyed. A shield came down, blocking the platform from the scan as a series of lights flashed over them, sweeping them for parasites and viruses from parallel worlds.

"Sterilization complete. Welcome back, Dr. Walter. Welcome back, Sans Ariella. Please move to the orange door."

Instead, Sebastjan went to the wall monitor and brought up Ariella's stats. Studying them, he grinned. "The inter-dimensional travel worked. You're fine. Whatever was in your system is gone now."

Ariella touched her temple. "I wouldn't say fine. I still feel the effects of the drinking sickness."

"That is easily cured. I'll find a syringe we can use." He pulled her with him. "If we hurry, we might be able to get out of here before my father comes to lecture us for not returning yesterday."

Chapter Twenty-One

Ariella wasn't one to press her luck when it came to the Medical Supreme, but even she was a little worried when he didn't seek them out at the hospital and wasn't at home. It wasn't like the man to miss an opportunity to lecture. Was it possible Walter had decided to stay out of Sebastjan and her lives? Somehow, she highly doubted it.

"He probably does not wish to face us before we leave for the research facility," Sebastjan said, tossing her travel bag inside the transport.

"But, you have to admit it is strange." She looked up at the mansion, almost unable to believe she was really free. "It's not like him to run away from a problem."

Sebastjan followed her gaze. "You're right, but it's just as well. If I saw him, I'd most likely hit him for what he's done. And as much as I hate it, he is Medical Supreme."

"You can't fight the king," Ariella finished for him with an old saying from her homeworld. "He's too powerful. I'm just happy to be getting out of the city with our lives and our health."

"We can't fight him, but we can be a nuisance," Sebastjan said. "This isn't finished."

"I think the best punishment is to never visit, never speak, never transmit to him. He thrives on the attention. Let's not give it to him." Ariella let him help her into the transport.

When he joined her, giving one last glance at the tall mansion, he said, "At least until we have enough evidence against him to do damage. This time he's gone too far."

As the transport door closed, Ariella sighed and settled against her husband. "Can we discuss revenge later? I just want to enjoy—"

"Sebastjan!" A loud knock sounded outside the transport. "Wait!"

"Who is that?" Ariella asked.

Sebastjan reached to open the transport door. "Dr. Lu? What are you doing here?"

"It's your father," Dr. Lu answered.

"What has he done now?" Sebastjan grimaced.

"He's sick," Dr. Lu said. "Something new we haven't seen before. He collapsed soon after you left. Dr. Swift was called back from his ambassadorial duties and has the Medical Supreme isolated in a private care center. We don't want to cause any panic. That's why they sent me to come find you."

Dr. Lu stepped into the transport, nodding once at Ariella before entering new coordinates. Soon they moved through the city streets.

"What's wrong with him?" she asked. "You don't have any idea?"

Dr. Lu opened his mouth, but gave Sebastjan a hesitant look and didn't speak.

"Talk frankly," Sebastjan said. "We both know what my father has done."

Dr. Lu studied Ariella briefly before nodding. "We suspect whatever he had given you, Sans Ariella, has mutated. We've tested the off-plane doctors and all other recent visitors, but they show no signs of the disease. So far, it is contained. Dr. Swift has recommended full lockdown quarantine. That is all I know at this time."

The transport moved through the city toward the edge of town and stopped before a small square building. The place looked like a warehouse unit with plain exterior walls, flat roof and nondescript stone walkway. Dr. Lu glanced around before stepping quickly out onto the quiet street. He lifted his hand to help Ariella down before leading the way into the front door.

Dimly lit pathways were formed between stacks of wooden crates. They were marked with strange symbols she couldn't read. After taking several turns, they finally came to a dead end. Dr. Lu reached for the crate blocking their path and opened it. Inside stairs led down into the floor.

"Where are we going?" she asked.

"The quarantine laboratory," Sebastjan answered. "We cannot risk keeping the Medical Supreme where he will be seen by others. If word spreads that he is sick, and sick with something we have not seen before, people will panic."

"The problem with a medical plane," Dr. Lu interjected, "is that we do not handle the reality of an epidemic well. In theory, we are invaluable as doctors. In practice..." He lifted his hand to the side in a helpless gesture.

"In practice, it has been so long since our world has seen an epidemic that the people tend to panic at the very idea," Sebastjan said. "The concept is practically unheard of."

"We pride ourselves on our health," Dr. Lu added.

"I see," Ariella said, though their admission hardly surprised her.

At the bottom of the stairs, Dr. Lu opened a door. Light streamed in from the laboratory. In the center of the large room the Medical Supreme rested on a bed surrounded by thick plastic. His ashen features were pulled tight, but his eyes remained as sharp as ever. She could feel the displeasure pouring off him. He didn't like being trapped.

Ariella felt a strange sense of power and fear wash over her— power to see him helpless as she'd once been and fear that whatever was happening to him would eventually happen to her. What if she wasn't cured? What if it didn't matter if she was? Would the people of Chiron let her roam free? Or would they lock her up out of fear?

Sebastjan took her arm. "He can't harm you. Nothing will harm you. I promise."

She quickly nodded her head in understanding, believing her

husband meant what he said. Whispering, she asked, "What if I have what he has?"

"It would have shown up on your scans when you arrived through the portal," Dr. Lu answered.

"Don't stare at me as if I'm on my deathbed," the Medical Supreme ordered. "I still have my wits about me."

"That has always been debatable," Sebastjan answered, walking closer to the isolation booth. "I'm assuming you sent for us?"

"You were supposed to be back yesterday," Walter said.

"I will leave you in privacy to speak," Dr. Lu said, walking quickly through the doorway and up the stairs.

"And yet we came back today," Sebastjan said. Ariella felt the tension in his back and felt sorry for him. For all that the Medical Supreme had done, he was still Sebastjan's father. "The great thing about you being in there, Father, is that we don't have to stay and listen to you. So, tell me, what is it you want?"

"Would you speak to me like that if you knew I was dying?" the Medical Supreme demanded.

"You're not dying, at least not yet." Sebastjan walked over to a monitor and began scrolling through the data. "You're just contagious and have to stay in here." Stopping on a screen, he enlarged a photo of a microscopic organism. "They've isolated the abnormality. There is nothing I can do for you."

"You can act in my stead as Medical Supreme Proxy until I am better. You can live at the mansion while seeing to my duties. You can even fund your precious facility. We'll tell people I have gone on a trip to another plane for medical collection and research and you are training for your future position."

Sebastjan sighed. "No."

"No?" Walter repeated, clearly shocked.

"No," Sebastjan affirmed. "I have told you before. I have no desire to be Medical Supreme."

Walter's pale features filled, becoming flushed. He pushed up on the bed. "Enough of this foolishness. It is your birthright, your duty to be Medical Supreme."

"Did you bring me here to discuss my future or your cure?"

Sebastjan inquired. Ariella didn't move as she watched the interplay between the two men. Walter didn't answer. Sebastjan touched the monitor. "I'm sending a copy of the records to my office. If you want my help, you'll send your private records to me as well. I'll help you from my facility. That is all I can do for you."

"That's all you *will* do." Walter fell back on the bed, glaring. "You have always been your mother's son. She too was an ungrateful—"

"Enough!" Ariella yelled. Both men turned to her, surprised. She gave Sebastjan an apologetic look. To the Medical Supreme, she said, "You are a miserable person. I can honestly say I've never met a more miserable person. That said, the goddesses do not allow me to watch you die. What about taking you through the portal? Will that help?"

"No," Walter said. To her surprise, a snarky comment didn't follow.

"Then there is nothing more we can do for you here," she said. "Your son has offered to work on this problem from his laboratory. Do you want his help?"

For the longest time, the Medical Supreme didn't answer. Then, when she didn't turn her gaze away, he nodded once. The gesture was stiff with anger.

"Very well. Then you will send the files my husband has requested." Ariella moved toward Sebastjan and took his hand. "If you need anything else, perhaps you can find compassion with someone you didn't wrong. But, as you look at these plastic walls, locked away like some tree from the rest of the world, know that the goddesses have laid their justice upon you."

"Goddesses." The Medical Supreme snorted.

"Call it fate, then, if you like," she said. Walter didn't speak again. "Remember me when the insanity of captivity creeps in on you and there is no one you can talk to about it."

"I never locked you up like this," the Medical Supreme said bitterly.

"Gilded bars are still bars," Ariella answered. She saw the light in his eyes darken. There was some grim satisfaction in knowing he was imprisoned by a disease, jailed by his own body and unable to do anything about it. Turning her back on him, she walked away.

Sebastjan finished transmitting the files he needed before making a move to follow his wife. The symmetry of his father's punishment wasn't lost on him, especially since it was done by his own hand.

"Sebastjan," his father said. Sebastjan thought about ignoring him, but something in the man's voice made him stop. "You will work for a cure, won't you? Aside from you, doctors Lu, Swift and Fauchet are the only ones who know. I need you, son."

"I'm not sure you deserve the consideration, but, yes, I will work toward a cure." Sebastjan glanced back to see his father staring at him, the man's eyes pleading. "Unlike you, I would never willingly keep anyone imprisoned if there was something I could do to help. As you said in the past, I take my role as a doctor very seriously."

When he was once more in the transport, Ariella was alone. She said, "Dr. Lu went back to the hospital. Since there is nothing more we can do here, he's wished us well on our trip home."

Sebastjan nodded and began resetting the transport's coordinates. "Part of me wants to let him rot in there."

"You're too good of a man for that." Ariella reached for him, but a light smoke filtered into the transport. Frowning, she covered her mouth and looked as if she would speak. Sebastjan felt his limbs become heavy before his whole world went black.

Chapter Twenty-Two

Ariella blinked, stirring against the thick mattress beneath her body. It took her mind time to focus, but once it did, she shot up on the bed. The smooth walls of the chamber held no decoration, nothing that would set it apart from any other room on dimensional plane 187.

"Hello?" she called only to hear her own voice echo back. "Sebastjan?" Then shivering, she whispered, "Medical Supreme Walter?"

What had Supreme Walter done? Why was she here? Was his illness just a trick to control Sebastjan? And, when it didn't work, did he poison them both with the smoke-filled transport? Dr. Lu had been alone with the unit while the Medical Supreme spoke with them. He would have had time to sabotage their vehicle.

"Sebastjan!" she called louder. Ariella rubbed her arms. Her heart-beat sped and the sudden tension caused her stomach to tighten. What if they'd been separated? What if her words to the Medical Supreme about his own just imprisonment caused him to react to her insolence with a new prison home?

Breathing hard, she went toward the door. It slid open, allowing her out of the room. A long, empty hall with doors lined up on each side stretched before her. She slowly walked toward the end, glancing from side to side.

Touching the smooth, metal wall, she leaned around the corner. The adjoining hall was wider and split into two directions. A couple of doctors with electronic clipboards strode down the hall. They both glanced at her as they passed, but didn't speak and didn't try to stop her.

An arm wound around her waist, jerking her back. She gasped, instantly moving to fight.

"There you are," Sebastjan said. "The computer said your room door had opened and that you were finally awake."

Ariella turned in surprise, hitting his arm. "You scared me. I thought your father had drugged us and carted me off again."

"The dose must have been too high for you. Everyone else has built an immunity to the sedation." He placed a kiss on the tip of her nose. "I had to carry you to our room—not that I minded."

"What happened exactly? One second, we're getting ready to drive. The next I'm blacking out." Ariella glanced around the empty halls.

"You mean transport sleep?" Sebastjan asked. "It's an automatic transport feature to make long-distance trips more tolerable. But now that I think about it, you might never have had occasion to use it. No wonder you slept so long."

"Where are we?"

"Come. I'll show you." Sebastjan threaded his arm in hers and led her down the hall. "This is my research facility. I know it's not a mansion, but—"

"I don't need a mansion," Ariella assured him. "I'm just happy to be out of the last one I lived in. You could move me to a tiny one-room house for all I care."

"I was going to say, but..." He paused as he reached the end of the hall and swept his hand over a scanner next to a narrow door. As the door slid open, a wave of cool air hit them. It carried the scent of nature and the loud roar of falling water. Yelling, he finished, "But I hope you'll find this place has its charms."

Ariella stepped out onto a balcony platform. A cool mist hit upon her face from a nearby waterfall. She smiled, lifting her hand. The air smelled like air should smell, not sickening sweet with sterilizers. "We're on a different plane, aren't we? The trees aren't behind windows."

"No, we're in a perception room." He lifted his hand to the wall. The waterfall and balcony disappeared, replaced by metal grate floors and walls. "We're helping to test them before they're offered to the population. The technology was traded though the Divinity portal. We call them relaxation retreats. I thought, perhaps, you might want to work with a couple of the developers to maybe make a scene from your home world. We could use the input of someone who wasn't born here. Several of the scientists keep trying to change the smell of the air."

Ariella nearly teared up at the thoughtfulness of the gesture. She nodded. "Yes, I would love to recreate my home world very much."

Sebastjan pulled her close to him. "You know, I meant what I said on Staria. I was not suffering from the drinking sickness."

"The part where you said you think you love me?" Ariella asked.

"I know I love you."

"I love you too, Sebastjan." Ariella leaned into his embrace. "Are there security monitors in here?"

"Yes." Frowning, he glanced around. "Why?"

"Can you turn them off?"

"Yes." A slow smile curled on his mouth and lit in his eyes.

"Then lock the door and make the waterfall come back." She pulled his face to hers. "I want to show you just how in love with you I am."

The End

Seducing Cecilia

BOOK TWO BY MICHELLE M. PILLOW

Seducing Cecilia (Divinity Healers) © Copyright 2013-2017, Michelle M. Pillow

First Electronic Printing September 2013, The Raven Books

ISBN 978-1-62501-056-8

Edited by Suz Gower

The Raven Books
Published by The Raven Books

About Seducing Cecilia

DIVINITY HEALERS BOOK TWO

Alternate Reality Romance, Part of the Divinity Universe

As things heat up, the clock is ticking, and the time for seduction is running out.

In a world obsessed with medical advancement, Dr. Gerard Fauchet longs for something more. When he's assigned as the liaison to a dignitary from a parallel universe, he never imagined she'd be so stunningly beautiful or so damned frustrating. One second she's kissing him, the next she's pretending nothing is between them.

The passion is scorching, everything he ever dreamed of having with a woman. He'll make her admit she wants him—or die trying.

Dr. Cecilia Markos is keenly aware that she's been shoved through a portal to an alternate reality for one reason—to bring home medical advancements for the betterment of her people. Unfortunately, she only has two months to learn a world's complete medical knowledge base. It's an impossible task made even more so by the distractingly handsome Gerard who she can't seem to keep her hands or her mind off of.

As the clash heats up between Gerard and Cecilia, the clock is ticking, and the time for seduction is running out.

ut.

To My Awesome Readers.
Thank you for your emails, wall posts, tweets,
and for letting me do what I love by reading my books.

Chapter One

D r. Gerard Fauchet tried to hide the spark of jealousy he felt when he looked at his childhood friend, Dr. Sebastjan Walter. Sebastjan nodded politely as his guests moved through the receiving line to congratulate him on his new marriage. The son of the Medical Supreme, Sebastjan had lived an easy life. His family had money, position and political power. Medical Supreme Walter was easily the highest ranking official on the planet and he was in charge of allotting all of the planet's medical research funding. To a world obsessed with medical advancements, research funding was like air and bodily sustenance.

Gerard focused his attention on his friend. It wasn't Sebastjan's birthright or money or power or position that made the pang of jealousy filter over Gerard. It was Sebastjan's new wife—Ariella. A true, exotic beauty, Ariella came from an alternate dimension of reality. Ever since Gerard heard about inter-dimensional plane travel, he'd become obsessed thinking about it. He'd never really wanted to be a doctor. It was just what everyone on his plane was expected to become. He'd much rather spend his days reading and learning about culture and social history, than studying the readily available medical books that filled every home and office.

Like most nice homes in Asclepius, the front room of Supreme Walter's mansion was excessively sterile, each surface hard and unwelcoming but for a few engraved curls and wisps decorating the marble borders on metal walls. However, the Medical Supreme did have a vast array of items collected from other parallel universes. Gerard found himself staring at them, wondering about those other worlds. What kinds of places were they to dedicate so much time to books that told unreal stories, and to creating things of elegance and beauty for the mere sake of elegance and beauty?

When he looked at Ariella, he thought of all the things she knew —non-medical things, small facts that would mean nothing to her but would provide endless fascination for him. The women on his plane talked like doctors, thought like doctors, were mostly doctors. Not Ariella. She was a Sans, a non-doctor. Sans Ariella. And the very idea of her captivated him.

"Dr. Fauchet, how good of you to come," Sebastjan said.

"How could I not?" Gerard answered his friend. The loneliness that welled within him as he looked at Ariella became almost unbearable, so he hid it behind a playful smile and flirtatious wink.

"Couldn't miss my reception?" Sebastjan asked, skeptical.

"I couldn't miss the Medical Supreme's summons," Gerard corrected. "You didn't think everyone was here to see you, did you?"

Ariella gave a short burst of laughter at the insolent joke.

Gerard winked at her but continued talking to Sebastjan. "Apparently, I am to host two off-plane dignitaries coming here to learn our secrets. However," he turned his full attention to Ariella, "while I am here..."

He wasn't a fool. All the thoughts running through his head would never come to fruition. Though he found her very pretty, he didn't know her, not really. He simply liked the idea of her. He would leave the mansion and perhaps only cross paths with Ariella a handful more times in his life. Her tiny secrets would remain hers as she lived out her days as a doctor's wife.

"Sans Ariella," Sebastjan introduced, "my childhood playmate and local lawbreaker—"

"That is distinguished gentleman and dignitary host," Gerard corrected.

"Dr. Gerard Fauchet," Sebastjan finished.

"A great pleasure," Gerard said, playfully studying Ariella's face. "And it was only one tiny law fourteen years ago. There was a medication mishap, it was hot and it was only the male chairmen who complained about my nakedness. I swear I am a reformed man."

Sebastjan cleared his throat.

Gerard laughed, not showing a single second of remorse at having been caught flirting with the new bride. Leaning in to Ariella, he whispered, "An even greater pleasure to see you've managed to make Sebastjan jealous over you."

Ariella blushed. Sebastjan frowned at them. Gerard bowed his head and moved on.

"What? No present?" Sebastjan grumbled after him. Gerard laughed, but didn't turn back around.

Chapter Two

NEW ORDER SOCIETY, DIMENSIONAL PLANE 303

D r. Cecilia Markos stared at her foot, absently following the lines of her citizen number with her eyes. "One. Zero. Eight. Seven. Five." She didn't need to read it to know it. The tight, neat script had been inked into her flesh the day she was born. It concealed the newer implants the government had instated as an enhancement to the anti-chaos movement. She still remembered the day, as a child, she had watched the government trucks pull into her school armed with brightly colored animal costumes and silly songs. The characters danced and sang as the coded implants were injected beneath every child's number.

One. Zero. Eight. Seven. Five.

Those numbers were everything—her money access, her workout logs, her doctor credentials, her purchasing rations, her identification. Everyone living in New Order Society had a designation. It was the only way a society could thrive. There had to be order to avoid chaos. Citizens needed to be monitored and watched. Control needed to be maintained.

Cecilia knew this, agreed with it fundamentally. Yet, despite her political beliefs, at moments like this when she was alone and unmonitored she couldn't help but wonder what chaos would be like. She didn't want wars or anarchy in the streets. That would be insane. But what about a night of passion that didn't include consent forms and planning? She knew it was wrong and she could *never* tell anyone her most secret thoughts, but when she closed her eyes she imagined spontaneity.

Just thinking about it made her heart race. What would it be like to break free? To kiss a man without waiting for an exchanging of permission? To feel passion, true chaotic passion that didn't make sense. It was something she could never act on. If she did, if the man she kissed complained or anyone found out, she would be fired. Her life would be over and she would spend the rest of her days in disgrace...if not jail.

Living in such a controlled world, it seemed strange then that she would be going to a place where those numbers on her foot meant nothing. A tiny shiver of fear washed over her. A few months ago, she'd never dreamed that visiting an alternate universe was possible. Now, she was to be one of two women going to a new world—another plane of existence, another reality, their world but not their world. Excitement mingled with fear, but she didn't allow herself to fantasize about the kind of men and sex laws this new reality would have. It wouldn't matter. On her plane or any other, she would be expected to exude anti-chaos values. She represented her people to the rest of the known universes.

An entity called Divinity Corporation had mastered the science of inter-dimensional travel and, two years ago, they had made contact with Cecilia's plane. Already a few of her people had gone through the portal gates to new dimensions. When Politician Shinclus first approached her, she'd thought he needed medical attention. The existence of the portals wasn't common knowledge amongst her people. But she'd since seen it for herself. She watched as people appeared out of nothing, carrying strange objects traded from other realms.

A few short months and so much had changed. All the waiting and planning, reading and studying, worrying and pretending not to worry, had all led to this day. Today, she would be traveling to an alternate reality.

The New Order Society plane was only one of four-hundred-thirty-six mapped dimensions used by Divinity—each as different as the last. Some had vampires and werewolves, some had faeries and gnomes, and some had humanoids so alien her dimension's species were hardly compatible. Many of them, like hers, had never even heard of dimensional travel or portals until Divinity arrived. Some societies were obsessive to the point of compulsion and some so brutal they enjoyed watching gladiators fight to the death. One thing many of them seemed to have in common was chaos. Utter, uncontrolled chaos. New Order Society thrived on anti-chaos—no unconformity, no inappropriate behaviors, and absolutely no crime. Well, minimal crimes anyway. There was definitely no tolerance for criminal activity.

Looking at an alternate reality was supposed to be like seeing your world had history unraveled differently. There were many similarities. Languages were comparable. Some people had the same appearance, but were not the same people. Certain events like natural disasters could be shared. People were human-like in appearance and functions, though she had been told of a race of people that didn't have toenails.

Cecilia wiggled her toes, wondering what they'd look like without nails. Then, sighing, she stood and reached for her best one-piece suit. Red material belled around the legs and led up to tightly-fitted hips and a looser bodice. The sleeves were long, falling past her hands. She brushed her hair back from her face, trying not to think about the fashionable crimson red streak she'd been forced to get rid of. Apparently, this medical plane she was going to didn't have the same fashions. In New Order Society everyone sported a bright streak of color in their hair. Just because they were orderly didn't mean they couldn't be fun too. Well, that and the streak proved the wearer had been to their mandatory grooming appointment by the lack of a line of demarcation where the new growth came in.

Taking a deep breath, Cecilia pulled on her boots, whispering, "It's only for a couple of months. It will be fine. It's only two months. I'll be able to make it back. Everyone else has made it back home."

Despite her words, she wasn't so sure.

Chapter Three

A couple of months looked like an eternity when staring into a Divinity portal. A pyramid roof set atop four square columns which framed a platform. Cecilia had memorized the literature on the device. The columns were constructed of a dense material which created its own gravitational field and drew objects to it. They hid a complex configuration of liquid crystals, electrical currents, mirrors and vacuums. It was held in check by the wavelength of a specific blue light, which kept the portal inactive. Should the light change, a dimensional shift would occur, taking whoever stood on the platform to a new parallel universe.

Cecilia didn't move. All the facts in the world were doing little to calm the increasingly fast beat of her heart.

"You know, Politician Shinclus told me that people sometimes get rematerialized into solid objects when going through these things," Linnea Nel, Cecilia's new assistant said.

Cecilia glanced at the woman. Such occurrences had been reported in the early day of portal travel. Now Divinity sent out microscopic probes first. Even so, it wasn't exactly what she wanted to think about at the moment.

Linnea hugged a stack of papers to her chest a little too tightly.

Cecilia had only known the woman for a few weeks, but already she didn't care for her. Before this assignment, Linnea had been in and out of trouble with the authorities. Plus, she was a non-conformist. For some reason, the New Order Society implants didn't work inside Linnea's body. They believed it had to do with her natural magnetism and electrical current—not that she shot lightning out of her fingertips or anything absurd, just that for some reason computers didn't always work around her. Without an implant, Linnea was like a ghost, uncontrollable, untraceable, chaos waiting to happen. Sure, she had the identifying tattoo, but one had to look at her foot to see it.

"He was just trying to scare you," Cecilia answered, refusing to let any fear show. She was already nervous enough about traveling through the portal. "Politician Shinclus is known for his bad humor. It is true accidents happened in the past, but that is why they send out the probes first. Besides, where we are going is a known destination and an opposite portal will receive us on the other side. Everyone there works for the central hospital government in some capacity. It should be like going to a giant hospital." She turned to study Linnea. The blue light from the portal reflected in the woman's eyes, giving them an eerie glow. The woman's black hair was shorter with a streak of dark purple to match the purplish grey of her eyes. Her bodice was tight, less conservative in design. A thick, black belt wrapped her ribs, dark purple over black material. "Weren't you supposed to change your hair?"

"I didn't make it to my appointment. Something else came up." Linnea arched a brow. "I don't really think it matters all that much. I'm sure they'll make allowances for our alien customs."

"The plane we're traveling to does not know of our fashion customs. We might unintentionally insult them. Did you read the recommendations report put together by the Committee for Inter-plane Diplomacy?"

"I was going to," Linnea drawled, "but I was in the middle of a different book at the time. I wanted to finish it before we left."

Cecilia closed her eyes, too weary to argue at the moment. She had too much on her mind. She had to represent her entire planet in what could possibly be the most important trade agreement ever negotiated in the history of their society. Who knew what kind of medical advancements this plane would be able to show them? What if they could advance their medical technology by years, hundreds of years, thousands of years? She would need to focus and learn and observe. Glancing at Linnea, she frowned. And by all evidence she would be busy apologizing for the controversial woman they were sending with her. How Linnea managed to get sent on such an important mission was beyond Cecilia's reasoning.

Linnea smirked as if she hadn't a care. Workers began filing out of the room, leaving them alone with the portal. Cecilia frowned, saying, "It's too late to do anything about your hair now. We will be leaving soon."

Without waiting for Linnea to speak, Cecilia moved toward the platform. Her luggage had already been sent ahead. It had been strange to see it disappear into seemingly nothingness. A low, steady hum sounded moments before a voice could be heard overhead, ordering, "Dr. Markos, Citizen Nel, please report to the platform."

Cecilia concentrated on keeping her legs steady and her chin up. She was in charge. This job, this mission, would open so many doors for her career. If she worked really hard and kept the delinquent at her side in line, she could do great things. Such an opportunity for advancement would not show itself again.

Once on the platform, she turned her attention toward the source of the light beam. It hurt her eyes, but she knew behind it would be the control booth's window where technicians would be manning the controls and the politicians in charge of this secret project would be looking down at them.

"Prepare for portal travel," the controller announced.

"See you on the other side, Doc," Linnea said softly.

The light began to change color, shifting into a pale green. Cecilia's flesh tingled, tightening as if being pulled away from the bone. She braced herself, knowing that portal travel was reported to hurt. Nerves bunched in her stomach and she held her breath. The humming grew louder. She closed her eyes to the bright light.

Heat burned her flesh and she felt heavy, but she didn't move. Cecilia would have screamed, but she had no voice. Her body pulled apart at a molecular level. Then, as quickly as it started, it stopped. She fell to her knees, gasping for breath. Linnea collapsed on the floor next to her, coughing as she dropped her papers.

Cecilia took several deep breaths, not bothering to get up as she looked around. A sweet scent filled the air, subtle and not exactly unpleasant, but different. Blue light shone on them, not looking as bright as the one on their side of the portal. A loud alarm sounded, blaring over them.

"So loud!" Linnea said, her voice lifting as she covered her ears.

"Sterilization commencing," a male voice announced, louder than the alarm. When she looked, she didn't see anyone. "Please stand and move away from the platform."

Linnea gathered the papers and pushed to her feet. Reaching down, she pulled Cecilia up by her arm.

"Please stand and move away from the platform," the voice repeated, even louder.

"I think that's us," Linnea yelled over the alarm. Both women obeyed. Linnea didn't let go of her and Cecilia found that, for the moment, she was grateful to not be alone. The room was constructed of shiny metal—from the floors to the walls to the ceilings. A shield slid down from the ceiling, blocking the platform. They both turned, startled, watching it.

"Welcome, dignitaries from New Order Society, Dimensional Plane 303, to Central Hospital and Optimal Health Centre in the City of Asclepius, Country of Chiron, Dimensional Plane 187. We are now scanning you for foreign dimensional parasites and viruses. Please do not move until scanning is complete." A series of lights followed the male's orders, flashing over them. The alarms stopped, leaving her ears ringing. "Sterilization complete. Please state your clearance code."

"Dr. Cecilia Markos," she answered. "New Order Society dignitary."

"This is tedious," Linnea muttered. "I hope they don't all talk that loud."

"Voice recognition accepted. Please move to the orange door."

The door was actually metallic gray with a series of numbers and letter written in orange across the front. It opened automatically.

"It's only for a couple of months," Cecilia said under her breath. She led the way through the door, forcing herself to be brave.

"Yeah," Linnea answered, "but two months of what?"

Chapter Four

Gerard walked through the secured halls of the Central Hospital and Optimal Health Centre building toward the Divinity portal hidden within. Studying his electronic clipboard, he checked over the visitors' sterilization scans results before signing off on them to let the visiting doctors inside the main complex. This assignment was more like a child-watching mission, but he didn't care. He'd lied when he told Sebastjan he was summonsed to meet the dignitaries. The truth was he'd volunteered. How could he resist the opportunity to meet off-plane visitors?

The overhead alarm would continue to buzz until he signed his name. Doing so quickly, he relaxed as the buzzing stopped. He hurried through the metallic gray corridors of the hospital. It looked like an endless maze with only the orange lettering on the walls to give directions. Any unauthorized visitors would be lost.

"It's only for a couple of months."

Glancing up, he started to smile. The look faltered.

"Yeah, but two months of what?"

He glanced back down to the clipboard to gather his wits. His information didn't say anything about the doctors being pretty. The slightly shorter woman carried a stack of papers. Her shoulder-length, black hair was streaked with dark purple and matched the strange shade of her purplish-grey eyes. Gerard wondered if it was a genetic anomaly or common for her people. But then, as he studied the other woman, all thoughts stopped. She was tall and proud with just a hint of disdain and fear in her voice as she'd spoken.

It's only for a couple of months.

Clearly she didn't look forward to this assignment. Gerard found himself fascinated. Though, if he were completely honest with himself, he'd admit that his fascination also had to do with the fact that this off-world woman caused a sudden surge of hormones to run rampant through his body. He shifted his hips, glad that the standard-issue facility uniform, a long, blue coat with red trim, hid his growing erection.

Knowing he had to get his wits about him, and fast, he cleared his throat. "Welcome..." Gerard hesitated, suddenly unable to remember their names. The tall one looked directly at him. Her brunette hair was pulled away from her face, giving him a clear view of her blue eyes. Her clothes were a strange style, but that was to be expected considering her origins. "Welcome, doctors."

"I'm the doctor, Dr. Cecilia Markos," the object of his sudden attentions answered tersely. Her hard tone only served to pique his interest more. She motioned to the woman with the papers. "This is my assistant, Linnea Nel."

Linnea gave a rueful smile at the other woman's introduction.

"Welcome, Dr. Markos, Sans Nel," Gerard amended.

"Thank you," Linnea answered. Cecilia nodded once.

"I am Dr. Gerard Fauchet. I will be your guide while you're on our plane. Anything you need, all you have to do is ask." He motioned to the papers. "Would you like me to carry that for you?"

"No, I've got it." Linnea glanced at Cecilia and added wryly, "I am the assistant, after all."

"We don't work with parchment, but I can have one of the doctors scan your documents into a clipboard if you like." He lifted his electronic clipboard to indicate the device he was talking about. "In fact, I understand supplies are waiting for us at the assigned research facility."

"You mean," Cecilia glanced around. "We will not be working here? Near the portal?"

"Afraid we might keep you here against your will?" Gerard teased. Cecilia didn't appear to appreciate his humor. He let the playful smile fall from his lips. In a more businesslike manner he stated, "Please, follow me."

Chapter Five

Cecilia tried to smile, but the more nervous she became, the harder it was for her to act pleasant. All around her was a parallel world. It was not lost on her how impossible it would be to just run home and pretend none of this ever happened. Now this stranger—someone who until recently she would have said was the figment of an overactive imagination—wanted to take her away from the portal? What was she doing here? Was she crazy to agree to this? No one from her world ever stayed away so long.

Dr. Gerard Fauchet made her nervous. She wasn't sure about the way he looked at her. It was almost too familiar, too friendly, too interested. And she wasn't sure about the way his attention made her feel. How could she maintain a sense of professionalism if the man in charge of showing her around stared at her like she was already naked and in his bed? This wasn't the first time a man in power tried to play that game, and like the others she would quickly put him in his place. Only here, he wouldn't need her to sign consent to be in his bed. Or did he? She wasn't sure what their laws were. They were civilized doctors. It was entirely possible plane 187 would require informed consent before Dr. Fauchet could act on his leering expressions.

Oh, but what if he didn't have to? What if he could do what he wanted, when he wanted, how he wanted? Her breathing deepened.

Concentrate, she thought, *anti-chaos, anti-chaos, anti-chaos...*

She took another deep breath, proud of herself for maintaining control.

So why, exactly, was she looking at his ass while he walked?

Cecilia's eyes darted up to his back. Next to her Linnea chuckled knowingly, or in a way Cecilia translated to be knowingly. She took a deep breath, almost choking on the sweet air freshener the hospital utilized.

"Doctor?" Gerard inquired at her cough. He looked at his clipboard and then at her.

Cecilia touched her chest lightly. "I am still adapting to the air."

He arched a brow and she found the expression slightly infuriating.

"It smells like we're walking near a confectionary," Linnea observed. "The air is very sweet."

"That is the air-filtering sterilizer," Gerard said. "The air is continuously tested for abnormalities and purified. You have nothing to fear here. We haven't had a serious illness for, well, some would argue for centuries now, depending on your particular definition of serious." He gestured absently toward the ceiling. "I am told that after a time you will become accustomed to the scent. We tried modifying the formula to be unscented, but it lost two-point-three percent potency."

"No illness for so long?" Cecilia questioned. She gave a meaningful look to Linnea. The woman's face was a blank mask. Then, realizing that maybe she expected too much of a reaction from a nonconformist semi-criminal, Cecilia turned her attention back to Gerard. She watched the shift of his shoulders beneath the lab coat. It was a subtle movement, but she found herself staring at the hypnotic play of muscles. "That is quite the accomplishment."

He glanced back at them. "Indeed."

Gerard led them through the hall, turning several times until Cecilia gave up trying to remember their path. Monitors on the wall showed their life signs as they passed, very similar to the scanners on her home plane. Only, instead of reporting a picture ID, it reported heartbeats and temperatures. Her heart was beating a little fast.

When he stopped, Gerard turned his attention to her. His voice was low as he observed, "Your lidec levels are elevated. Would you like me to alleviate your..." he paused, "*symptoms?*"

The way he said the word "symptoms", all low and warm, caused a sudden shock of pleasure to spread through her stomach. It radiated over her pussy and thighs. His eyes seemed to smolder with intent. Lidec? Symptoms? Did that mean her arousal? Was he propositioning her? Did the monitors reveal her interest in him?

"Ah, Dr. Fauchet." The abrupt sound cut into her thoughts and directed her attention to the older man coming down the hall. By the self-satisfied look on his face, she assumed him to be the man in charge.

"Dr. Markos, Sans Nel, may I present Medical Supreme Walter, his son Dr. Sebastjan Walter and Dr. Walter's wife, Sans Ariella."

"Doctor," the Medical Supreme acknowledged, glancing only briefly at Linnea. He had a smooth, youthful look to him that contrasted the intelligence in his blue eyes. A foreshadowing of gray salted the black hair at his temples.

"Welcome," Dr. Walter said. Ariella nodded.

"And this is the hospital coordinator, Dr. Lu," Gerard finished. Dr. Lu stayed back behind the others and she didn't get a good look at him.

"Welcome to Asclepius," the Medical Supreme said. "We look forward to a mutual exchange of knowledge. I have chosen Dr. Fauchet to be your guide. He will remain at your side. Should you need anything, please speak directly to him or to Dr. Swift. I will be unable to attend you at the research facility. I am a very busy man, after all."

Cecilia began to answer, but the Medical Supreme cut her off.

"Here he is!" The Medical Supreme lifted his hand, motioning behind them. "May I present the esteemed Dr. Swift, Director of Central Hospital."

Dr. Swift nodded at the visitors. His gaze lingered on Linnea's hair a long moment but his expression gave nothing away.

"It is good to meet you, doctors," Cecilia said.

"Dr. Markos," Dr. Swift acknowledged. Behind him Sebastjan slipped away with his wife. The quiet Dr. Lu soon followed. Cecilia thought their abrupt departure odd, but chose to ignore the obvious plane custom. "I've ordered your transport readied. Your belongings have already been loaded. Dr. Fauchet will show you where to go. I must attend to a few matters here but will join you later at the facility."

"Sans Nel has parchment to be transferred to a clipboard. Perhaps she should work here and arrive later with you when she is finished?" Gerard suggested.

Dr. Swift didn't spare Linnea a look as he nodded. "Very well. Sans Nel, follow me. I will show you where you can work."

"Where did my son...?" The Medical Supreme began to question, glancing around. Then, as a severe frown crossed his features, he said, "Excuse me. I have urgent business to attend to."

Before Cecilia fully realized the implications of what was happening around her, she found herself alone with Gerard. He smiled at her, a playful, almost achingly seductive look. There was an ease to his mannerisms that took her by surprise and didn't seem to fit with the others she'd just met.

"You're very pretty," Gerard said.

Cecilia opened her mouth to answer, but no sound readily came out.

"Are you with someone? Married? Taken? Do you have such customs on your plane?" he questioned.

"Ah, no, I'm not taken," Cecilia managed, not sure she should answer such a personal question but unable to think of anything else to say.

"Brilliant. I'm pleased to hear it." His smile didn't fade. And was it just her imagination, or was he leaning closer? The thoughts racing through her mind were anything but anti-chaotic.

Cecilia watched his lips move as he said something more but she didn't pay attention to the words that came out. The sweet smell or sanitized air was temporarily overwhelmed by the scent of his body. He smelled clean, fresh, not like the cleansers on her plane, but exotic and new. She found herself breathing deeply. With each inhale she shivered, and with each exhale she found her senses focused more fully upon him.

"Dr. Markos?" Gerard inquired, arching a brow. "Are you ready?"

"Ready?" she repeated. What had he been saying? For the life of her she didn't know. All she could think about was kissing him without permission. She cleared her throat and forced her eyes away from him. "Yes, yes, of course I am ready to leave."

Chapter Six

Cecilia stepped slowly toward a box-shaped vehicle Gerard called a transport. It hovered over the ground outside the hospital. She took her time as she glanced over the carved stone landscape. The streets, sidewalks and buildings seemed connected by one smooth formation of rock. Statues rose up from the ground, their stiff lines and symmetrical features just as clean and orderly as their surroundings. Aside from the small plants encased in large glass boxes, they were the only visible pieces of life in the area.

The Central Hospital and Optimal Health Centre dominated the street like a centerpiece. Thick columns and oversized stone arches were mimicked by the smaller buildings. The outside architecture was nothing like the metal corridors within.

Gerard waited for her by the transport door. As she approached, he held out his hand, offering to help her up. Instead of steadying her when she placed a hand in his, he tugged her off balance. Cecilia fell toward him, landing against his chest. She blinked in surprise, gasping.

Warm lips found hers, pressing hard against her mouth. The kiss took her by surprise and she didn't pull away. Her knees weakened. Gerard held her to his chest. Firm muscles pressed into her softer breasts, making her very aware of the intimate moment. Heat filled her, radiating down her stomach and thighs.

Cecilia moaned softly, her lips moving of their own accord to accept his inappropriate embrace. In the back of her mind a thought whispered that this couldn't be happening, that it couldn't be real, that she wanted it too much and was delusional. He answered the movement of her mouth, deepening the kiss. His tongue slid into her mouth, gliding between her lips and teeth. She knew she should pull away, but part of her wanted to see what he'd do next.

Gerard's hands slid down to the small of her back and he turned, pressing her against the transport. The solid feel against her back and the sudden thick arousal hitting her stomach caused her senses to come crashing back to reality. Gasping, she ripped her face away and pushed against his chest. His hand was lodged against her ass, frozen in a squeeze. For a moment, he didn't move as confused eyes stared into hers.

"Doctor!" she hissed in warning, keeping the word low. Drawing up her hand, she slapped his cheek, not so hard as to leave an imprint but enough to snap him to his senses. The action came from years of living in anti-chaos. It was how she was supposed to react to such a presumption. Had he done that on the city street back home, they would have both been arrested. He let go and she pushed harder, forcing him to stumble back. The ache of withdrawal hit her like a cold rush of air. She shivered, resisting the urge to rub her arms. "What do you...? It is not..." she hesitated. "I am unfamiliar with your plane's customs, but you are taking liberties I am not willing to give. In my reality we have certain customs that must be followed to avoid any chaos or confusion. I certainly did not sign a consent form for your advances before coming here."

Cecilia hoped her words sounded properly diplomatic, even if the tone did not. Gerard's expression lost its playfulness. Slightly under his breath, he mumbled, "I am unfamiliar with your plane's customs, but generally if a woman is not interested she does not kiss a man back."

Gerard stepped into the transport, not waiting for the visiting doctor to go first. He wasn't really angry at her so much as he was irritated with himself. He didn't know what came over him—grabbing and kissing the visiting dignitary like that in front of Central Hospital where anyone traveling by could see. It didn't matter that the streets were mostly vacant this time of day.

He'd wanted her from the first moment and his desires had only grown. When she took his hand, he'd just reacted—without reason or sense. He'd meant the kiss to be short, but she'd responded to him. Her lips had parted. Her body had pressed, so warm and soft and feminine. She smelled exotically sweet, like the celebratory desserts his grandmother used to sneak him before the full enforcement of medical contraband laws. She had wanted him, if only for the briefest of moments.

Cecilia was slower to enter, but she did, taking a seat across from him. She pointedly looked everywhere but at his face, pretending to study the inside of the transport as he pressed a button to activate it. The coordinates had already been entered. Since the address was typed into the transport's computer, the occupants were free to enjoy the ride—no driver needed. It only took a few seconds for the door to slide shut and for them to be on their way. The vehicle moved soundlessly, hovering above the ground as it sped along Asclepius's self-navigating streets.

"You might want to get comfortable for the journey," Gerard instructed, stretching out his legs and shutting his eyes.

"Do all your cities look like this one?" Cecilia asked. When he opened an eye he found her staring out of the window. "Everything seems very orderly and quiet."

"No. Not all cities."

"Is it true everyone here works for the central hospital government in some capacity? How do you feed everyone if you all work for the hospital?" She turned her attention to him. "Don't you need farmers? Laborers?"

"Biologists provide sustenance with enhanced properties," he answered. "Agricultural doctors deal with plant production and nutrient compounds."

"What about the crime rate? It seems quiet here. Our streets are very busy at all hours, though crime is low due to the anti-chaos laws. Do you have a way of tracking your citizens? Is that a function of the wall monitors?"

"You have a lot of questions and there will be plenty of time to answer them all. Are you nervous?" Gerard didn't move. "Is that why you are speaking so fast?"

Light smoke began to filter into the transport. It would help them to sleep for the ride. Cecilia coughed, covering her mouth. His limbs felt heavy as the drug filled his lungs. Her wide eyes turned toward him and her mouth opened in panic but she slumped over on her seat. Darkness crept over his vision and he let sleep take him.

Chapter Seven

Waves lapped against an unseen shore, creating a constant, tranquil rhythm. Cecilia yawned, stretching in her seat. For a moment, she blinked heavily, forgetting where she was. Nothing looked familiar. Bringing her hand to her mouth, she yawned again.

New plane. Work. Dr. Gerard Fauchet.

Her attention turned sharply to the man sleeping in the seat across from her. He appeared completely relaxed, breathing evenly. She looked out the transport windows, finding nothing but an expanse of wilderness on one side and ocean on the other. They weren't traveling very fast and the unit even halted a few times, rocking the occupants. She looked out the window toward a large expanse of forest. The thick trees were so dense she couldn't see deep into the forest. Wind stirred the purplish foliage littering the unmarred forest floor. There were no paths, only dense underbrush. On the other side, a beach led toward an ocean. The sand was perfectly rippled by nature, unmarked by human feet. They were away from civilization. The transport stopped moving. She held her breath, waiting.

"Dr. Fauchet?" she whispered, reaching for his knee when the transport didn't move. She shook him gently. "Dr. Fauchet? Can you wake up?" The transport turned in a circle. "I think something's wrong with this vehicle. We're, well, I don't know where we are but we're moving precariously."

The vehicle jerked suddenly, tossing her forward into his lap. She braced her weight with her hands, managing to stop her fall before their bodies pressed tightly together. His knee wedged between her thighs. She breathed deeply, studying his face. He didn't move. Her eyes moved to his mouth. He'd kissed her without permission. It was clear such things as filing consent forms weren't needed on this plane, not like in New Order Society. What if she kissed him? Exhilarated by the privacy of the transport, she leaned forward and brushed her lips against him for the briefest of seconds.

Cecilia slowly pulled back, almost frightened by what she'd done. She quickly untangled their limbs and sat on the seat next to him. She tapped his cheek lightly, waiting to see if he knew of the liberties she'd just taken. "Dr. Fauchet? Gerard?"

He didn't react.

Cecilia frowned and tapped him harder, worried something might really be wrong. Here she was acting on sexual instinct and he could have a medical issue. She felt for his pulse, holding his wrist as she pried open one of his eyes. The steady beat of his heart didn't change and the vacant stare didn't waver. She knew when someone was sedated. "Dr. Fauchet? Can you hear me?"

When he didn't move, she let her hand rest against his face. He didn't appear ill, just sleeping. The texture of his skin was stubbled lightly by beard growth. Her lips tingled and she wanted to kiss him again. His attraction to her had been clear, eloquently expressed in the pressure of his mouth and the tight push of his body. She remembered the outline of his arousal pressed against her stomach. Desire leapt up inside her, heating her belly and moistening her thighs. She wondered what he'd feel like against her, naked and strained.

This was not supposed to be happening. She was on assignment, a dignitary for her people. Spontaneously sexing up the first doctor she saw wasn't very dignified. Yet, as she touched his cheek, she felt herself inching closer to him. She breathed deeply, noting the exotic scent of his flesh.

Cecilia closed her eyes, forcing control over her body. Sex was not the first thing she should be thinking about. She reached for her hair and pulled it loose, scratching nervously at her head. "You really need to wake up now."

Fingering a hairpin, she grabbed his hand and poked it with the tip in effort to stimulate a response. He moaned softly, the first sign of consciousness since she'd awoken. Heartened by the reaction, she poked him again, harder.

"Ow." He jerked his hand from hers, blinking rapidly. "What are you doing?"

"There is something wrong. We're—" The transport jerked, starting up again.

Gerard pushed up from his seat, looking out the window. "We're only halfway there. Why did you rouse me? What are you doing awake?"

"I don't know. I woke up and the transport had stopped. We're in the middle of nowhere and I thought..." She looked helplessly at him. Now that he was awake the transport seemed really small. "I thought we were in trouble."

"Splendid," he drawled. "There isn't enough of the sleeping agent to put us back out. We'll be aware for the rest of the trip." He studied his hand, examining the dot of blood on his skin. Then, as if deciding he'd live after such a tiny wound, he stretched his arms over his head.

"You say that as if you've never been on a trip." She frowned. "How long is it until we get there? A day? Two?"

"I've been on several trips and have only been awake for a few of them." He suppressed a yawn. "As for this one, we probably have a little over two hours left."

She laughed. He looked troubled as he said it. "Hours? Unless that word has a much different meaning here than on my plane, I hardly think a few hours in a transport will do us harm."

"Harm, no. Boredom, yes." He closed his eyes, leaning his head back.

Cecilia realized she was still next to him on the seat, but didn't move away. Instead, she adjusted her body to mimic his pose. "You didn't find me so boring back at Central Hospital."

"That was before you slapped me," he answered. "You weren't boring when you were kissing me."

"You took liberties."

"Yes." He grinned. "I did and you enjoyed it."

His expression was slightly infuriating and yet sexy at the same time. "I suppose we could talk about what is going to happen while I'm here."

"We could. Or you could kiss me again."

Cecilia felt his heat radiating down her side. She was very aware of where his sleeve brushed against hers. Her nerves seemed to stand on end, reaching for the next light contact. "You kissed me."

Cecilia wasn't sure what made her debate him, or even talk about it. Maybe it was the new plane, the isolation of the transport and surrounding location, the subtle scent of his flesh, the heat from his body, or maybe it was the unexplainable rush of attraction that seemed to seize hold of her to the core. Doubts filled her. What if people found out? What if he told the other doctors and they didn't take her seriously? What if the tension knotting her stomach didn't go away and she was left with a sick feeling and bad memories of her time in this other world?

"I assure you, Doctor, you'll know when I kiss you."

"Why? You'll give me notice in writing?" he teased, not bothering to open his eyes.

Not knowing what exactly fueled her into action, Cecilia pushed up and leaned over him. He barely had time to look at her before she grabbed the sides of his face and kissed him. A low moan of surprise escaped him, as if he'd only been bantering with her and was stunned by her actions. For a moment, he didn't move. Then, slowly, a hand crept over her hips, testing the breadth of her resolve with that one touch.

"There are no, ah, recording devices of any kind in here, are there?" she asked when she pulled away, glancing around. Her lips tasted of him and she was breathing hard. She was in spontaneously unfamiliar territory but she didn't want this moment of insanity to come back and haunt her later. "No one is watching or listening?"

"No one." Gerard breathed just as hard. "Our trip is logged. If we do not arrive they will send help. If we need help before then we can trigger an alarm. There is an emergency medical kit on board, so you have nothing to worry about—"

Cecilia kissed him again, quieting his words. If they only had a few hours, she wanted to take full advantage of it.

"Otherwise, we are completely isolated," he continued, as if not really paying attention to his words. His eyes roamed over her body.

"When we step out of this transport, this never happened," Cecilia said. "Agreed?"

He met her eyes and hesitated before nodding once.

"Good." This time Cecilia let her tongue slide slowly along the seam of his mouth. His hands ran along her back, exploring the line of stitching along her spine. She unfastened his long coat, pushing the material off his shoulders. The thin undershirt he wore molded to his chest. He looked to be in fine shape, but then everyone on this plane looked to be in fine shape—even that politician they called the Medical Supreme. Politicians on her plane tended to be a bit more on the gluttonous side. These people had to have some kind of easy fitness secret. If she discovered that little gem, Politician Shinclus would probably assign her to the highest medical councils. She'd have her pick of jobs.

Why was she thinking of Shinclus at a time like this?

Cecilia pulled back, feasting her eyes on the man before her.

"What is it?" he asked.

"Nothing." She pulled her clothes off her shoulders and tugged the one-piece suit down around her hips before standing to finish undressing the rest of the way. Gerard followed her example, shrugging out of his coat. His undershirt was longer at each hip than at the stomach. He grabbed the sides and slowly peeled the material off his muscled chest.

The transport turned again before building speed. Trees blurred as they zipped past. Despite this, the ride became smooth and even as if the vehicle stood perfectly still.

Naked, she came over him, straddling his body. He still wore pants, but the unmistakable outline of his cock greeted her. It brushed against her pussy, causing a shiver of anticipation to run through her.

Gerard caressed her arms, reaching upward to cup her face and pull her mouth back to his. At least kissing seemed to bring them both the same kind of pleasure. If she closed her eyes, this plane almost felt normal.

The smell of him was muskier than the sweet sanitized air. She leaned in, breathing deeply, enjoying it. Heat radiated from his body, centering down between her spread legs. A small fear crept into the back of her mind. What if he wasn't built like the men she was used to? Curious, and a bit apprehensive, she brought herself more fully against his pants. He groaned. The thick arousal felt normal. Actually, it felt...

Cecilia rubbed more fully against it. The firm length stroked her clit. She'd been so tense. The pressure of this trip had been building inside her. Now that the travel was over and she was here, that tension came rolling out of her. Everything inside of her became primitive and instinctual. She wanted him on the basest of levels, a place beyond reason and logic. Her body ached, needing to be filled.

They didn't speak, even as their lips pulled apart. He touched her everywhere his hands could reach. He kissed her neck, moaned into her chest.

She threaded her fingers through his thick hair, jerking his head back. Cecilia licked at his neck, tasting his flesh. He smelled so clean, yet very masculine. Beneath her, his thighs flexed. Gerard lifted from the seat and tugged the pants from his hips. She instantly reached between their bodies to examine him, to see if he was shaped as she knew men to be. This would be an awkward encounter if she found out he had hard spikes on his penis or some kind of abnormality. Pleased, she discovered the smooth length of his arousal filled her hand. She sighed heavily in relief.

Boldly, she stroked him, massaging the full length of his member. He adjusted his hips. The seats didn't allow for the kind of exploration she wanted.

Cecilia lifted over him and angled his cock toward her. She paused. "We're given birth control on my plane and my health checkup is clean."

"You were scanned when you entered. I'm not worried." He

leaned toward the control panel. "I can show you my health scans. I'm—"

"I trust you." She pushed down onto his lap. "You are all health obsessed."

"Obsessed?" His handsome face captured her attention—the straight line of his nose, the firmness of his perfect mouth.

"Focused," she amended, needing him too urgently to argue over word choice. Cecilia wanted him inside of her. Pushing down more, she slid fully onto his naked shaft and moaned as the thick length of his cock stretched her pussy. It had been so long since she'd been sexually gratified, and it had never felt like this.

Cecilia gasped and trembled, keeping him deep even as her legs strained. She moved over him and the pleasure outweighed the discomfort of their position. She needed this too badly.

Gripping her hips, he helped to control the rhythm. He whispered something, but she couldn't make out the words. Her heart pounded heavily. She lifted and fell, pressing down hard and fast. In and out, in and out, they set a desperate rhythm. The transport turned, rocking her on top of him. The stimulation caused her to jerk. Gerard pressed her to the side, mimicking the movement. She jerked again, stiffening as he hit sweetly inside her pussy.

His feet braced the floor and he pressed up. She couldn't fight it. Her release came in a hard, ungraceful, stiffening jerk of muscles. Even her toes curled. She couldn't control her body. Gerard didn't appear to notice as he too came, finding release deep inside of her.

When his hands slipped from her hips, she fell back onto her seat. The slick material stuck to her ass. For a long moment, she didn't move, simply gasped for air.

Gerard's entire body hummed with energy. He hadn't expected such a reaction from the woman. Sure, as a man, he had hoped something would happen between them. She was a very attractive specimen of female kind, after all. What man wouldn't want to fuck that?

But it was more than a simple attraction. He felt a connection to

179

her. It burned deep inside of him. It was impossible to explain, especially after such a short time together. Perhaps it was her eyes. She tried so hard to look calm and controlled, but he had the impression it was all an act. The way she kissed him proved there was more to this woman than her anti-chaos regulations and rigid way of talking. The coldness she exuded when she arrived he could well attribute to nerves. Gerard had seen her monitor readings. Her heart had been hammering out of control.

He smiled at her, liking the way she lounged naked, unashamed of her form. Not that she had a reason to be. She was beautiful, by any plane's standards. It was on his lips to tell her as much when she spoke first.

"You must emit some kind of pheromone," Cecilia said, as reasoning slowly came back to her. "That is the only explanation for it."

"The only?" he repeated, a little shocked by her tone. The cool dismissiveness of it didn't match the passion of moments before. She reached for her clothes and started to dress. He pulled his pants up to cover his waist. "Yes. Pheromones are a natural part of attraction." It was true, but it wasn't what he wanted to say. What he felt in those moments of pleasure went well beyond simple pheromone attraction.

"You remember our agreement? No one knows of this. What just happened between us," she gave him a pointed look, "never happened."

He nodded, hurt by the matter-of-fact tone.

"I didn't mean it like…" Cecilia hesitated.

The vulnerability was back in her eyes and she fought so hard to be in control. He felt a little sorry for her. It must be difficult trying to be so good all the time. Life on his plane was controlled, everyone was a doctor and followed protocols, but her world must be stringent if she was so terrified of anyone knowing they had sex.

"I'm a dignitary and I don't want anyone knowing that we came together in such an inappropriate way," she explained, needlessly. "I should have demanded you sign a consent form. I didn't even bring consent forms. If anyone finds out, I'll… It should not have happened.

It's either pheromones, or a side effect of plane travel, I'm not sure, but whatever it is, it will not be happening again. I can't let it."

"And I am your host. I assure you, it is not in my best interest to make this known either." It was a lie. No one would care. Sex was sex. Humans had needs, and fulfilling those sexual needs was actually good for your health. As long as the dignitary was willing, he could fuck her as often as they wanted and none from his world would so much as lift a brow.

Yet, her stinging dismissal of him, of what they shared, caused him to lie. He hated lying, hated himself a little for letting it slip past his lips. Her words had been a defense. Gerard knew that and could even understand and sympathize with it. Knowing did not make it easier. So, doing what he did best, he pasted on an easy smile as he righted his clothing and pretended as if nothing in all the known planes mattered.

Chapter Eight

"Welcome to Biosphacility Three. It is the largest biosphere facility on our plane and where you will be working while you are here. Computers have complete access to all public records and this place is equipped with some of our most advanced technologies. You will be permitted to work and learn. A laboratory has been cleared in anticipation of your arrival." Gerard spoke, but did not lean up from his seat. "For the first month you will work in the laboratory and with the public records. In the second month, if a doctor in a field of interest is available, you will be permitted to tour the biosphacility research labs and observe experiments." He gave a small yawn. "May your stay on our plane be productive and educational, and may it lead to many future dealings between our people."

Cecilia had the impression he'd made that speech before. He glanced at her, smiling easily as if nothing had transpired between them. Okay, she knew what she had said to him and his actions were in accordance with the discretion she'd demanded from him. Even so, the emotional woman inside her began to feel a little used. The logical doctor slapped the emotional woman and reminded her that this was how things had to be. She didn't need coddling by her one-time lover.

In fact, she needed him to remain professional. The easy, carefree smile was hardly professional as she would define it, but at least he wasn't pawing her and acting like they were a couple.

Pawing. She closed her eyes and took a deep breath. The feel of his hands was still burned into her flesh. If anyone found out, she could be arrested or fired. She would definitely be censured. The embarrassment of law-breaking would be mortifying. "I assume now that you have escorted me here, you will be leaving?"

The words were colder than she'd intended, and almost a little desperate. How was she supposed to concentrate around him, knowing him as intimately as she now did? What in the name of anti-chaos had she been thinking?

"No, sorry, you're stuck with me." The words were light and his smile never wavered. She looked back out the window. In the trees she saw people wearing large white suits over their entire bodies. They touched leaves with gloved hands and picked plant samples off the ground to put into specimen containers. They worked leisurely, unfazed by the transport coming past. Behind them a robotic unit lifted a scientist into the taller trees to collect from the dense tree tops. The figure disappeared into the high branches. As the transporter turned, she could no longer see them.

A glance at the man beside her was a mistake. He watched her through shaded eyes. A tiny shiver of desire went through her. She needed out of the enclosed space. Her fingers skimmed the window, already knowing there was no way to open it. They were sealed inside. No wonder she couldn't fight her desires. She was locked in a box with his pheromones.

As they turned, she was able to see the biosphacility. It curved high from the ground in a large dome surrounded a good distance away by high security gates constructed of a ring of solid stone topped by several rows of thick metal bars. Covered walkways snaked out from the center facility toward the gates like tentacles, releasing into the surrounding forest. They moved down an incline and the view became blocked by the wall.

"Are we in danger?" The transport stopped and made a series of fast beeps. The gate slid open just enough to let them slip through the wall. For a moment the transport became dark as they moved into the biosphacility. "What exactly is this wall meant to keep out?"

"Nature," he said. "The magnetic fields above keep out birds and insects. The thick wall keeps out other forest creatures. Sterilization protocols deal with any pollens and things we can't see."

An uneasiness crept through her. She felt isolated in this place. If they had to wear suits into the forest, and they were worried about whatever was in the forest getting in, she was going to be trapped there until they took her home. The more fearful she became, the more self-disciplined she tried to make herself appear. She had to maintain at least the façade of control. Her people expected her to represent them properly. It wasn't as if her travel companion Linnea was going to be much help in the inter-dimensional dignitary department when it came to representing their people.

Inside, the ground was covered with loose stones. A strange wave started under them, running in a foot-wide strip along the ground to the gate and then came back to the facility. The movement seemed to be rotating the stones on the ground and evening out the mark of footsteps. The transport drew them closer to the dome. For as large as this place was, it felt very, very small. She took a deep breath. This was her home for the next few months.

The transport stopped and the door automatically slid open. Gerard moved from his seat, hopping through the door onto the ground. He turned, offering his hand. She didn't take it, afraid of what she would feel if she touched him. Instead, she used the steps that slid out from the unit. When she vacated, the transport shut and slid along its way toward the biosphacility gate. She watched it briefly before turning her attention to her temporary home.

Chapter Nine

Gerard didn't wait for Dr. Markos to examine the entire building, not that there was much to look at beyond the white, shiny plates of the exterior walls. Just being around her was hard, and not just hard on his emotional well-being, but damned hard on his throbbing cock. One fuck hadn't been enough, but he'd been unwilling to try for a round two when she'd hardened toward him as she did. Now, she barely looked at him, treating him like a complete stranger. Okay, so he was a stranger, technically, but they'd fucked. The least she could do was acknowledge what was between them.

Even as her cold demeanor irritated him, it made him want her all the more. He wanted to see her face soften again in passion. He wanted to push her to her knees and watch her take him into her mouth. He wanted to drag her to the nearest laboratory, bend her over a worktable and pound her hard until ever last bit of cum drained out of his cock.

He widened his easy smile and continued down the long, metal corridor. Doors lined each side. Bringing her into section one, he paused by a laboratory's entryway. "This will be where you work."

She leaned past him, careful not to touch. A few of the facility staff came down the hall. They paused, curiously eyeing their newest guest.

"Dr. Markos," Gerard automatically introduced. "This is Dr. Sunn, Dr. Frank, Dr. Jonns. Doctors, this is Dr. Cecilia Markos from New Order Society, Dimensional Plane 303. She is here to study."

"Ah, initial contact," Dr. Candra Sunn said, dismissively. She didn't think much of most inter-dimensional dignitaries and found them useless because only rarely could they provide their world with any kind of real medical advancements. She often vocally spoke out against teaching their secrets to so many other planes. "We will not be seeing each other again. I return to my arctic facility today." Then, to Gerard, she added, "I will stop by before I go." Though her tone gave nothing away, she glanced meaningfully at the clipboard she carried. She was probably reading his arousal levels and offering to take care of him before she left. The woman had sucked him off a couple times, and was quite good at it, but he didn't feel like taking her up on it this time. No, he wanted Cecilia on her knees begging for it. Without further acknowledging Cecilia, Dr. Sunn continued along her way.

Frank and Jonns were more polite. Cecilia smiled at them, warmly took their hands in greeting, and even invited them to her assigned laboratory any time they wanted. Gerard stiffened, jealous. Franks clearly took her to mean more than she had been offering—at least she had better not be offering sex to the man. Jonns appeared interested as well. If this woman thought she was going to sample her way around the men, she had another think coming.

Where was all this possessiveness coming from? His testosterone levels were way out of control. He blamed all the fantasizing he'd been doing about off-plane women since attending Sebastjan's wedding.

He waited while Cecilia went into her lab to look around. He pointed out a few of the devices before handing her a training clipboard. "If you read this, it will tell you everything you need to know about running the devices and will allow you to access any information you desire."

She took it. "Thank you."

"I'll show you to your private quarters. Your luggage should already be there." He didn't wait to see if she would follow. If he couldn't live out the fantasies pounding in his brain, he needed to get away from her to clear his mind. The wide hall split off into a narrower one which would lead to private quarters.

He stopped at her door and waited for it to slide open. The smooth walls of the chamber held no decoration, nothing that would set it apart from any other room on dimensional plane 187. A thick mattress with silver covers had been placed on the platform in the middle of the room. A health monitor turned on with the lights. There was a small area for personal needs, a row of drawers built into the wall, and items to cover every basic necessity she might have. The dark red of her bags stood out against the monochromatic interior so there was no need for him to point them out.

Stepping inside, he said, "You sleep here. Settle in however you like, read through some of the tutorials and I will be back later to bring you to the daily sustenance."

"Thank you." She stepped around him, keeping her distance as if she thought he might grab her.

Gerard turned abruptly and left, unable to stand being in her frustrating presence a moment longer.

Cecilia was finding it much harder to act controlled than she would have preferred. How did Gerard do it? Smiling as if he was completely unaffected by what they'd done. Was fucking dignitaries a normal thing for him? And why did she care?

Oh, yeah, because she was so hot she wanted nothing more than to tear off his clothes and go for a round two...and three...and four...and...

Cecilia groaned. The door slid shut behind her and she hoped it would stay that way. She dropped the electronic clipboard on the bed. Her clothes had the faint scent of sex on them, or at least she imagined they did. She pulled out of the one-piece suit, feeling as if the material was an extension of his hands on her body.

Her sex ached, begging for another climax. It would be so easy to slide a finger inside her wet pussy, though she knew that would hardly satisfy what she needed. Instead, she began opening drawers and digging through the contents. Some she could speculate as to their purpose, other objects were foreign contraptions she didn't even want to guess at. Finding a set of local garb, she tugged the material on, figuring it would be best for her to blend in. Then, still aching, she sat on the bed and began figuring out how to run the electronic clipboard. She was there to work and that was exactly what she was going to do. Hopefully, these two months would pass by quickly and if she tried really hard, she could avoid Dr. Gerard Fauchet.

Chapter Ten

Cecilia closed her eyes and pressed her fingers to her temples. Two weeks of staring at the electronic clipboard, trying to translate what equated to some kind of ancient medical cipher, had caused a dull ache all the prescribed shots in the neck couldn't seem to get rid of. Even as she thought it, the wall monitor dinged for her attention. She glanced at it and frowned. Apparently it had read her headache and had dispatched another prescription. She knew from past attempts if she didn't take the medicine they would send someone to check on her, reciting something about protocol. Still, she didn't move. She wanted to figure out their basic formula for curing seasonal illnesses.

"Can you shut that off?" Cecilia's tone was more of an order than a question. Linnea glanced at her from where she stared at a handheld unit and nodded. The assistant went to the wall monitor and punched in a dismissal code. The woman didn't speak much, at least not to Cecilia. When Linnea wasn't performing a required task, she was reading.

The laboratory was spacious, more so than her private quarters. She'd managed to figure out most of the equipment. Though much different in design, it functioned a lot like the technology on her plane did—only more advanced. There were work tables, dozens of pieces of medical testing equipment and sterile tubes lining one of the walls. In the corner there was a sleeping cot.

The laboratory door opened and Dr. Franks appeared. He smiled, holding up a shot. "I'm here to administer your medicine. The computer sent me an alert."

"That's not all he's here to administer," Linnea mumbled as she walked back to her seat to resume reading.

Cecilia ignored her. She much preferred when the woman didn't speak. Every word that came from Linnea's mouth seemed to drip with sarcasm. Though, in this instance, Linnea did have a small point. Dr. Franks had made his intentions toward her very known and her gentle rebuttals had met with friendly ignorance. His eyes invited her attentions. However, whereas Franks was a very attractive man, she couldn't help thinking of Gerard Fauchet.

It wasn't lost on her that she'd been determined to avoid Dr. Fauchet when she'd arrived at the biosphacility. At the time, she'd thought it would be difficult. However, as days turned to weeks and she didn't see him, she was beginning to feel slighted. How could she pointedly ignore a man who didn't show himself?

Then there were the nights—the long, long nights. Alone in her quarters, the work done for the day, all she could think about was the transporter. Strong chest. Firm flesh. Gripping hands. Heavy breath. Thick, pounding coc—

"Doctor?" Franks asked.

Cecilia blinked, realizing she'd begun daydreaming of Gerard during the day now. Heat warmed her features and she found it hard to recover her self-control. "Sorry? I'm in the middle of..." She held up an electronic clipboard, completely unable to recall what she'd been reading moments before.

"I understand," Franks said, lifting the shot. She leaned her head to the side to give him access to her neck and closed her eyes. He gave her a quick injection. It did lessen her headache. He then deposited the dispenser into the wall unit to be sanitized. "Perhaps we can talk later, after you're done with your work?"

Linnea gave a small laugh. Both doctors turned to her. She held up her clipboard and motioned to its contents. "Funny stuff."

"Perhaps," Cecilia said, "but there is a lot for me to learn and only a couple of months for me to do it in."

Franks grinned, clearly taking her words to mean there was hope for his suit. She sighed as he left, only to stiffen as the object of her desires entered. Gerard was the last person she'd expected to see. For a moment, she blinked, thinking she hallucinated him. When he didn't disappear, she gave a slight nod.

"I've come to see how things are progressing. My reports say you've accessed many of the public databases." Gerard's voice was low. Even though his easy smile gave her no hope of a repeated transporter trip, she couldn't help the shiver of anticipation and longing that filtered through her. She'd had time to think and was a little ashamed she'd been so quick to deny what had happened.

"I wouldn't say *many*," Cecilia said, glancing at her work. Was he having fun at her expense? She'd only accessed a couple of the basics and was still trying to figure out equivalent expressions for the same things on her plane. "But I'm managing."

Linnea cleared her throat and stood. She held her clipboard to her chest. "If you no longer need me?"

"Yes, fine," Cecilia dismissed. Her assistant left.

When they were alone, he continued, "The reports also say you've had several headache injections since I've been gone. I've come to see if you have an underlying medical problem. Are such headaches normal?"

"You were gone?" she asked, surprised. That would explain why she hadn't seen him. She'd thought he'd been staying away from her because she'd told him to. Almost every day she'd regretted it.

"Didn't someone tell you? I was called back to Asclepius by Dr. Lu. There was a matter that needed my attention." Gerard's eyes dipped, not meeting hers.

"Asclepius?" Cecilia put the clipboard down and took several steps toward him. She breathed rapidly. "It's not the portal, is it? We're not...?"

"Trapped?" he finished for her. "No, it's not the portal. It was a medical issue."

"Oh." Cecilia felt a little silly for her panic. "I hope everything worked out favorably?"

"Not yet. Hopefully soon." His tone dismissed the subject. "We were discussing your head."

This was not the conversation she wanted to have, but she was unsure how to start something more intimate. "They're tension headaches, nothing more. There is a lot of information to absorb and very little time to do it. I was hoping that you would let me bring the files home with me to further study—"

"Let me stop you there. No, I apologize, but our medical knowledge does not leave our plane. It is the law. You are welcome to the public information while you're here, but anything that leaves has to be pre-negotiated between the Medical Supreme and your politicians." Gerard smiled, the irritatingly easy look she'd remembered all too often while alone in her quarters.

Cecilia knew as much. Still, she'd been instructed to try.

"Is there something I can assist you with to help with the headaches?" His smile remained intact. He went to the door and pushed the scanner next to it. The unit beeped once, indicating the door was locked.

"What are you doing, Dr. Fauchet?"

Gerard laughed. He arched a brow. "Really? You have to ask?"

"I mean, of course I know what you're doing." Cecilia became flustered and she didn't like that he could make her feel like an idiot with just one playful look. "What happened to remaining professional?"

"Most of the laboratories are closed for the night. Your assistant is gone. I can think of nothing more professional than a doctor trying to cure another doctor's headache."

The man was incorrigible, and yet she found herself unable to suppress a small laugh.

"You can't tell me you haven't considered fucking me again?" he persisted.

"I wanted to apologize for how I left things last time. I reacted badly." Cecilia had to admit his confidence was sexy. "Still, what you are suggesting is not..."

"What?" He came closer. "Please don't say prudent."

"Logical," Cecilia finished.

"Which is exactly why I prescribe it for you." He came to a stop in front of her. The smell of him was familiar. A shiver worked down her spine. Her breathing deepened. Gerard lowered his tone to a seductive whisper. "The only way to cure logic is by doing something illogical."

"They do say that doctors should never diagnose themselves." What was she doing? This man was chaos. She was about control. Still, no one would know. No one would see. He was her one chance to give in to something wild and crazy. "No one can know about this."

"You made your terms clear." Gerard pressed his mouth to hers, stopping any last-second protests she might make.

Cecilia liked to think she would have made such protests, but in truth she doubted it. The second she saw him, she wanted him again. She wanted a release from work, from feeling like a complete, inept idiot who couldn't read a basic medical book. Basic inter-dimensional communication was the same, but their advanced medical language had a nuance to it she couldn't quite grasp.

"Now let me tell you my terms," he whispered.

When she would have pulled away, he moved forward and deepened the kiss until all reason faded into that blissful moment. She grabbed his hair briefly before running her hands down to his lab coat. Eagerly she tugged it open, fumbling with the material to get to the flesh underneath. He finally let her escape his kiss. She gasped for breath. The intensity of his eyes pierced into her, holding her gaze captive. She couldn't close her eyes and she couldn't look away.

"You can keep your secret, Doctor," he allowed, "but no more denying what is between us."

Their breaths mingled, heavy, passionate pants of air. His hands artfully unfastened her lab coat to expose her skin underneath. She did not wear the customary undershirt beneath the coat, finding the practice of layering multiple pieces of clothing odd and uncomfortable.

Gerard ran his hands down her chest. He caressed her breasts, his fingers tweaking her nipples.

"And what is between us?" Cecilia asked with a small moan of pleasure. What was it about this man? She'd never reacted so strongly to a lover before.

"Passion, attraction..." He thrust his hips against her so she could feel the hard outline of his cock. "Sexual chemistry."

Sexual chemistry wasn't exactly the most romantic thing he could have said, but the way he said it caused her to shiver in anticipation. The tension eased out of her, melting away into oblivion. Even so, she refused to give over the last bit of control. She turned him so that his ass pressed against a work table.

Cecilia undressed him, freeing his cock from beneath his pants. Boldly, she stroked the length, running her hands over his shaft. His breath caught. She did it again, tightening her grip.

Gerard reached for her face, but she dodged his kiss. His lips curled up at one side in a half smile. Challenge lit in his gaze. His lab coat was open, hanging on his arms. She grabbed hold of it and pulled him with her toward a small cot in the corner of the room. When she released the material, the coat fell to the floor.

Cecilia pushed the pants from her hips, kicking them off her feet. She fell back onto the cot. Gerard followed her, naturally settling between her legs. The smooth, firm texture of his skin felt so good against her hands. She wrapped her legs around his, hooking her feet on the back of his knees to draw him forward.

"I'm going to fuck you, Cecilia," Gerard asserted boldly, "without written permission."

Cecilia moaned in response, thrilled by the naughtiness of it.

"You're my bad girl, aren't you?" Gerard kissed her.

She bit his bottom lip lightly. Her nails raked his back and he shivered, making a small noise of approval. She scratched harder while licking his lip. The hard press of his cock drew along her inner thigh. She trembled in anticipation, tensing ever so slightly while she waited for that first intimate slide of his body inside her. That first thrust did not come as hard and fast as she expected. Instead, he entered her slowly, forcing her eyes to meet his passionate gaze. "Look at me."

Cecilia obeyed. Her toes curled and she found it hard to catch her breath. He moved against her, his hips brushing her thighs before pulling back. Each movement was measured and drawn out.

There were no words, nothing beyond that look in his eyes and the feel of his body. Every part of her concentrated on him. Planes and worlds did not exist. The laboratory did not exist. Medical science, anti-chaos laws and annoying assistants did not exist. There was only now, him, this moment of perfection.

Cecilia pushed her hips, trying to force him to quicken his pace. He didn't, remaining in complete control. The rhythm was torment, sweet and utter torment. She wanted to shove him onto his back and take over, but he wouldn't obey her insistent pushes along his shoulders.

The pleasure built, racking through her body in a giant explosive release. Only after she'd found her climax did Gerard join her. He tensed, frozen at the pentacle of desire for the briefest of moments before collapsing over her.

Cecilia's bones felt as if they melted inside her body. Her legs fell limply to the sides. Gerard shielded her from his weight by bracing himself on his elbow.

"How does this keep happening?" she whispered.

He turned his face toward her neck, nuzzling her. "Simple. I'm irresistible."

She weakly hit his arm.

He pulled back, giving her the charming smile he wore so well. "Because you are irresistible."

"This can't go anywhere. As soon as my assignment here is over, I have to go home." Cecilia didn't want to face reality, but it came crashing in around them anyway.

Gerard kissed her neck and ear. "Unless your plane has some kind of future-telling ability we don't know about, you have no way of predicting what will happen. Stop trying to define everything. Just let it be what it is. Let it become what it will become."

"I need us to be honest. My plane has logic. Logic tells me nothing will come of this. My heart tells me I don't belong here and that I want to go home. I would never be able to accept a permanent post here. I have a life on my world that I will not leave behind." Cecilia wasn't sure why she needed to make sure he understood. Maybe she needed herself to hear the words aloud.

"We don't offer permanent posts."

"My point exactly. And from what I understand of the agreement, none of your medical technology can come back. I'm assuming that includes the doctors as well. You can't come with me." She reminded herself to remain in control of her emotions. Chaos brought with it a myriad of problems. When Gerard touched her she became mindless. This second encounter proved as much.

"No. Doctors do not accept permanent posts elsewhere. Normally other planes come to us. We do not go to them." He kissed her again, sending shivers over her. "But there is no reason for you not to have some fun while you're here."

Beyond the way he made her feel, the only thing she knew of this man came from how those at the biosphacility spoke of him. They respected him, that much was clear, but there was little said beyond that.

"It's late and I have a lot of reading left to do tonight." She pushed at his shoulder.

"Are you sure? I could follow you back to your quarters." He let her guide him up.

"Linnea is going to meet me there later to finish up our logs," she lied. She moved to gather her clothing, glancing at the door. It was locked, but that didn't stop her from thinking someone might come in and catch them.

"That is unfortunate. Though I suppose there are things I should attend to. There will be plenty of paperwork to sign from my absence." He stood, pulling on his lab coat. "However, now that I'm back I'm sure we'll be seeing much more of each other. I'll come by tomorrow evening. Try not to make plans with Linnea."

Cecilia was much slower to move as she fastened her coat. He waited while she righted her clothing. Then, coming to her, he gently kissed her mouth and caressed her cheek.

"Dream well, Dr. Markos," he whispered.

Cecilia watched him go, trying to look calm. Inside, her emotions erupted into chaos.

Chapter Eleven

Gerard had not planned on making love to Cecilia again. Yes, he'd thought about her endlessly while away, but he hadn't expected a repeat of their time in the transport. There was just something about her that drew him to her and silently begged for his kisses. He felt the pull as strongly as that first moment, if not more so. Even now he tasted her on his lips.

But her shame of their sexual encounters had not changed. Why was he doing this to himself? She was right. There was no future in it.

It didn't matter. He was taken by her and he would go back to her again and again, as often as she would have him, until their story together came to an end.

"Dr. Fauchet, I heard you had returned. What news? Is it true? Has there been an outbreak?"

Gerard frowned, quickly glancing behind him to make sure no one heard Dr. Jonns's panicked questions. He was under strict orders that no outsiders should know of their situation. Dr. Jonns only knew because he'd intercepted a message meant for Dr. Swift. Unfortunately, the man's level of panic would only be magnified if the full truth were known. Jonns wasn't exactly the most composed of researchers, preferring botany science and food production to human infectious diseases even though he was technically qualified to help with the problem. Should others find out before they had more facts, there would be worldwide terror. With their medical advancements came a false sense of security that they could cure anything.

"No. There is no outbreak," Gerard assured the man.

Jonns did not look fully convinced. "Then the illness is contained? How many infected? What is it?" Looking at Gerard, he stepped back. He glanced up at the wall monitor, as if Gerard himself might be carrying a new virus.

Gerard lifted up his hands. "I'm clean. I've been scanned many times."

Jonns nodded, but did not reclose the distance between them.

"Privacy Code Six has been enacted. We're not allowed to discuss it with anyone. Since you're privy to the information, you will be tasked as one of the members working to find out what it is we're dealing with. Currently, there is only one infected, but we're concerned the virus is airborne. Sanitation protocols have been enacted as well."

"Who? Who is infected? A traveler? Are they quarantined? What about the portal? Have they suspended travel?"

Gerard heard the door behind him and gestured Jonns to hurry down the hall. They ducked into an empty laboratory. Seconds later, Cecilia walked by the door. She did not look in.

"Is it..?" Jonns motioned toward the door in horror. "Dr. Markos and Sans Nel? They're the carriers, are they?"

"No." That was the last rumor Gerard wanted circulating around amongst his peers. If Jonns thought the virus was inside the local facility, the man wouldn't be able to keep his mouth shut about it. "I am not at liberty to discuss the patient, but he is local. You will get a copy of the report. Dr. Swift will personally deliver the information when it is ready. Until then, you are to clear your cases and prepare a private laboratory to work. Assign your current projects to another doctor. This is top priority."

Jonns nodded in understanding. "It is one of the facility directors, isn't it? They're always overseeing experiments they shouldn't be." The man was merely guessing. "Dr. Sebastian Walter? The Medical

Supreme's son? That's why the secrecy. Or Dr. Hattu? They found something at the underwater biosphacility. They're always bringing up samples they should leave on the ocean floor."

Gerard was careful not to give anything away with his expression. "I cannot say more."

Jonns gave him a knowing look, though Gerard doubted the man knew the full extent of what they were dealing with. In truth, Jonns was not the man Gerard would have picked for this job. But it wasn't his decision. It was Swift's.

"You have your orders, Doctor." Gerard reached to open the door. He glanced out, making sure the halls were empty. His eyes lingered in the direction where Cecilia disappeared. "And I have a stack of paperwork waiting for me."

Chapter Twelve

Gerard had come as promised that first night, and every night since. Cecilia found herself looking forward to his visits, even going so far as to send Linnea away early. He never said much, beyond the charming nothings that seemed to come so easily for him. He asked if she needed supplies, if the food was to her liking, if he wanted to let him follow her back to her quarters to stay the night. The laboratory was well stocked, the food was bland but palatable—not that she told him as much—and the answer to his last question was always, "No. I have much work to do."

Passion wasn't a problem. One look, one touch, one kiss and she fell willingly into his arms. The problem came afterward, when she watched him leave, and she realized each night she fell deeper and deeper into chaos. The more she was with him, the more she thought about him when he was away. Her mind drifted from her work. Every nerve ending tingled until the damned wall monitor beeped and forced her to take shots for her levels.

"Levels," she muttered. Half the time she didn't understand what the unbalanced levels were that the computer was telling her to fix. If the desire stirred too fierce, a shot to the neck numbed it back to manageable levels.

Cecilia rubbed her neck. She was really tired of injections. As if on cue, the wall monitor beeped. Frustrated, she grabbed the electronic syringe, pressed it to the wall unit and stuck it in her neck. The knot in her stomach eased, but it was just a physical relief, not a mental one. The stress remained.

There was one very glaringly obvious fact about this plane—citizens were obsessed with immortality. There were numerous references to the pursuit of escaping death. Some tried to find the path to ascension, electrocuting themselves in the process, the rest of them just tried to cure everything and block out what they couldn't.

She looked up at the ceiling. They'd been trapped inside since they arrived.

"Over half," Linnea said. The woman hardly ever spoke to her but when she did the words were tipped with an emotion akin to indifference.

"Half of what?" Cecilia asked.

"You were mumbling out loud again," Linnea said, not glancing up from her work. "You said we were almost halfway done. In fact, we are over halfway done. As of yesterday, we are starting month two."

"It's this place. With no daylight, it's impossible to keep track of the hours." Cecilia studied the woman, part of her wishing Linnea was someone else, part of her wishing Linnea would look up and smile at her in some kind of same-plane camaraderie.

Linnea did look up, but it wasn't to smile. "Go up to the top level. There's plenty of sunlight."

"The top level?" Cecilia again looked up, as if the ceiling would part and show her something new.

"Haven't you wandered around at all?" Linnea asked.

"No. I've only gone where instructed, as should you. They showed us our quarters, the dining hall and our laboratory."

"Not surprising this," Linnea drawled. "You're one of those true believers in the anti-chaos, aren't you? One of the devout."

"No," Cecilia denied, not liking the comparison to being a monk.

"Really? Then why all the shame about Dr. Fauchet?" Linnea chuckled.

Cecilia stiffened. "I don't know what you mean."

"All right then. Whatever you say, Doctor." Linnea laughed harder. "It's about time for you to kick me out for your..." The woman paused, giving her a meaningful look. "Your nightly serious platonic anti-chaos discussions with Dr. Fauchet."

Cecilia felt heat rising to her cheeks at the sarcastic tone. "My professional medical conversations with Dr. Fauchet, our inter-dimensional contact, are not of your concern. You haven't been to medical school, so I understand you have no idea the level of complicated maneuvering and paperwork involved in a mission such as ours."

Linnea set down her electronic clipboard and moved toward the door. "A little hint, Doctor." She ran her hand over the wall unit and smiled. It wasn't lost on Cecilia that she'd been wishing for that very look just moments before. Now she wished it would go away. Linnea's smiles weren't comforting. "As you've pointed out on many occasions, I'm not a doctor, but in my experience, anti-chaos conversations work much better if you keep your clothes on."

The woman left and seconds later the wall unit beeped for her to correct her levels. Cecilia glared at the monitor. Linnea's words left her mortified. Everywhere she looked reminded her of making love to Gerard. Perhaps having an affair inside her laboratory wasn't the best of ideas.

Instead of correcting anything, she slammed her hand against the counter and stormed out of the laboratory. She wanted to be in control. There was comfort in control. Control was safe and good and right and...

Her breathing deepened. She needed to monitor her emotional output. If she kept on as she was, in a month she'd be an embarrassing wreck returning home. Cecilia wasn't sure where to go. She couldn't be in the laboratory and she couldn't roam the areas of the biosphacility where she'd not been explicitly told she could venture.

Her feet carried her to her private quarters. Perhaps it was best she hid where no one could see her. Once inside, she paced the floor like a caged animal.

A strange beep sounded by the door. She ignored it. It was probably just a warning to take her shot. Seconds later the door slid open.

She inhaled sharply and turned, lifting her arms up in fright.

"What's happening?" Gerard asked, coming in without being invited.

"I locked the door." Cecilia pointed at the monitor.

"And I overrode the lock," he explained. "Now, what is happening? The computer said you were agitated and that you did not take your shot. Are you ill? What are you feeling?"

"You need to go. I can't concentrate when you're near." She waved him away when he stepped closer. "I need to concentrate. My assistant hates me, which is fine, because she's rude and sarcastic, but she's not a doctor so I can't really discuss medical stuff with her beyond telling her what to log for our paperwork. Your plane's medical knowledge is so vast, yet I'm still stuck trying to decipher that what we call Firghelm Syndrome you call Policompititen-something."

"Policompition Ten," he supplied.

"Yes, that!" She resumed her pacing. "We cured Firghelm years ago, but I just spent a day translating your documents to try to understand what I was looking at, only to discover it was chronic itchy feet. I thought it was the basic formula for curing seasonal illnesses. But no, itchy feet."

He smiled that damned charming look that made her all tingly. Her frown deepened.

"There is no way I'm going to get much past the basics at the rate I'm going," she continued. "My government is depending on me to bring back something fabulous. If I don't, I could very well lose my job, or if I'm lucky, simply be demoted. What is worse, if that happens, I can't tell people why. I can't say, well I was in an alternate reality and only given two months to conquer the impossible task of trying to learn a new language and get a secondary medical degree. They'll think I'm insane." Cecilia turned her attention to Gerard. "Then there is you. You make me all chaotic inside."

"Cecilia, take a breath." He reached into his pocket and pulled out an electronic syringe. He leaned toward her and injected her before she had time to swat his hand away. He dropped the syringe in a nearby disposal. "Better?"

Yes, she did feel better physically. She felt calmer and able to focus. However, warmth flowed through her veins, unlike the previous injections, giving her the sensation of being tipsy. "You shouldn't be in here."

"Neither should you." His hand brushed her cheek. "We had a meeting scheduled in your laboratory. I was looking forward to it. Seeing you is the highlight to my day."

A shiver worked over her. She couldn't pull herself away from him. His eyes held such emotion, beautiful and passionate. His charming smile drew her closer. This man had a power about him. If she believed in magic, she would have called it that.

Gerard fingered a strand of her hair. His eyes stayed on hers, as if something about her fascinated him. Heat built inside her. Electricity snapped between them, silent, invisible and strong. It always happened like this. Whenever he was near, she was pulled deeper and deeper into his chaos.

There was a surety to his actions she did not have. He knew what he wanted and wasn't ashamed of taking it. The backs of his fingers fell against her neck. The hair he held tickled her as he drew a line down the neckline of her lab coat. The lock slipped from his grasp and he turned his hand to begin unfastening the coat.

"I enjoy your smell," he whispered. "Is it a special scent from your home plane?"

"It is government-approved soap," she answered. "All citizens are issued the same kind."

He breathed deeply and sighed. "I like it."

Gerard's hand brushed over her naked breast as he continued unfastening the coat. The action caused her nipple to tighten in anticipation. As the material was lifted from her skin, the cool room air puckered her flesh, erecting the tiny hairs.

"Some planes call horripilation bird flesh." He hummed thoughtfully and lightly touched her chest. "Or goosebumps."

"How do you keep all the words in your head?" Her mind followed the path of his fingers instead of concentrating fully on his words.

"They say I have a talent for languages. If I read it, the words seem to stay in my head."

"I hate feeling stupid."

"No one here thinks you're stupid. The fact that your plane trusted you enough to send you here proves your intelligence." Then louder, he added, "Computer, dim lights."

The lights dimmed in the room. She gasped, looking up. "They didn't tell me the room was voice activated."

"It's in the tutorials file package you received on the handheld when you arrived." His lips swept along hers.

"The tutorials were organized horribly. The workflow was completely sideways compared to what I'm used to."

He chuckled.

"I shouldn't complain," she amended quickly. "On behalf of my plane, we are very grateful for this opportunity to learn from you and I will try harder and work longer hours."

"Shh," Gerard urged. "Try to quiet your mind. Thinking about something too hard makes it harder to understand."

Shadows cast over his features. His words drew her full attention to his face while he undressed her. Her clothes slipped easily off her body. He ran his hands down the small of her back, over the curve of her ass. When she stood completely naked, he stepped back, studying her form.

Gerard leisurely pulled off his clothes, letting her watch. His fingers followed the stripe on his coat, unfastening the hidden buttons. She licked her lips in anticipation, watching the show of flesh unfold. His erection lifted his pants. He pulled the waistband forward, freeing his cock.

She moved to her bed and lay on her back. Naked, he crawled over her. She lifted her arms to accept him and her hands glided over his strong chest, rising and falling along the ridges of his muscles. The intimacy of the dimmed light contrasted that of the bright laboratory. Her eyes caressed him, following her hands.

Gerard settled between her legs. His hips forced them open. The hard length of his arousal stroked along the wet folds of her pussy. He parted his lips and his mouth hovered over hers. A light moan escaped her, turning into a gasp when he pressed his hips more firmly against her.

Fingers skimmed her nipples before making their way down her stomach. He gently opened the lips of her sex, readying her body to take his. She tensed, taking his breath into her lungs as she waited for that perfect moment.

Gerard's mouth claimed hers as he thrust forward. His tongue glided through her lips as his cock entered her sex. He braced his weight to the side as he moved within her. His free hand found her breast, massaging the globe deeply. He rocked his hips against her and soon the steady rhythm became frantic and pounding. Their limbs tangled in a series of frenzied movements. She flipped him over on his back and raked her nails down his chest. He groaned, rolling her back around to thrust harder.

Bedding bunched under her thigh and she lifted her leg. He hooked the back of her knee with his arm. The move let him go deeper still.

"*Apolloa*, you are sweet."

"I'm Cecilia," she corrected, instantly pushing at his shoulders.

"It means goddess," he assured her, kissing her deeply before she could stop and think too much.

The pleasure built before exploding within her. She gasped and tensed as the climax overtook her body. Gerard's release joined hers. He jerked his hips, trembling violently above her.

He fell next to her on the bed. She lay beside him, relaxed and sated, not thinking, just being. That was, until he spoke.

"I am sorry the translations are proving difficult. What if we extended your visit?" he asked.

She turned her head to look at him. His face was close, his nose almost touching hers. The smell of him radiated over her. Cecilia almost said yes in a moment of weakness—yes to him, not to work. "My government would not allow it without better reason. There is protocol that must be followed to change a mission order. My people don't like surprise and change. I can't guarantee I'd find enough reason with a little extra time, unless your government would be willing to give me the answers?"

"They don't know you well enough. My government is not too trusting, especially on a first mission."

"Are you allowed to help me translate the text?" she asked. "I would appreciate the assistance."

It was hard for her to ask it. She was so used to doing things on her own, for herself. On her plane she was in a competitive field.

"I'll do what I can." Gerard pushed up and sighed. "Are you sure you won't reconsider and stay longer?"

"I told you, it's not up to me. It would take a minimum of two months to fast-track something through the government channels."

"I'm sorry to hear that." He turned his back to her.

"You knew my stay was temporary," Cecilia whispered. She reached to touch him but merely let her hand hover near his back, not making contact. "We both knew the arrangement going in."

"I'm sorry, because I was hoping you would stay voluntarily and this next conversation could be avoided." He stood and grabbed his lab coat. He slipped it over his shoulders, not bothering to put on the undershirt.

Cecilia grabbed the blankets and pulled them to her chest. "Explain yourself."

"We cannot allow you to leave our plane at this time."

"You are kidnapping us?" She pushed up from the bed. Panic filled her. The biosphacility was in the middle of their planet, far from the portal. The portal was in the middle of their most prestigious hospital, hidden by a maze of hallways. She'd never find her way back there, not without help. "Why would you do such a thing?"

"The decision has been made for reasons I cannot discuss with you. But, for the time being all inter-dimensional travel has been suspended. All dignitaries will remain at their assigned facilities until further notice." He didn't look at her so she forced him to by stepping in his way. She stared at him until his eyes met hers. "There has been a medical incident at Asclepius. Until such a time as it passes, we cannot permit any travel outside of our plane." She arched a brow, not moving. "Cecilia...Dr. Markos, please understand that this is hope-fully a temporary situation and is incredibly rare. It is possible this will be resolved before you were supposed to leave."

"Possible but not likely." Her expression was stiff and her breathing too measured.

He tried to comfort her, but she saw he doubted his own words. Her mind whirled with thoughts. A medical situation that these people were not equipped to handle? Not only was she trapped in an alien world, they were under medical containment. What if they never let her leave the biosphacility?

"Leave." Cecilia's heart beat hard in her chest.

"I told you. Not until there is portal clearance."

"Leave," she repeated. The wall monitor beeped. He lifted his hand as if to indicate she needed medicine. "I said get out of my quarters."

"Oh, you mean leave your room." He quickly pulled on his pants. Gerard paused beside the door. He opened his mouth to speak but she cut him off with a hard look as she pointed at the door in warning. He nodded once and left her alone.

Cecilia gasped for breath, trying not to cry out. Her knees weakened and she collapsed onto the bed. She panted, trying to get oxygen into her body, but she found it hard to breathe. Fear trapped her mind. She couldn't live like this, forever, here, forever...

"Forever?" She stared at the sterile walls, feeling as if they grew smaller. A couple of months was one thing, but now? She hugged her legs to her chest. "Please don't make me stay here forever."

Chapter Thirteen

The relationship with Cecilia wasn't going according to Gerard's plan. Well, honestly, he didn't really have a plan, but if he did, this would not be it. Every time he went to her, he ran through his mind what he wanted to say to her. None of it ever made it past his lips. One look at her and every logical thought left his brain.

"I could have handled it better," he told himself, not for the first time that morning. He knew he'd said too much about their situation, but that hadn't stopped him.

"Dr. Fauchet?"

Seeing Dr. Sam Swift, Gerard turned his attention to the man. He didn't try to make excuses for why he was pacing back and forth along the long corridor. "Dr. Markos does not want to take us up on the offer to stay longer. I plan to take her outside and try again. Maybe a walk in the forest will pique her scientific interest. What about Sans Nel? Did you get a chance to talk to her last night?"

"I did. Instinct tells me they are not responsible for this." Sam hesitated. "I received a communication early this morning. The Medical Supreme's condition has worsened. A couple of his staff are now showing symptoms. It's spreading. If we can't make the dignitaries want to stay, then we have no choice but to inform them or imprison them. I have no wish to imprison them."

Gerard let loose a long breath. He didn't tell the Medical Director that he'd already told Cecilia too much the night before. For some reason he found it impossible to lie to her. "There are other options. I can break protocol and ask her to help us with this problem. Or I can show her something that is not in the public dignitary archives, something she will not be able to resist."

"The Medical Supreme will never approve opening up the secure knowledge bases to strangers. Even sick, I doubt he would give up any future bargaining chips. However, he might agree to have another doctor work on his illness. If we don't tell her it's from our plane, and we don't mention that the Medical Supreme is sick..." Sam rubbed the bridge of his nose thoughtfully. Gerard wondered at the man's tone. Sam was normally very decisive. "Let me speak with Dr. Lu."

"If it helps, Dr. Markos has accessed more of the records in a short time than most dignitaries do in most trips." He didn't mention Cecilia's doubts in her ability to understand that material.

"I remember seeing a report for her login. I didn't think her accesses high in number. In fact, I think they were average."

"Check her assistant's code," Gerard assured him. "I think she has Sans Nel bring up the reports for her."

Sam stretched his fingers wide, studying his hands. "All right. I'll discuss it with Dr. Lu."

Gerard knew that was the best answer he was going to get. In order to give her access, Dr. Swift needed a second doctor with high level clearance to sign off on the plan. "So I have your permission to take her outside?"

Sam nodded. "I'll sign off on it as soon as I get to my office."

Gerard hoped Cecilia would be agreeable. Her stress levels were getting worse and her injections more frequent. That worried him. Unlike Linnea, she didn't seem to leave the visitor's section of the facility. She needed to see there was more to his plane than labs and medical texts. The last thing he wanted was to imprison her here. If they did that, she would never forgive them, or him.

Chapter Fourteen

Cecilia blinked as the bright sunlight hit her face for the first time in over a month. The brightness did not bring the expected warmth, though. Inside the large, white, plastic suit her body temperature was regulated. The clear plastic shield over face separated her from the fresh air. As her eyes adjusted, she looked up at the tall trees. Behind her, the biosphacility door slid shut, closing off the maze of dim hallways they'd walked through to get to the outside border.

For a moment, she didn't move. Gerard wore a matching suit. His movements were stiff as he turned to her. When he spoke, the small click of a communicator preceded his words. "Try to breathe normally. You will get used to the suit."

"I am breathing normally," she answered, though it was a lie. Her panted breaths filled the helmet, fogging the bottom edge of the face shield.

When she moved to follow him over the dirt path, the suit swished in time with her steps. Her thighs were forced open by the bulk of the material.

"This is ridiculous," she muttered.

"What?"

"I said this is ridiculous," she stated louder.

"No," Gerard corrected, "I meant, what is it you find ridiculous?"

"What are we doing out here?" Cecilia stopped walking. She couldn't learn anything stuffed inside a human-shaped bag. "Don't we need a specimen container?"

"We're not collecting specimens," he said.

"Then what?" She was forced to continue on after him when he didn't stop moving into the forest. The trees towered over them. She glanced back at the biosphacility. It wasn't far away, but the denseness of the forest obscured it from view within a short distance. "I should get back to my work."

"It's just a little further this way," he said, waving his arm forward.

"Are you going to help me find information useful to my plane?" she asked.

"No. I told you, the Medical Supreme would never allow it."

"You're not going to..." She hesitated, trying not to give in to the thread of fear curling insider her. "Are you bringing me out here because I refused to stay longer?"

"What?" He turned sharply. His hands lifted and he jerked the helmet off his head. "You honestly think I am capable of hurting you?"

"Gerard!" Cecilia rushed forward, her heart hammering in her chest. "What are you doing? Your helmet!" She grabbed to take it from him. The gloves made her hands clumsy as she tried to lift it up over his head. "Try not to breathe."

Gerard laughed. He snatched the helmet from her hands. "I'm rather partial to breathing."

Cecilia stared at him, confused.

His laugh faded and he gave her an endearing look. "Trust me." Gerard reached for her head. She pulled back. "Cecilia, trust me."

Slowly, she nodded. He unfastened her helmet and pulled it off her head. She took a deep breath as the cool air hit her. It felt nice and fresh, more like home. The scent of trees filled her nose. She pulled at the neck of her suit, craving the feel of air on her skin. The sweet sterilizer couldn't be detected in nature, but she knew it permeated her body. She ran her fingers through her hair, pushing it back from her face.

"Why would you lock yourselves away from this?" she asked.

"Fear does many things to people. When I was a child there were still a few people who were unafraid of nature and walked in parks without the protective gear. One year the pollen count was high and set off allergies. A few people who didn't walk outside were made sick by those who did. The Medical Supreme ordered new nature protocols and it became illegal to breathe unsanitized air."

"I'm breaking the law right now?" Cecilia wasn't sure why the idea didn't terrify her as much as it should have. "Won't the order-keepers come for us?"

He placed their helmets on the ground and began shrugging out of his protective suit. "You have nothing to fear."

"But there can be no society without control." The mantra sounded a bit hollow when she said it. "I am sure the Medical Supreme understands this and enacted the anti-chaos protocols for the good of society."

"I will tell you a secret if you promise not to repeat it." He waited for her nod of agreement. "The Medical Supreme has some of the worst allergies I have ever seen. He was one of the few affected by the secondary pollen exposure. Instead of inconveniencing himself with daily injections, he changed medical protocol."

"He is that sort of politician." Cecilia frowned. "This is why we are suddenly trapped? Something happened to the Medical Supreme that he does not like and everyone must now bend to his whim despite the chaos it causes."

"I never said it was the Medical Supreme who was sick." The surprise in his voice at her astuteness confirmed just that.

"It's an easy deduction even if your expression did not give you away. Considering what he did over allergies, I'm not surprised he closed down a portal for whatever this new thing is that he's contracted, especially if he thinks off-plane dignitaries are to blame for bringing it." Logic did not give her comfort. "Gerard, he's not going to let us go home, is he? He's blocking the portal."

"No," he assured her. He set his suit on the ground next to the helmets. "The portal is too important to this plane. They might make the travel protocols more stringent, but they will never cut off portal travel completely. I promise you, you will see your home world again. We have some of the best minds working on a cure. You just might go home later than planned."

"I want to see the medical reports. If my going home is contingent on discovering what this is, I deserve a chance to help." She glanced at his hands as he reached for her suit. He unfastened the shoulders to help her out of it. It didn't completely register what he was doing as she was more concentrated on her predicament. "Depending on what this is, it could take months, *years*, to understand it."

The weight of the suit slid off her shoulders and she stepped out of it. Gerard motioned around them. "I thought you might like to get out of the biosphacility. Normally, I would have offered you a tour before now, but this crisis has me occupied."

"I want to help," she repeated emphatically.

"I already asked for permission, but at this point it is probably too late to stop you. I've seen the number of documents you've had your assistant access on your behalf. You must really have a grasp on our medical knowledge by now. However, I must ask you to keep your suspicions about the Medical Supreme to yourself."

"My assistant?" She frowned, confused. "I don't have Linnea access documents for me. She does a few logs. I assume she's spending most of her days reading fiction novels."

"We don't have pretend novels," he said. "I have heard of such things being popular on other planes, but here if you write fiction it is punishable by death, since faking research results is a grave offense. Our records show she's accessed several medical documents."

Cecilia wasn't sure what to say. "But...she's not a doctor."

"Should we be worried? You don't think she's doing something with the information, do you?"

"No. I don't think she..." Cecilia frowned. She didn't want to lie, but she didn't know what the truth was. "Linnea and I only met for this assignment. My people would not send someone they did not think would act as a dignitary should."

A bird call sounded over them. Gerard glanced to the trees and smiled. "Come explore with me. I brought you out here to relax, not discuss politics."

"Relax?" The concept was strange. "We're in the middle of a medical crisis and you want me to relax?"

"Nothing can be done at this moment." Gerard reached his hand out. "Walk with me. Let me show you there are things on this plane beyond laboratories and sterile rooms."

Chapter Fifteen

Gerard had told Cecilia too much. She knew about the Medical Supreme. He told her there was a chance she could work on the medical crisis. Dr. Swift hadn't given permission for it yet. But how could he deny her? How could he lie to her? He was in love with her.

Gerard stopped walking. The sounds of the forest echoed around them. None of the scientists would be out collecting today. The solitude helped to clear his thoughts and focus his emotions. His heart beat faster in his chest. He was in love with her.

"What is it? Gerard?" Cecilia touched him. The press of her fingers to his arm was like shot of the best illegal pleasure drugs.

"I would have to check my levels with a monitor to prove it to you, but I am certain." He covered her hand with his.

"Certain—?"

"I love you, Cecilia. I am in love with you. I—"

"You love me?" She cut off his decree. "This isn't logical. We don't even exist on each other's worlds. I shouldn't even be here. Sometimes I question my own sanity in believing that alternate realities exist."

"Yet here you are," he countered.

"This is too chaotic." She shook her head even as she leaned closer to him. "There is too much going on. I keep expecting a doctor to wake me from a dream. That is the only explanation for how I feel for you, for how I've fallen..."

"Fallen?" he prompted.

"Fallen...into your...bed so easily," she finished weakly.

"Fallen in love with me," he corrected. "Say it. Say you love me. Admit it. I know what I feel can't just be one sided. You love me. I know you do."

"Gerard." Again she shook her head in denial. A small part of him twinged in agony at the gesture, but he didn't give up hope.

"If you really think this is a dream then what is the harm in admitting the truth?" He cupped her face with both hands, drawing her mouth close to his. Against her lips, he whispered, "I love you, Cecilia."

"This can't work," she protested.

"I love you."

"It's illogical and chaotic."

"I love you."

"It makes no sense. It can't go anywhere."

"I love you," he shouted enthusiastically.

Her eyes shut. "I love you, too, Gerard. It makes no sense, but I love you too."

He closed the distance between them, kissing her with all the passion in his heart. Nothing else mattered. The future was uncertain. He didn't know how they would make it work. All he knew was that he loved her, wanted her, needed her. For the rest of his life he would never regret any of it. Cecilia completed him. She was what he'd been searching for his whole life.

He wanted to tell her as much, but her kiss kept his lips against hers. The taste of her brushed over his tongue. Hands roamed over his body, pulling at his clothes. He let her undress him, eager to explore her yet again. No matter how often he held her, he would never tire of making love to his woman.

Mine.

The reality of her filled his heart. He knew he'd forced her to say the words, but she meant them. He saw the love in her expression even as she tried to fight it.

"This is chaos," she said against his mouth, still kissing him.

Gerard pulled back to study her face. Her lids fell heavy over her eyes, as if she was entranced. Her moist lips parted as she gasped for breath. For a moment, he couldn't move. She was so beautiful. The texture of her full lips captured his notice. He reached to run a finger over the bottom length. They were warm from the kiss.

Her fingers tapped along his arms. The scent of nature surrounded them. He loved the outdoors, but not as much as he loved her. Heat filled him, centering in his loins. Every part of him focused on her. Before he realized what he was doing, he had her stripped of her clothing.

When she was naked, standing before him, he took a step back. He quickly rid himself of his remaining clothing. She smiled at him, letting him look at her. Spots of sunlight came through the trees. The sterile suits and clothes littered the forest floor. A breeze whipped over them, rustling the leaves and chilling the skin. She shivered, her nipples budding.

His cock tightened and he shifted his weight. Lifting his hand, he beckoned her to him. She came willingly. Their fingers threaded together as he led her deeper into the trees to a patch of softer grass. His desire for her only increased.

He kneeled on the grass, taking her with him. When he lay on his back so she could straddle his waist, she came over him with sunlight dancing around her. He liked this position. It freed his hands to roam the length of her body. Soft skin and supple flesh pressed to his.

Cecilia ran her hands over his chest to his neck. She cupped his face tenderly as her body lifted to take his cock inside. They came together, making love in the gentle sanctuary of the forest. Gerard could never remember being so happy.

Cecilia tensed, her pussy tightening along his shaft. He answered the call of her body, finding his release in unison with hers. Afterwards she lay on his chest. Her breath tickled his neck. Gerard became aware of a rock digging into his ass but he didn't dare move and break the tranquility of the moment.

Chapter Sixteen

"You're limping." Sam frowned, eyeing Gerard.

"It's nothing. I'll take care of it." Gerard resisted the urge to rub his bruised ass. He'd managed to hide the injury from Cecilia when they walked inside. He'd thought he was alone when Dr. Swift joined him from a side office.

Sam automatically started leading Gerard to an exam room. When they were alone, he motioned Gerard to pull down his pants. "I spoke with Dr. Lu. He had a meeting with Dimensional Plane 303's politicians. They are not happy with the change in plans and threatened to inform Divinity Corporation if their dignitaries are not returned on schedule. The Medical Supreme neglected to inform us of an Anti-Chaos treaty he signed with them. We have no choice. Health risk or not, we have to send the women back in two weeks."

"Two?" Gerard stiffened. His heart beat hard. Just moments before he'd had an indefinite amount of time. "They were not scheduled to originally leave for almost four weeks."

"Apparently the fact we even requested an extension for their dignitaries has given 303's Politician Shinclus the idea that he has negotiating power. He has started making demands."

"Negotiation power? Why? Because we want to give them more information? You figure he'd be grateful."

"The Medical Supreme authorized some personal trades so he thinks he can make demands."

Gerard frowned, thinking of all the artifacts the Medical Supreme had in his home. He'd admired them on many occasions. "Politician Shinclus thinks he has power over us based on a few cultural artifacts the Medical Supreme wants to decorate his home with?"

"I don't understand the politician's reasoning. It must be a 303 cultural trait. Dr. Lu is handling the situation, but it's been decided to end their stay as soon as possible." Sam reached to the medical panel and filled a syringe. He jabbed it in the middle of Gerard's sore muscle. The bruise began to heal as the medicine repaired the muscle tissue beneath it. Sam continued, "It is the only power play we have to show 303 we're in control."

"Surely the Medical Supreme will not allow..." Gerard pulled up his pants and turned to face Sam.

"The Medical Supreme is the one who ordered it. Lu convinced him to give us two weeks. He reluctantly agreed." Sam didn't look happy about the news. Why would he? They locked down the portal for a reason.

"We need more time. What if it spreads?" Gerard shook his head. "We can't risk infecting another plane."

"The Medical Supreme has spoken."

"He's sick." Gerard lowered his voice. "He may not be in the best position to make that decision."

Sam held up his hand, stopping Gerard from saying more. Already the words bordered on treason. "We have no medical proof of that."

"Sam, please." Gerard's eyes fell. He took a deep breath. "I can't send her back. Not yet. Don't ask me to."

"I suspected there may be more to you two when I saw the dirt on your back." Sam gave a long sigh. "Are you petitioning to have her stay as your wife?"

Gerard hadn't thought of that. "She doesn't want to stay. She is very attached to her home. As much as I care for her, I can't force her to stay with me. She may come to resent me if I did. I need more time to convince her to love this place or to find a way to go with her."

"You know the Medical Supreme would never agree to letting you go. With your knowledge, it would be seen as a medical database walking through the portal." Sam went to the monitor and scrolled through Gerard's medical readings. "You really do love her."

"I don't need the monitor to tell me that." Gerard gave a soft chuckle, but he wasn't really amused.

"I did," Sam answered. "We have two weeks. I feel for your plight, but our first order of business will be to find out how this disease is spread and how it mutates. If we can prove that it's contagious we can override the Medical Supreme's order and keep them here."

As much as Gerard wanted more time with Cecilia, he couldn't wish their mystery illness to be highly contagious. He loved her, but he didn't want her harmed. A war waged inside him, selfish desires against moral duty. Duty won. It had to. "And if not, at least then I will know she's safe."

Chapter Seventeen

Cecilia wasn't sure what to think. She stood alone in her room, feeling as if her body were spinning in circles even as she remained still. Nothing made sense. A lifetime of anti-chaos warned her against falling in love with a man who didn't exist on her plane of reality. But it was too late. She had. She'd fallen in love with Gerard.

Her logical mind tried to analyze the situation, desperately wanting to reason how it happened. He was kind; she saw that in how he talked to others. He was smart. He made her laugh and smile, and somehow convinced her to break the law of her host plane and make love in the forest. He made her heart beat faster and her head forget everything she'd ever known to be true. He was chaos and she loved it, loved him.

She hadn't meant for any of it to happen. Cecilia was keenly aware of the job she was sent to do. In that she was failing. The pressure of it dampened her mood. She doubted the politicians would accept, "My apologies, I didn't manage to bring anything of real value back from a medically advanced plane, but I had some great sex and fell in love. Thank you for trusting me to take the trip. It was fun."

Then there was the little fact that she might not be going home any time soon. The idea of it didn't terrify her as it had before, but she knew she didn't want to live in the world that was so narrowly focused. She missed her mandatory grooming appointments and non-work days having breakfast with friends in the trollypark. She missed workout wheels, watching panel debates, clothes without layers, and the smell of non-sanitized air. And she most definitely missed not having to listen to an irritating wall monitor ding, forcing her to take yet another shot in her neck.

With a low growl, she went to the wall and took the syringe. Not bothering to look at the doses, she stuck it in her neck and recycled the injector. She did not want to do that for the rest of her life.

Cecilia knew she should go to her laboratory and get to work, but she couldn't force herself to leave the room. What did it matter? She was trapped on this plane until they developed a cure. It wasn't as if she understood half of what she read of their records anyway. For a smart woman, with an intelligence level to be proud of on her world, she felt completely useless and stupid on this one.

"At least I have time to figure this out," she told herself.

Chapter Eighteen

"What do you mean two weeks?" Cecilia was very aware she'd spent most of the day cursing the fact she was going to be trapped on a different level of reality. She had tried to focus on reading the files she'd been given access too, but her mind had wandered. Linnea was nowhere to be found, and Cecilia was actually glad for it. Now, as Gerard told her she was going home early, she wasn't ready to leave. "We were scheduled for four more."

"I thought you would be pleased. With the threat..." He didn't come to her, barely looked at her.

She searched his face, trying to bring froth the man she'd made love to in the forest. "I'm confused. One moment it's not safe to go. The next moment we have two weeks."

Gerard tensed, as if he didn't know what to say.

"You are right. My going is logical." Her brain agreed, but her heart didn't feel the same. "I should be grateful. What changed?"

"One of your politicians tried to renegotiate the terms of your agreement when we offered to extend your visit."

"Shinclus," Cecilia concluded, frowning. The man had a lot of power and even more lack of tactfulness.

"With our plane's current situation and the political climate between our worlds, it was deemed best that we send you home with the hope of trying again in the future."

"The future," she repeated. "So after two weeks, I may never see you again." Cecilia didn't bother to hide the tears entering her eyes. Her nose burned with the desire to cry. She closed the distance between them. "What if I want to stay the four?"

"You want to stay now?" He finally met her eyes.

"No. Yes. No." She lifted her arms helplessly. "I don't know. I miss my home. I miss my friends. I miss the food and the music. I miss color. Everyone here dresses the same and has the same hair and same smell."

His eyes softened.

"But you're here," she whispered. "If you could come with me..."

"That's not possible. No medical database is allowed to leave here. With what I know, it would never be allowed." He pulled her closer. "We'll figure something out."

"It's not like we can send communications to each other or visit each other on work breaks." She pushed weakly at his chest. "I told you from the beginning this couldn't go anywhere, that it couldn't mean anything. There will be this invisible wall between us, keeping us apart. We will spend our entire lives waiting on the whims of our politicians that I can someday come back."

"You would wait?"

"What do you think love is?" Cecilia responded, her voice rising. "You think I'll just go home through the portal and it will all go away?"

"Doctor."

Cecilia stiffened, startled by Linnea's intrusion. "What!" she answered, a little too harshly.

Linnea's face hardened. She stood in the doorway.

"What is it?" Cecilia said, softer, trying to amend her tone.

"Dr. Swift sent me to inform you we're leaving the facility in the morning." Linnea's voice was flat and emotionless.

"I didn't mean to yell at you." Cecilia looked helplessly at the woman then Gerard. "I'm overwhelmed at the moment."

Linnea appeared cautious, but her expression did lighten. "I understand." She nodded once and left them alone.

"Cecilia." Gerard pulled her into his arms. The tight muscles of his chest pressed into her. She shivered, taking in his comfort. She didn't want to leave him. "I love you. I don't have answers for the rest, but I love you."

I love you. There was nothing more to say beyond that. Words would not change their reality.

"Spend the night with me," she said, forgetting all about trying to find something useful for her plane. "You'll leave with me tomorrow, won't you?"

"Of course. I'll stay with you every second I can."

Cecilia took his hand, not caring who saw them as she led him out of the laboratory into the hall. Her steps quickened. She pulled him into her room not wanting to waste a single moment. Barely waiting for the door to close, she kissed him. She poured everything she had into that kiss, holding nothing back.

Passion always simmered beneath the surface, and now it raged between them. A feeling of desperation and sadness filled her. She tried to grab on to the moment, but felt it slipping past. Soon they were naked and his hands were on her body, urging her to her back. They made love slowly, savoring what they could.

As they climaxed in unison, his cock deep inside her, she whispered, "I love you, Gerard." What else could she say?

Chapter Nineteen

The transport stopped before Central Hospital. Cecilia lifted her head from Gerard's shoulder. For the majority of the transport ride they'd worked on compiling the research of each individual scientist on the virus. Even though all the records simply referred to the patient as Infected Subject One, Cecilia knew it was the Medical Supreme. Subject Two and Subject Three were part of his medical staff who had been working closely with him.

Cecilia didn't readily move to get out. "I don't think I can help you with any of this. You have some of the best medical minds on any plane of existence. I feel stupid compared to your doctors."

"I don't know why you say that. You comprehend much more than most dignitaries who visit." He kissed her cheek. "Our system is not the fairest. You come, are given very little information and training, and then are sent home. Very few planes have left after one short dignitary mission with anything valuable. What you've done has set the tone for future dealings. That makes your time here a success."

"On my plane I can read something and I instantly understand it and can apply it practically. Here, I feel like someone handed me cave markings." She closed her eyes briefly as he kissed her cheek again. The transport door slid open, as if the unit wanted them out so it could go along its way.

"We have to hurry." Sam appeared at their open door.

"Hurry?" Gerard repeated, surprised.

"Dr. Lu informed me unofficially that the Medical Supreme has changed his mind. He's not letting them go home." Sam gestured for Cecilia's hand to help her down. "We must hurry and get you home before I receive the order and the portal room is sealed shut indefinitely."

"Changed his mind? Again?" Gerard shook his head. "But..."

"There is no time." Sam practically pulled Cecilia from the transport. She stumbled. Gerard was right behind her, grabbing hold of her arm to steady her. As they walked, Sam continued, "It appears airborne. If the Supreme's staff is infected, the incubation period is short. We would see more cases outside of quarantine. Now is the only chance you have. Once that order comes through—"

"What about Linnea?"

"She wanted to finish up some logs at the biosphacility and asked that we go ahead. She took a later transport and will be along in a couple hours. It's just you. You can't wait for her. You have to go now." Sam glanced at Gerard, giving him a strange look she didn't understand. He didn't give her much time to think but her first instinct was to protest. Two weeks was bad enough, but now it looked as if she had two minutes. She stopped walking. Sam continued on, talking as if they followed him.

"Gerard..." She shook her head. "This can't—"

"Gerard," Sam insisted.

Gerard leaned closer to her, lowering his voice. "This is your chance. If you go now, you can go home. Who knows when you'll have another opportunity? Things are uncertain here. I don't want your health at risk. If you go now, I'll know you're safe."

"What if I never see you again? They keep taking time away from us. How can the Medical Supreme do this? He can't keep changing his mind." She needed time to think and logic and decide. How could she when they were pushing her through the portal?

A beep sounded.

"The official notice," Sam said, looking at the monitor. "They know we're here. I can't wait too long to read it."

"I can't ask you to stay," Gerard said to her, almost desperate. "I know how important your world is to you. This world is not safe, not right now."

She felt as if her heart was breaking. "Come with me."

"I need special permission." Gerard looked helplessly at Sam. She didn't care if the other doctor listened.

"Come anyway." Her heart beat faster. "I don't care about the anti-chaos laws. I'll deal with my politicians."

"There is no more time." Sam reached into his lab coat pocket and pulled out a syringe. "This will boost your immune system just in case, but it will also make you tired." He jabbed it in her arm before she could protest. "You must go now. For the sake of both our planes. Your world will be upset if we keep their doctor."

"But, Lin—" Cecilia swayed as the medicine fogged her mind, unable to voice her concern over Linnea.

"I'll take care of her. I promise." Then to Gerard, he said, "You can't go, no matter how you want to. You don't have permission and your plane needs you here. The virus..."

Sam kept talking, but Cecilia didn't hear the rest. The man made sense, but she wanted to find something to say to protest the words. Her head swam with the shot he'd given her and the rush of emotion churning inside her body.

Family, life, world or Gerard?

Cecilia opened her mouth to say she wanted to stay but no words came out. She again swayed on her feet.

"The medicine might be strong. Linnea mentioned how much the inter-dimensional travel hurt their particular biology. This will make it easier on her. Help her," Sam insisted. "Go."

Gerard took her arm and rushed her toward the portal door. Her feet stumbled but she managed to stay upright. Everything was happening too fast.

Sam stayed back. When she looked down the hall, she saw the man answering the monitor summons.

Gerard walked her into the portal room. He pulled her into his arms and kissed her hard. "I thought we'd have more time."

"Ask me to stay," she whispered. Her head swam. The words were slurred.

"I can't do that. I know how much your home means to you." He went to a control panel and began pushing buttons.

"Ask anyway." She felt her lips move, but she didn't hear the words. Her vision became very narrow and focused. She stared at Gerard, not wanting to leave him. She willed him to understand her thoughts, as she tried to hold on to them.

"I promise. As soon as I can, I will petition to have you brought back here. I love you, Cecilia. I will never forget you. I will wait." Gerard kissed her with a sense of urgency. She could tell by his body's response he wanted to do more, but they were out of time. He walked her to the platform. Her legs weakened and she sat on the floor. He let her go. She tried to grab on to him. Gerard pried her hands from his wrist and stepped back toward the door. "There is so much I want to say to you. I'll wait forever."

Cecilia reached for him but couldn't move. Tears came down her face. "Please," she mouthed.

They were out of time. Four weeks became two became none, all within the course of a day. She felt her heart breaking. That combined with the medicine made her incapable of speaking or moving. She begged him with her eyes to make time stop. There had to be a way.

He reached his hand behind him for the door. If she had known she was leaving, she would have said more in the transport. The blue light became brighter. The moment before it blinded her, she saw Sam join Gerard through the crack in the door. The burning in her flesh as she was ripped through the portal was nothing compared to the pain in her chest. Whatever Sam had given her helped the bone-shattering, muscle-disintegrating pain of portal travel, but it left her limp.

The portal tore her apart and put her back together. She fell to her stomach and didn't try to move. Her head swam, part from stunned grief, part from the shot she'd been given. The cool floor pressed to her cheek and a hot tear slipped over her face.

"Identify yourself."

She drew her head up to look at the control booth. Cecilia took several deep breaths. This was her world, but it felt surreal. She weakly lifted her hand in the green light, trying to block its brightness.

"Dr. Markos?"

She didn't recognize the voice. Feet shuffled toward her as the light dimmed. She was surrounded by private orderkeepers. Someone grabbed her foot and pulled off her shoe. She heard her identification number being read and a voice confirming her identity.

"Get her up," someone ordered.

"What happened to you?" another asked.

"Why are you back?" She recognized Shinclus over a speaker.

It was one voice she was compelled by a lifetime of law-abiding to answer. "They sent me." It wasn't much of an answer, but it was all she could manage in her drugged state. Someone repeated her words louder.

"And the other one?" Shinclus asked.

Cecilia shook her head.

"Just as well. Linnea Nel is untraceable," Shinclus said, giving no more concern to Linnea. "Someone help Dr. Markos to her feet. Call the government groomer and get her presentable before anyone sees her and she makes the news for not being sanitary. She looks terrible. Make sure the groomer wears protective gear. Then get her into quarantine and have her health checked."

Chapter Twenty

Gerard stared at the door, unable to move. His hand shook, and he pressed it against the metal. He imagined he could feel the exact second she was pulled through the portal to her home world.

"I'm sorry. There was no time." Sam put a hand on his shoulder. "The order came through. If I had waited, she wouldn't have been able to leave at all. You told me how important it was to you that you didn't force her to stay."

"I didn't get to say all I needed to." Gerard felt as if he were dying. How could he live on the hope of maybe seeing her again when losing her hurt so badly?

"You did what you had to." Sam sighed. "I'm under orders to lock down the portal. We should go."

Gerard started to answer but saw Linnea stumbling down the hall. "I thought you said Sans Nel missed the transport."

"I..." Sam tried to lie. Gerard saw it on his face. The man looked to the floor.

"You trapped her here. You made me give up Cecilia and you trapped Linnea?" Gerard balled his fists. Anger built in him and he struck out, pushing Sam in the chest. The man fell back into the wall and didn't fight back.

"What is...?" Linnea's voice was weak.

"I had to," Sam whispered.

"I love her!" Gerard yelled. "Look at me. We just sent the most vital part of who I am through that portal." He pointed at a nearby monitor to his readings. It dinged several times demanding he take a shot to calm himself. "Look!"

Sam glanced behind to Linnea as she stumbled closer. "Then go. Take your chances. Go. Follow her. Just go. I'll say you were sent as a dignitary. I'll say it was to maintain peace." Sam reached for the wall and grabbed a clipboard. He handed it to Gerard along with a medical unit from his lab coat. "These will help ease your way with the 303 politicians once you get there."

Gerard didn't think. His rage turned instantly to excitement and fear. What if Cecilia didn't want him to follow her? What if her plane rejected him? Feared him? Locked him away? It didn't matter. He would risk any punishment for her.

"I'll take Linnea," Gerard said, making a move to help the woman.

Sam grabbed his arm and shook his head in denial. "No. That's the deal. She stays. She will be invaluable to helping stop this disease. Now go. They'll be watching to make sure this section is sealed. If I don't do it, they'll do it for me offsite."

"But..." Gerard frowned. He read the man's expression. Linnea would be safe. "Thank you."

"We'll meet again," Sam assured him. "As soon as this is all over I'll send word."

"Good luck." Gerard pushed through the door and into his future.

"You too."

Chapter Twenty-One

Cecilia stared at the quarantine wall, through the clear plastic, to the man at the other side. She'd given her accounting of what had happened. They only asked once about Linnea, seeming less concerned about the woman's fate than the lack of medical knowledge Cecilia brought back with her.

"It has been two weeks. Why are you keeping me in here?" She didn't bother to keep the commanding tone out of her voice.

Dr. Tregeo looked up from his paper and frowned. She hated looking at him directly. Though he looked nothing like Gerard, Tregeo's eyes were brown. Gerard had brown eyes. Beautiful, deep, soulful brown eyes. The memory of them hurt her deep inside. She missed him. At night she fought the urge to cry out for him.

"As I have explained before, you will be released when we are satisfied we know everything that happened," Tregeo said.

Cecilia refused to talk about Gerard. It was none of their concern and she wouldn't sully the memory of him by having them write his name in their records as her lover. Whenever a new mission came up, *if* it came up, that would keep her name off the return list.

"I don't know what else I can tell you. The food was bland. They all wore the same color. The air smelled so sweet from sanitizer, it can be hard to breathe. They are dealing with an unknown virus of unknown origin. It is quarantined, but they ended all missions until further notice. The Medical Supreme is a very cautious man. I only met him once, but he—"

"You have told us all that," Tregeo interrupted. "Numerous times."

"Then what else do you want?" Cecilia leapt to her feet and yelled.

Tregeo jumped at the chaotic display and dropped his papers. She saw he'd been drawing a very poor likeness of her and not taking notes.

"What is going on?" she demanded.

Tregeo rushed away from her, hurrying down the corridor. Cecilia gave a small laugh. She pressed her head to the plastic and watched him disappear from her line of sight.

Chapter Twenty-Two

"You're a very lucky lady."

Cecilia opened her eyes to look at Politician Shinclus standing opposite her quarantine wall.

"Lucky?" It wasn't the sarcastic comment she wanted to make. She wanted to reference her fine accommodations and offer to trade places with him.

"Tregeo insisted you be brought up on anti-chaos charges for your little display." Shinclus waited, as if watching for some terrified reaction. She merely stood, watching him in return. "I intervened on your behalf, though the man had every right to charge you. I assured him that your outburst toward him would not happen again, but he has been transferred for his safety out of your presence."

Had her plane always been so overly dramatic? She frowned. Then, belatedly, she nodded at Shinclus and mumbled, "Many thanks."

Shinclus smiled, the kind of benevolently irritating look people got when they thought themselves powerful and bestowing. "If you assure me you can behave yourself, I'll let you out of there."

"Tregeo is dramatic," Cecilia said very calmly. "Did you see the papers he left on the floor?"

"I did. They don't look like you at all. Your endowments are smaller." Shinclus lifted his hand to give the command she be released.

The sliding door brought with it a rush of cool air. She took a deep breath. "Has there been any word from Plane 187?"

"Not since your arrival," he answered.

"Linnea Nel? Should we attempt to make contact to get her back? I can go since I know everyone." She kept the hope out of her voice.

"I think it's for the best they keep her. She can't be scanned, you know." He didn't meet her eyes as he walked faster.

"She was an asset," Cecilia insisted. "We can't leave her there."

"It has been handled." He refused to look at her.

"Wait, that's why no one asked me about her? You made arrangements that they should keep her." Cecilia stopped in disbelief.

"The Medical Supreme agreed that he would find a place for her in his home," Shinclus said. "It's more than someone like her could hope for. I daresay the crime rate will drop by fifty-five percent now that she is gone. Do you know how many times she was caught reading in the library? Medical texts even. She is not authorized to study medicine. An untraceable woman cannot be given such knowledge. Who knows what she would do with it. Order must be maintained, and with her permanently off plane it has been."

The fact the elections were coming up and Politician Shinclus would personally take credit for the fall in crime probably had a lot to do with it.

"Don't look so stricken," Shinclus scolded. "She knows all about it. She was ordered not to tell you and distract from your mission. She'll be much happier there. She wants to read medical texts, and there she can."

The man's words made sense, though she didn't trust him completely. Linnea had seemed fairly comfortable at the biosphacility and she hadn't come to Central Hospital with Dr. Swift.

"What I want to know is why you haven't told us more about Dr. Fauchet." Shinclus paused at the end of the hall, waiting for someone to open the door for him. A guard grabbed the handle and pulled it open. She followed Shinclus into a small waiting area that would take her outside the facility.

Cecilia tried to remain calm. How could they know about her relationship with Gerard? Had she given something away? Cried out his name in her sleep? "What do you mean? I listed him as a contact in my reporting of events."

"You did." Shinclus didn't stop. He kept going, past the chairs to another secure door. A guard held it open when he saw them coming. Cecilia noticed the man eyed her as she passed, as if her crazy reputation with Dr. Tregeo preceded her. Why hadn't she noticed her plane's anti-chaos extremism before? No wonder Linnea wanted to leave.

As much as she'd wanted to come home, now it felt empty. She didn't belong on 187 but now she felt displaced on her own world. She looked at the people she passed. They had no idea what she had been through, what she had seen, what was really out there. She looked at the walls and imagined she could see Central Hospital's walls. It shifted from reality. Was Gerard standing where she was now? Unseen? Untouchable? As much a ghost to her as she was to him?

"Dr. Markos?" Shinclus looked at her expectantly.

"Where are we going? I'm ready to go home. My family—"

"Your family does not expect you for another two weeks." The politician led the way into the secure hall, away from the waiting area, deeper into the facility. He went through several doors.

"There is nothing more I can do," she said, hesitant to follow him. It was possible they'd lock her in another cell.

"Nothing?" Shinclus asked. Then stopping, he frowned. "I understand now. Your psychological work-up did not have you marked for political shrewdness, but now I see we underestimated you. They wondered why you were withholding key information about your contacts, but I see how you want to negotiate. Well done, Dr. Markos. I see my choosing you for this mission was well done indeed. So, what do you want?"

"What do I want?" she repeated slowly, trying to figure out what he meant.

Shinclus gave a small, knowing smile. Cecilia had never been more confused. "I can offer top-level housing. The movers will pack your belongings and have you in the new south tower complex today."

"I—" Cecilia began, only to be cut off. South tower was very high end. People would spend a lifetime on a waiting list just to get in to a place like that.

"No, before you try to negotiate, hear the rest." Shinclus stopped walking. "This alliance is important to us. You more than anyone understand that. You'll get an executive office and laboratory at your disposal in the most secure facility. You will be provided with a key to the private tram."

The private tram? Only top-level government officials used the tram. It had spa services and fine dining and delivered its passengers to private decks at the most luxurious places in town.

"You are a hard negotiator," Shinclus said at her silence. "This of course will mean you receive more compensation, trip allowance, and your own staff."

"Thank you." Cecilia tried to sound assertive, but really she was more worried now than before. They thought she knew more than she did.

"This way." Shinclus seemed pleased with himself. "You begin work immediately."

"Immediately," Cecilia protested. "What exactly is it you expect me to do?"

"Your job." Shinclus motioned to a guard. The man stepped to the side.

Cecilia slowly walked into the room, not sure what to expect. Seeing a man with his back toward her, she first noticed his lab coat. It was 187 issued. Her breath caught. Her eyes flew up toward his head. It wasn't Gerard.

"Dr. Swift," she acknowledged, racked with disappointment.

"Dr. Markos." The man smiled. "I'm pleased to see you are well."

"Cecilia?"

Cecilia turned, gasping at the sound of Gerard's voice. He stood in the corner of the room. She made a weak noise. All thoughts left her. She rushed forward. She didn't care where she was, or who watched. Once she put her hands on him she was never letting go again.

"Gerard," she whispered, reaching for him. She wound her arms around his shoulders. The depths of his brown eyes caught hers and she knew she never wanted to look away. She kissed him, deep and passionate. She heard words around them but she ignored them. His hands found her hips, pulling her close. The last two weeks disappeared. Tears filled her eyes. When she leaned away from his mouth, one drop slid over her cheek. "How?"

"I understand now," Shinclus said behind her. "Well played, Dr. Markos."

Cecilia touched Gerard's face, ignoring Shinclus. "How?"

"Cecilia," Gerard whispered. He smiled at her and she felt her insides melt a little.

Sam cleared his throat. "Dr. Markos, I came with good news. Your proposal was accepted by the Medical Supreme. You made a fine argument."

Cecilia blinked, glancing over her shoulder. She pulled out of Gerard's arms but took up his hand and held it in both of hers.

"We are very grateful for your plane's hospitality. Dr. Fauchet's two-week quarantine, though inconvenient considering our stringent health guidelines before travel, is understandable. I came to check up on him just as soon as I could get away. I'm happy to hear he will be staying with you."

Two weeks? Gerard had followed her through the portal? Why hadn't anyone told her? She opened her mouth to respond, but there was a seriousness to Sam's words and expression, an insistence that she go along with what he was saying, so she stayed quiet.

"Yes," Gerard said quickly. "Completely understandable."

Cecilia didn't speak, finding it best to try not to look too confused. It was then she noticed the streak of purple in Gerard's brown hair. He'd been groomed and he smelled of government-approved soap. Then she noticed his clothing—a one–piece, pale blue suit that looked very much like her quarantine garb.

"There are some formalities, naturally." Shinclus puffed out his chest. "An identification number will be assigned and a chip implanted immediately. We will also need you to file papers regarding your sexual relations status. 187's consent forms cannot be entered into public record, as 187 technically does not exist. I am assuming you filed all of the correct forms before initiating contact?"

"Of course," Gerard said mimicking Shinclus's serious tone. "Dr. Markos is very thorough with her paperwork. It is my intention to conform to all 303 laws and regulations."

"Dr. Markos will be your liaison." Shinclus gave a small laugh. "I assume that is agreeable. As long as you abide by all our anti-chaos laws there will be no issue. Will you require your own home?"

"He'll stay with me," Cecilia said finding her voice.

"Very good," Shinclus agreed, looking at Sam. "Dr. Markos will keep him from wandering into the wrong neighborhoods. Now that is settled, I will leave Dr. Markos to begin orientation. Dr. Swift, I believe you mentioned something about technology."

"Yes, but we have very strict guidelines as to how and who may use it. All devices will be biocoded to Dr. Markos and Dr. Fauchet." Sam glanced in her direction and gave a small smile before moving to follow Shinclus out of the room.

"Wait," Cecilia beckoned him. "Sans Nel? Is she...?"

"She is well. She has agreed to stay with us as part of the exchange program." Sam looked sideways at Shinclus. "As you proposed."

Cecilia nodded. When Shinclus turned his back, Sam mouthed, "She is well taken care of."

"Thank you, Dr. Swift," Cecilia held Gerard's hand tighter.

"Until we meet again, Dr. Markos." Sam left, closing the door behind him.

When they were alone, Cecilia pulled Gerard closer. "What is going on? Is the virus cured? When did you get here? How did you come through the portal? They were closing it down. I saw you disappear when I was pulled through. How did you manage to convince the Medical Supreme to let you come? I thought he would never agree to it. I thought I would never see you again. How is this possible? Is the Medical Supreme dead? Is that why you are allowed to be here? And is Linnea really all right with the trade? I didn't get a chance to talk to her. Though, I'm not giving you back. They can't take you. They won't try to take you back, will they? How long can you stay?"

Gerard's smile only widened until finally he cut off her rush of words with a quick kiss and a laugh. "Are you nervous? Is that why you are speaking so fast?"

"You said the same thing to me in the transport my first day on your plane." Her body heated at the memory. They had made love for the first time on the trip. It felt so long ago. So much had changed.

"I remember. You were so flustered."

"How are you here, Gerard?" She stroked his face and neck before touching the colored streak in his hair.

"Do you like it?" he asked, clearly excited. "I couldn't decide which kind to get, so I let the groomer choose. Did you know that I could have my whole head green?"

Cecilia nodded. "Yes, I did know that."

"Of course you did."

"Gerard? My questions? How much time do we have?"

"Only forever," he answered. "I am 303's new permanent liaison, thanks to Sans Nel's excellent work on 187. She is very well, by the way. You have no need to worry about her. The Medical Supreme is alive. The virus is under control. I came through about two seconds after you did. They wouldn't tell me where you were and I refused to talk to anyone but you. Strange though, they wanted to groom me before a health check. We should probably work on getting that protocol changed. Then Sam showed up with a trade agreement two days ago. Aside from the required trips back, I'm now a member of New Order Society."

"Only forever?" she repeated. Her heart beat fast. "I don't know if that is enough time."

"We better not waste it then." He playfully brushed his nose against hers. "I remember the first day you came to my plane. You couldn't keep your hands off me and I knew that first second I wanted to be with you."

"You kissed me," she protested, trying not to laugh. "It was very presumptuous of you, Dr. Fauchet."

"You kissed me back, Dr. Markos."

"Mm." She lifted up on her toes and let her mouth move against his. "Yes, I did. I will always kiss you back, Gerard. I love you. Only forever."

"Only forever, my love." His lips met hers in passion.

The End

Linnea's Arrangement

BOOK THREE BY MICHELLE M. PILLOW

Linnea's Arrangement (Divinity Healers) © Copyright 2013-2017, Michelle M. Pillow

First Electronic Printing November 2013, The Raven Books

ISBN-10: 1625010648

ISBN-13: 978-1-62501-064-3

Edited by Suz Gower

The Raven Books
Published by The Raven Books

About Linnea's Arrangement
DIVINITY HEALERS BOOK THREE

Alternate Reality Romance, Part of the Divinity Universe

Beautiful, highly intelligent Linnea Nel wants what most women want—a career, love, respect. But coming from a plane where order and all things anti-chaos reign, the untrackable, untraceable and highly rebellious Linnea is considered a threat—to her family, society and her world. When her numerous arrests for reading library books become a public embarrassment to her politically minded sister, Linnea is forced on a dignitary mission to an alternate reality.

There are only two classifications of people on plane 187: Doctors and Not Doctors (Sans). Dr. Sam Swift is one of the highest ranking officials on the medical plane, answering only to the Medical Supreme. When the Medical Supreme becomes ill, it's up to him to find a cure. Nowhere in this equation is there room—or time—to fall in love. And then he meets the exquisitely frustrating Sans Linnea Nel.

In the midst of the worst outbreak 187's society has faced in decades, two people who never should have met fall in love. How can Linnea stay where she may be in danger? But how can Sam let the love of his life go?

To the Manfriend. Yes, you, Manfriend.
I'm kind of thinking that a book dedication should be about equal to
you bringing me a giant plate of pasta for every book sold. Mmm, pasta.
Oh, and dressed as—why are you shaking your head at me?

Chapter One

NEW ORDER SOCIETY, DIMENSIONAL PLANE 303

L innea Nel eyed the bars of her cell. The New Order Society government wouldn't keep her locked up long. They never did. For every second she stayed in jail, the higher her offender ranking number would go. Since all number statistics were reported to the public, they would prefer she was ranked as a misdemeanor disturbance as opposed to anything major—like thievery or, worse, public chaos.

As one of the few people whose body's natural magnetism didn't allow for the anti-chaos implant, she was on every government and societal watch list. As a child, she'd managed to blend. Linnea had been a good student, a model participant in societal functions. Then came graduation. No higher learning institutes would take her. They didn't even bother to give her a good reason why she was rejected. Without an implant, they had no way of ensuring she did her own coursework and followed institutional policies. So it didn't matter how good she was or how smart. Unlike all other students, she would never be under their complete monitoring and control. They couldn't risk putting her into a position of power. They couldn't risk educating her. So she'd educated herself.

"Come on out of there, Nel," Orderkeeper Delkin said. The man should have instilled fear in her with his Goliath size, but Linnea had been in his cell way too many times. "And don't let us catch you in the library again without permission."

"Wouldn't dream of it," she answered dryly.

"Yeah," he muttered. "You know what to do. When you're checked out of the system, there's some people here waiting to talk to you."

People? Linnea frowned. Her own parents barely spoke to her—the uncontrollable one. Since she moved into New Order City, they hadn't really spoken to her. Why should they when her older brother and sister both did the family proud? Her genetic fluke only caused them embarrassment. To society's way of thinking, since she couldn't be watched, she was destined to cause trouble. She'd stopped trying to impress her parents years ago. Some battles couldn't be won, so there was no point in fighting them.

"See you next time around, keeper." Linnea typed in her identification number and made her way toward the front of the Order-keeper Station. The tracking monitors made a familiar beep as she was scanned and found without a chip. They had tried making her wear a few around her neck, but her body's natural energy made them glitch. Once the monitor even read her as the wrong person—a dead singer, to be precise. That little event had raised a lot of alarms. There were still rumors that Silev had faked his own death and was really alive. What could she say? Diehard fans would believe anything. The only reason the orderkeepers didn't lock her up was because the authorities were fearful word of her condition would get out. Societal control depended on society trusting the implants implicitly.

"Linnea."

Linnea paused by the open door and slowly moved to stand in the doorway. Out of all the people who'd come to the station to get her, she never expected to see her sister. When they were little, Jinna had been her best friend. Now, looking at the woman, she couldn't see that little girl. Instead, she saw the pristine and orderly countenance of Politician Nel, new leader of the anti-chaotic task force.

"Jin," Linnea answered. Like everyone else on the planet, her sister wore the one-piece suit. Material that belled around the legs led to tightly-fitted hips and a looser bodice. Her black hair had been streaked along the side with a bright, unnatural red, and tiny jewels had been adhered in a swirl pattern along the inside of it.

Linnea preferred to keep her black hair shorter with a streak of dark purple to match the purplish grey of her eyes. Her bodice was tight, less conservative in design. A thick, black belt wrapped her ribs, dark purple over black material.

"Leave us," Jinna ordered her two guards. Linnea didn't back away as they passed, even as they stared at her like she was about to attack her own sister.

When they were alone, Linnea stepped into the room.

"This needs to stop," Jinna said. "I can't have a sister who's constantly being arrested for petty chaotic crimes."

"I'm great, thanks for asking, Jin," Linnea answered, moving to the long bench next to the wall. She took a seat and stretched her feet forward in easy repose. Smiling pleasantly, though she hardly felt pleasant, she inquired, "And you?"

"Always a child." Jinna frowned.

"Ah, Jin, I think you're being too hard on yourself. You've done well. I wouldn't call you a child." Linnea smirked. The look was a mask, a way of keeping the true depths of her hurt to herself. She wanted so badly to live a normal life, to have a family, find love and marry, have a career and a well-earned respect. Instead, she was arrested for daring to better herself.

"I didn't mean me," Jinna answered, flustered. "You are always a child. This proves my point. Do you ever think of anyone but yourself?"

Dropping all pretenses, Linnea drew her feet in and placed her elbows on her knees. "I was reading a book, not running naked through the streets."

"Not this time," Jinna grumbled.

"Once. I ran naked through the streets once. I was angry. You would be too if your application to medical learning was denied because of a stupid inability to take an implant. My grades were better than yours. I passed all my tests. I had recommendations and—"

"I'm not here to debate the past," Jinna interrupted.

"It's not the past," Linnea said. "It's my present, my future." She leaned over, jerking off her boot to expose her bare foot. A black numbered tattoo stared back at them, her identification number. Normally, the implants would be placed underneath the visible mark. Those numbers were everything—her money access, her education and work history, her purchasing rations, her identification. Everyone living in the New Order Society had a designation. When they were children, the government trucks had visited their school. The technicians wore costumes as to not frighten them. They danced and sang as the coded implants were injected beneath every child's number. Linnea's body rejected the implant, and every one after that. Her scarred foot attested to it. "It's not like I'm unwilling to be part of the system. I almost lost my foot to infection because I had the damned chip implanted too many times. I know the law. I know that this is the only way society can thrive. There must be order to chaos. You all just won't let me be a part of your society! It's not like I can help some natural electrical magnetism in my body—a current your doctors can't even define. Maybe if you let me go to school I could figure it out. I could design a better implant."

"Funding will not be granted to cure one person, Linnea. The needs of the many will be met first."

"The needs of the many? Like using chemists to make better-smelling grooming products?" Linnea wanted to scream, but knew that would do no good. "I could do that too."

"I'm here to discuss your future." When Jinna looked at her, Linnea didn't feel as if her sister actually saw her.

"You're letting me go to school?" Hope filled her.

"You know I can't do that."

The hope died. Though she should have been used to it by now, the disappointment physically hurt. "Then what?"

"I've secured a position for you with Dr. Cecilia Markos as an assistant." Jinna smiled for the first time.

"Assistant?"

"Don't look so disappointed. You clearly want to be in the medical field since you're constantly sneaking into the library to read medical textbooks."

"I read fiction too," Linnea said, just to be contrary. "Perhaps I really dream of being make-believe."

Even as part of her wanted to jump at the chance to be near medicine, another part knew that to be merely an assistant would eventually wear her down. To be so close and not be able to succeed. It would be torture.

"Dr. Cecilia Markos is fast becoming one of our greatest assets. You're lucky she's willing to take you with her."

"With her?" Linnea stood. "Where? Are you banishing me? New Order City is my home."

"Dr. Markos has been assigned to the off-plane program. You will be joining her on a trip through what we call the Divinity portal to a medically advanced dimensional plane in a parallel universe. It's primarily an ambassadorial journey, a basic trading of goodwill while gauging the plane's medical knowledge and their usefulness to our world."

"Portal travel?" Linnea felt a shiver work over her body. "I was joking when I said I wanted to be make-believe."

"When have you ever known me to joke?" Jinna arched a brow.

Good point.

"What do you mean a portal to a parallel universe?" she asked.

"Exactly that. You're smart, so I know I don't have to explain the concept of alternate realities and parallel universes to you. So take the theories you know and suppose they are real. Suppose someone found a way to move between the veils, so to speak. Looking at an alternate reality is like seeing our world if history had been altered in some way. Languages are similar, so you will not have a problem in that department. I'm told some people will look the same, but do not mistake them for being the same people. Humans will look like humans, save a few minor differences."

Linnea opened her mouth to speak, but said nothing. Jinna was serious.

"An entity called Divinity Corporation mastered the science of inter-dimensional travel. About two years ago they made contact with us. Since then, we've allowed a portal gate to be placed on our world. We're one of four-hundred-thirty-six charted universes, with infinitely more out there. We plan on staking a big claim in Divinity's project. Several ambassadors have been sent through and have come back successfully. Dr. Markos will lead the medical team. You will be her assistant."

Linnea frowned. "Team?"

"Well, a team of two. You and her."

"Why haven't I heard of this?"

"And cause societal panic? No. The public will not be made aware of these developments. There is no need to concern them. The government knows what is best for them."

"What if I say no? What if I tell? Your secret would be out."

Jinna laughed. "Do you still believe you can make people listen to you? Lin, Lin, Lin." Jinna shook her head in amusement. "You don't have a choice. You're going. It's what is best for societal harmony. I'm sure you understand."

"And when it's over? When I come back?" Linnea stiffened, a strange feeling of dread unfurling inside her. But, this was her sister. She didn't want to believe that Jinna would do something to hurt her.

"Why don't you concentrate your efforts on dealing with today? My guards have the information you need." Jinna left, leaving Linnea to stare after her. No matter how fantastic her sister's words were, Linnea found the idea of an alternate reality easier to believe than Jinna actually teasing her with this ridiculous conversation.

Chapter Two

Portal travel was very real and Linnea had no choice but to experience it.

A pyramid roof set atop four square columns, which framed a platform. The columns were constructed of a dense material which created its own gravitational field and drew objects to it. They hid a complex configuration of liquid crystals, electrical currents, mirrors and vacuums. It was held in check by the wavelength of a specific blue light, which kept the portal inactive. Should the light change, a dimensional shift would occur, taking whoever stood on the platform to a new parallel universe.

"In the early days, before these platforms, plane travel had been a matter of trial and error. Many testers died when they materialized inside solid objects," Politician Shinclus said, his eyes on the Divinity portal. The man smiled, a large, almost toadlike expression. When he spoke, his great lips smacked together as if about to strike with his tongue at any moment. "Now they use microscopic probes before sending people through, so accidents are rare."

Linnea's eyes grew wide as she looked at the politician. She found herself unconsciously stepping away from him.

"Is my sister...?" Linnea paused. She hadn't seen her sister since the jail. In fact, she hadn't heard from any of her family, though she'd tried contacting them. "Is Politician Nel here?"

"No. She does not oversee this project," he said, and dismissed her question. Then, motioning back to the platform that was the center point of his story, he continued on as if she hadn't spoken. "It is not too late to change your mind." His smile widened. It wasn't the first time a man had looked at Linnea in such a way—eyes narrowed, lips parted, chest filling with heavy breath. "Other...arrangements could be made for you."

"Dr. Markos is expecting me. We've already discussed—"

"Other assistants can be arranged. There is no need for you to travel to another dimension." His eyes dipped over her chest, lingering on the tighter fit of her black bodice.

"I have reason to go."

"I can give your reason to stay. My home is quite large."

"It's a medical plane." Linnea lowered her eyes to the floor and lied, "I have hopes that they'll be able to cure...my...feminine..." She glanced up briefly, forcing a blush over her features.

Politician Shinclus cleared his throat. "Oh, yes, well, I haven't been through the portal myself, but I'm told it's quite an enjoyable ride." Motioning to a nearby woman, he said, "Here is the material Dr. Markos has requested."

Linnea took the stack of papers, glancing at the top. They were a compilation of basic medicines and known diseases.

"There is Dr. Markos. I must see if she requires me for anything before we leave." All too glad to have a reason to leave the lecherous politician's side, Linnea tried not to laugh as she hurried away. Shinclus apparently didn't like her enough to risk contracting a social illness. Then, seeing Dr. Markos, her smile faded. She didn't like the woman. Like everyone else, she was judgmental and a little condescending.

Dr. Markos wore a red, one-piece suit. The sleeves were long, falling past the woman's hands. Her brunette hair was all one color and had been pulled back from her face. Her features seemed overly pale in the blue light reflecting off the portal. When the woman looked at her, Linnea said, half conversationally, half to get a rise out of the fine doctor, "You know, Politician Shinclus told me that people sometimes get rematerialized into solid objects when going through these things."

"He was just trying to scare you," Dr. Markos answered tersely. "Politician Shinclus is known for his bad humor. It is true accidents happened in the past, but that is why they send out the probes first. Besides, where we are going is a known destination and an opposite portal will receive us on the other side. Everyone there works for the central hospital government in some capacity. It should be like going to a giant hospital." She turned to study Linnea. The blue light from the portal reflected in the woman's eyes. "Weren't you supposed to change your hair?"

"I didn't make it to my appointment. Something else came up." Linnea arched a brow and shifted the papers in her arms. Drawling sarcastically, she added, "I don't really think it matters all that much. I'm sure they'll make allowance for our alien customs."

Cecilia closed her eyes, appearing annoyed. "The plane we're traveling to does not know of our fashion customs. We might unintentionally insult them. Did you read the recommendations report put together by the Committee for Interplane Diplomacy?"

"I was going to," Linnea drawled, "but I was in the middle of a different book at the time. I wanted to finish it before we left."

Cecilia frowned, saying, "It's too late to do anything about your hair now. We will be leaving soon."

Linnea mimicked the woman's disapproving expression. The unspoken meaning in the doctor's tone was clear—her hair ultimately didn't matter because Linnea was only her assistant, a nonconformist, not a doctor.

Workers began filing out of the room. A low, steady hum sounded moments before a voice could be heard overhead, ordering, "Dr. Markos, Citizen Nel, please report to the platform."

Chapter Three

D r. Samuel Swift didn't move from his place on the narrow cot. The room was small, but he wouldn't be disturbed. It was practically the only room within the walls of the Central Hospital and Optimal Health Centre where he could find any kind of sanctuary and, if he was lucky, a few minutes of sleep.

As Director of Central Hospital, Sam had one person to answer to —the Medical Supreme. Unfortunately, Medical Supreme Walter had been especially demanding lately—not the least of which was using his laboratories in the middle of the night, something that required Sam's special clearance and attendance within the building.

Exhaustion and stress filled him from just thinking about it. He didn't like Supreme Walter's late night experimenting and he especially didn't like not knowing what those experiments were. But, his position was a delicate one. The Medical Supreme was in charge of funding and had power. To question him would be to lose not only his position, but his hospital's funding. With only a cheating former wife to call family, this hospital was all he had.

The former wife was pretty, he'd allow her that much. He'd been blinded by her physical charms—round breasts, soft flesh, thighs that would part as eagerly as her mouth. She'd sucked her way into his life, quite literally. Shamefully, that's what he missed most—not her, but the feel of her, the companionship, the release.

A light beep sounded. One of the benefits of living on one of the most medically advanced planes of existence was the constant monitoring of health. The room monitors constantly checked his system, anticipating his needs. Automatically turning his head to the side, he let the injector extending from the wall give him a shot in the neck. Instantly, his stress levels lessened and he felt better.

Another beep sounded and he opened one eye. He reached for his waistband a little too eagerly, tugging at it to pull his pants off his hips. The computer had sensed his borderline arousal and was instructing him to take care of it. Who was he to argue with science?

Sighing, he wrapped his fingers around his cock. No one in particular came to mind as he lazily stroked himself. Though he enjoyed it, he knew it was merely a physical function like eating or breathing. He'd heard of people finding great passion. Though he'd enjoyed the charms of his former wife, he hadn't felt any kind of mighty love passion. Through the Divinity portal, they had traded research with a plane of people who'd done extensive mapping of the brain. Emotions were easy enough to explain, read, even cure. Love was merely what they had called phenylethylamine, a trick of the brain, a chemical the body produced to create the emotion.

He found his mind trying to wander to work, to the mental checklist of things to be done. Off-world doctors were coming today. He'd have to greet and acclimate them. There would be tests to run, scans, checkups. Then he would be expected to escort them to whichever facility he deemed best for their trading purposes.

He glanced down his body, stroking harder. The dry rub of his hand on flesh caused his stomach to tighten. His breathing deepened. Pleasure rippled over him. So close. Almost... Almost—

"Dr. Swift, the dignitaries have arrived. They are in decontamination," Dr. Lu's voice interrupted. The man was the last person he wanted to hear at that moment. The shock of it jolted him back from his release. Though some substance did leak from the tip, the pressure remained inside his stomach.

With a frustrated sigh, he reached for the wall panel and pressed a button to answer, "Dr. Lu, I'll be there in a moment. Please see that they are cleared."

"Dr. Fauchet has already been dispatched to see to it," Lu answered.

"Very good." Sam took a deep breath before getting up to clean himself off. The wall panel beeped a reminder that he needed to do something about his levels. Unfortunately duty called and he hit an override code to ignore his current state of un-release for the time being.

As he was the director, the incident would not be reported to the others. It was one of the small perks of the job, a little bit of medical privacy. If the others knew how many times he ended up taking matters into his own hands without the aid of female companionship, they'd probably stage an intervention. Though, finding women in his position was hard. He didn't want them fucking him because he had power. He didn't want them thinking they *had* to fuck with him because he had power. The Medical Supreme didn't seem to have the same issue with power that Sam had. The man would seduce anyone he wanted—the more unattainable, the better. In fact, the Medical Supreme even hinted at using the Divinity portal to bring through virgins for their trainable pleasure. His cock tightened at the erotic idea of tight female flesh to plunge into. However, he found the Medical Supreme a letch. Sure, the idea of sexual vessels worked well for a healthy fantasy to get off when he was alone, but the reality of importing virgins was a sort of mental pathogen he wanted no part of. Fantasy women wanted to be fucked. Real women deserved the choice.

Besides, he never understood the obsession some men had with virgins. He hadn't held on to his own virginity, why should the women who came to his bed be expected to? Sam found himself pulling aside his lab coat and reaching to stroke his cock through his pants. And, furthermore, he didn't want to have to train his lover to fuck him. He had enough work to do as it was.

The reminder of work caused him to growl and drop the coat. The long length of the standard-issue facility uniform, a long blue coat with red trim, would hide his erection until it lost interest. Since he was expected to escort the visitors to a facility several hours outside the city, it would be a long while before he had a chance to take care of himself properly. The idea did nothing to his mood as he grumpily reached for a medical clipboard and hit his hand against the door scanner.

Chapter Four

Quite an enjoyable ride.

Q uite an enjoyable ride.
As the color of the light shifted to a pale green to pull Linnea through the portal, she cursed Politician Shinclus for his obvious lie. The pain of portal travel was unimaginable. The humming in her ears grew louder, drowning out all other sounds. Linnea closed her eyes to the bright light. She wanted to scream, but when she opened her mouth it felt as if her jaw was being ripped away from her skull. Flesh burned and her entire body was ripped apart at a molecular level. She should have been dead, or unconscious, but her mind stayed completely aware.

Those few seconds of pain were unlike anything she'd ever experienced. Then it was over, leaving her body numb and weak. She collapsed onto the hard platform, dropping her papers and not caring. She gasped for breath, coughing and choking as her lungs filled with a sickeningly sweet air.

Quite an enjoyable ride?
Bedlam and anarchy!

She was vaguely aware of Cecilia Markos on the floor next to her. The pale green turned to blue and her hearing came back in the form of loud, blaring alarms. Linnea covered her sensitive ears. "So loud!"

"Sterilization commencing," a male voice announced, louder than the alarm. "Please stand and move away from the platform."

Linnea didn't bother looking up. She crawled forward to gather the papers before pushing to her feet. Cecilia stayed on the ground, shaking. Reaching down, Linnea pulled the woman up by her arm.

"Please stand and move away from the platform," the voice repeated, even louder. No one was there. The voice came from a sound system. She looked around but couldn't see any viewing devices looking in at them. The room was constructed of shiny metal—from the floors to the walls to the ceilings.

"I think that's us," Linnea yelled over the alarm, not letting go of Cecilia's arm as they moved, afraid one of them would collapse again and injure themselves. They both turned, startled, watching as a shield slid down from the ceiling, blocking the platform.

"Welcome, dignitaries from the New Order Society, Dimensional Plane 303, to Central Hospital and Optimal Health Centre in the City of Asclepius, Country of Chiron, Dimensional Plane 187. We are now scanning you for foreign dimensional parasites and viruses. Please do not move until scanning is complete." A series of lights followed the male's orders, flashing over them. The alarms thankfully stopped. "Sterilization complete. Please state your clearance code."

"Dr. Cecilia Markos," her companion answered. "New Order Society dignitary."

"This is tedious," Linnea muttered. Her ears still rang from the blaring noise. "I hope they don't all talk that loud."

"Voice recognition accepted. Please move to the orange door." A metallic gray door with a series of numbers and letter written in orange across the front opened automatically and they passed through to the metallic gray corridors of the hospital. They stepped down the hall, not sure where they were going, but heading down the longest route. The orange letters on the wall seemed to indicate some kind of navigational system, but they weren't trained to read it.

"It's only for a couple of months," Cecilia said under her breath.

"Yeah," Linnea answered, "but two months of what?"

A man appeared in a long blue coat with red trim holding an electronic device in his hands. The device held his attention for a long moment. The women stopped, waiting for him to look up and give them some sort of indication as to what they should do next. Linnea shared a quick look with Cecilia, but the there was no camaraderie between their gazes. In truth, Cecilia was as much a stranger to Linnea as the man standing before them.

"Welcome," the man stated. "Welcome, doctors."

"I'm the doctor, Dr. Cecilia Markos," Cecilia answered, her tone clipped and frankly a little insulting. She motioned to Linnea. "This is my assistant, Linnea Nel."

Linnea gave a rueful smile at the other woman's introduction and suddenly regretted bothering to help her up off the floor. She had hoped, being from the same dimensional plane, Cecilia would show her some form of respect. Though why Linnea expected as much was a mystery even to her. She was used to people treating her poorly, and all because of a stupid tiny-little implant.

"Welcome, Dr. Markos, Sans Nel," the man amended. He smiled at both of them equally, unfazed by her non-doctor status. Linnea was inclined to like him instantly.

Cecilia nodded once.

"Thank you," Linnea answered politely.

"I am Dr. Gerard Fauchet. I will be your guide while you're on our plane. Anything you need, all you have to do is ask." He motioned to the papers. "Would you like me to carry that for you?"

"No, I've got it." Linnea glanced pointedly at Cecilia and added, "I am the assistant, after all."

"We don't work with parchment, but I can have one of the doctors scan your documents into a clipboard if you like." He lifted his electronic device to indicate what he was talking about. "In fact, I understand supplies are waiting for us at the assigned research facility."

Cecilia looked around, clearly taken aback. "You mean...we will not be working here? Near the portal?"

Linnea had the same question. A thin thread of fear worked through her at the idea. Of course, she knew this was part of her mission, but the nagging idea that her plane might just abandon her here wouldn't leave her. They couldn't kill her. They couldn't

291

monitor her. But they could trap her in an alternate reality and tell her family she'd suffered an accident. Who wouldn't believe it? Inter-dimensional travel just sounded dangerous. And that was if they even admitted to what they'd done to her. Her family might not even know she'd gone missing. They might even be relieved to never hear from her again.

"Afraid we might keep you here against your will?" Gerard teased. Linnea couldn't help but return the man's playful smile. However, Cecilia was far from amused. The open expression disappeared from the man's face. In a more subdued tone, he stated, "Please, follow me."

Linnea gave her companion a questioningly glance as Gerard led them down the hall. She caught the woman staring at the man's ass. This was who they sent as the dignitary? A displeased woman who lusted after the first male specimen they came across? Linnea gave a small laugh, feeling a tiny bit superior to the great Dr. Markos.

Cecilia began to cough.

"Doctor?" Gerard inquired, glancing at his clipboard then the women.

Cecilia touched her chest lightly. "I am still adapting to the air."

"It smells like we're walking near a confectionary," Linnea observed politely, trying to lighten the insulting tilt to Cecilia's words. This was getting ridiculous. As unhappy as she was by her plane's anti-chaos laws keeping her out of medical higher learning, she didn't want her people misrepresented by the rude doctor at her side. "The air is very sweet."

"That is the air-filtering sterilizer," Gerard said. "The air is contin-uously tested for abnormalities and purified. You have nothing to fear here. We haven't had a serious illness for, well, some would argue for centuries now, depending on your particular definition of serious." He waved his hand toward the ceiling. "I am told that after a time you will become accustomed to the scent. We tried modifying the formula to be unscented, but it lost two-point-three percent potency."

"No illness for so long?" Cecilia questioned, clearly trying to convey the significance of such a discovery when she looked at Linnea. "That is quite the accomplishment."

Linnea didn't react. Of course that was why they were here—to glean medical knowledge to cure diseases on their plane. She didn't believe for a second Jinna merely wanted them to spread some good-will and come home.

Gerard led them through the hall, turning several times until it became apparent the halls were an endless maze that would be impossible to navigate without a map. Linnea noticed monitors on the wall displayed their life signs as they passed, and if she walked too close to them they blipped, so she tried to stay toward the center of the hall. She stopped walking, staring at the monitor, trying to decipher what it was saying.

"Ah, Dr. Fauchet." The abrupt sound cut into her thoughts and directed her attention to the arrogant sounding man coming down the hall.

"Dr. Markos, Sans Nel," Gerard introduced, "may I present Medical Supreme Walter, his son Dr. Sebastjan Walter and Dr. Walter's wife, Sans Ariella."

"Doctor," the Medical Supreme acknowledged, glancing only briefly at Linnea. He had a smooth, youthful look to him that contrasted the intelligence in his blue eyes. A foreshadowing of gray salted the black hair at his temples.

"Welcome," Dr. Walter said. Ariella simply nodded and didn't look at any one person for too long.

Linnea noted that everyone talked louder on this plane, as if someone turned up the volume a couple notches. She was tempted to rub her ears, but refrained.

"And this is the hospital coordinator Dr. Lu," Gerard finished. Dr. Lu stayed back behind the others, more interested in his clipboard than his visitors.

"Welcome to Asclepius," the Medical Supreme said. "We look forward to a mutual exchange of knowledge. I have chosen Dr. Fauchet to be your guide. He will remain at your side. Should you need anything, please speak directly to him or to Dr. Swift. I will be unable to attend you at the research facility. I am a very busy man after all."

Cecilia began to answer, but the Medical Supreme cut her off.

"Here he is!" The Medical Supreme lifted his hand, motioning behind them. "May I present the esteemed Dr. Swift, Director of Central Hospital."

Linnea couldn't move. All thoughts left her as Dr. Swift moved closer to join their group. He nodded in acknowledgement. Dark brown hair framed his tanned face and green eyes. The cut seemed long compared to the other natives, but the look suited him. Well, honestly, she wasn't sure if the look suited *him*, but it suited *her* just fine. Attraction rocketed through her body, causing her nerves to come alive. It was potent and raw, as if he emitted some kind of sex pheromone all over her body. She shifted uncomfortably, her one-piece jumpsuit feeling very tight and oddly erotic. Moisture wetted her sex.

Linnea took a deep breath and pressed the papers closer to her chest. Her breasts ached in appreciation of the gesture, wanting to be rubbed. Unable to help herself, she stared at his strong features—deep eyes, proud nose, deliciously firm lips. As a highly trained doctor he probably knew all the right nerve bundles to touch inside a woman's body to make her orgasm. Damn, it had been way too long since she'd had sex.

And then she noticed his expression. It was one of disdain as he stared a long time at her hair. She resisted the urge to touch the purple streak. As quickly as it came, her desire left, replaced by irritation and indignation.

"Dr. Markos," Dr. Swift acknowledged, turning his attention from Linnea without bothering to greet her. Sebastjan slipped away with his wife, followed by Dr. Lu. "I've ordered your transport readied. Your belongings have already been loaded. Dr. Fauchet will show you where to go." He glanced at Linnea and shifted his weight. "I must attend to a few matters here but will join you later at the facility."

"Sans Nel has parchment to be transferred to a clipboard. Perhaps she should work here and arrive later with you when she is finished?" Gerard suggested.

Dr. Swift didn't spare her a look as he nodded stiffly. "Very well. Sans Nel, follow me. I will show you where you can work."

294

Cecilia gestured that Linnea should follow the man. Frowning, she had no choice but to go after the arrogant doctor.

"Where did my son...?" The Medical Supreme began to question, glancing around as Linnea passed by him. "Excuse me. I have urgent business to attend to."

With a few turns of the corners, Linnea found herself alone with Dr. Arrogant. The man didn't look at her and she couldn't help but think this was going to be a very long couple of months.

Chapter Five

H is dick hated him.

Sam tried to take deep breaths without being noticeable. Unfortunately, his uncompleted desires only grew more painful the second he looked at the visiting dignitary. Hell, by all rights he should have been attracted to Dr. Markos, the educated, tall, polished off-plane doctor. Instead, his cock pointed directly at her Sans assistant, Linnea Nel. Linnea didn't even have normal colored hair, or eyes—at least as they knew it on his plane. The shoulder-length black locks were streaked with dark purple and her eyes were a strange shade of purplish-grey. He found himself fascinated by their uniqueness.

Sam hated Dr. Fauchet.

At least, for the moment he did. The man's very reasonable assertion that Linnea transfer her parchments before transport made sense. It was protocol to enter new off-plane information into the universal database as quickly as possible.

However, reason aside, he did not want to be alone with this woman, not until he had a chance to finish masturbating. Even now he wanted to unwrap her slender body and discover what other strange colorings she carried. Was her nether hair streaked with purple as well? Did the color occur naturally? What about her nipples? Would they match the glossy color of her lips?

He almost walked past their turn and had to abruptly stop.

Linnea stumbled behind him. He turned and gestured to the door. "You may work in here."

She blinked those damn unique eyes as she looked into the room and then back at him. "Perhaps I should stick with parchment."

"I'll show you how to use the clipboard. The functions are quite easy."

"I'm not worried about figuring out the functions so much as inadvertently crashing your system." Linnea adjusted the stack of papers against her chest to free one of her arms. She lifted it and moved closer to the wall monitor. The screen blipped once, twice, before suddenly flashing faster the closer she came to the unit until the words were unrecognizable. When she pulled away, it went back to normal. "There is a reason my plane sent me with paper copies."

"Interesting," Sam said, studying her. Without thought, he reached to touch her free arm. She felt like he expected a woman to feel—warm and soft. "I don't remember seeing this phenomenon before."

Linnea's eyes dropped to his hand. "I'm not dangerous to people, just electronics."

"A rare condition," Sam agreed. He let go, not trusting himself to continue touching her. "Come with me. Let's see what we can do to counteract your affliction while you are here."

"Affliction," she repeated softly, not sounding too pleased.

Sam led her toward one of the private examination rooms. The square space looked like many of the rooms in the hospital, complete with a scanning booth. The door automatically shut behind them as they entered. "This is a medical booth. When you step on the platform, thin lights will come out and record your body's readings. It won't hurt."

"That's what they said about the Divinity portal." Linnea set her stack of papers on a metal counter. "That thing felt as if it ripped me apart. It will be much harder to step into the portal a second time, knowing what's coming."

"We can give you something for the pain before you leave to make it easier." Sam eyed her back. The tight material of her one-piece suit hugged her curves. Curiosity got the better of him, and he said, "It will be optimal if you remove your clothing for the scanners to get cleaner readings."

Linnea stiffened.

What was he doing? Okay, so technically it was true, but the accuracy difference only amounted to exactly point-two-percent.

"Lovely," she drawled, though the sound of her voice belied the definition of the word as he knew it. "Just like the Orderkeeper logs back home."

"Orderkeeper?" he questioned.

"Anti-chaos department." The answer was hardly helpful.

Linnea began undressing, her back toward him. She pulled the cinch from her waist and placed it next to the papers on the counter. Sam gripped his clipboard, watching the unveiling of her body. He tried to assure himself it was medical curiosity—a visual comparison of off-plane anatomy. His cock begged to differ with his motives. Fuck, it actually throbbed.

The clothing slipped off her shoulders to unveil smooth skin. A long valley ran down along her spine, shifting as she freed her arms. Slowly, she turned.

What color were her nipples? The question tickled his mind. He swallowed, desperate to find out the answer. Momentarily disappointed when they were not some strange shade, he quickly recovered. The large pink tips were perfect, punctuating two shapely handfuls. His eyes followed her clothing, down, over hips, down, over legs, down...

Sam breathed deeply before glancing up to meet her eyes. She stared at him, a brow arched. Unable to think of a better excuse for his unprofessionalism, he said stiffly, "You appear compatible with my plane. The machine should not have a problem reading you. Please, step into the booth for scanning."

The lasers turned on as she approached. She gave a small jump back before holding out her hand to touch the light. Obviously deciding it wasn't harmful, she went inside.

"Just stand still. It will only take a few moments." Sam watched the lights dancing on her flesh, touching where he wanted to. She stared at the wall in front of her, not moving, barely breathing. He wanted to say more to her, but was unsure how to start a conversation with a Sans woman from another plane.

Sam had never been sexually aroused by a scan before. The only explanation was he'd come into the situation already denied release. What he was feeling was simple physical need. By the looks of this woman they would have nothing in common on an intellectual level. He liked being a doctor and talking about medical things. When he spoke to a Sans, he didn't have much to say beyond the required niceties.

A loud blare sounded overhead, dragging him from his thoughts. Surprised, he turned his attention to the woman in the booth. Her wide eyes looked at him and she covered her stomach protectively with her hands.

"Containment," the automated system announced, as a plastic wall slid down from the ceiling, trapping her on one side of the room. "Containment. Exam One. Terminal. Containment. Security level one. Containment."

Needlessly, Sam looked at the door. They were in Exam Twenty. The alarm wasn't for Linnea. Who was in the hospital? Protocol demanded all exams for the day be cancelled due to the arriving dignitaries. Unless...

"What's happening? What's wrong with me?" Linnea asked.

"It's not you," Sam answered. The door had automatically locked at the containment alarm and he quickly punched in his twenty-five digit override code. "Stay here. Get dressed. I'll come back for you. There is nothing to worry about. This hospital is full of doctors who know what to do."

"But—" The slamming door behind him cut off her words. He hurried through the large facility.

The automated message repeated. "Containment. Exam One. Terminal. Containment."

The closer he got to Exam One, the stronger the sweet scent of sanitizer became. About halfway to Exam One, he met with Supreme

Walter. The man gave him a hard look and stated, "Don't you have a dignitary to escort?"

Sam was taken aback by the man's tone. "But..."

"It's a false alarm. I'm taking care of it. All exams have been cancelled for the day, you know that." As if catching himself, the Medical Supreme took a deep breath and instantly changed his sour expression into that of a politician. "Please, see to our guests. We don't want them frightened by this alarm, do we? I'll make sure Dr. Lu gives you a full report of the incident."

As the director, Sam wanted to protest, but there was nothing he could say when given an order directly from the Medical Supreme, especially when he had no justifiable reason as to why he should disobey and check the incident for himself. He nodded. "Of course. We leave immediately and I will be back by the end of the day. I'll expect his report on my return."

Supreme Walter quickly stepped away, leaving Sam to watch after him with suspicion. As he made his way back to Linnea, the alarms stopped. He relaxed a little, suddenly glad he hadn't pushed the issue with the Medical Supreme as he'd instinctively wanted to. They would not have turned off the alarms if it had been a real incident. He stopped at the wall panel, typed in his code and ordered a hospital-wide equipment check. The staff would hate him for it, but it needed to be done. He couldn't have alarms misfiring and scaring people.

When he returned to Linnea, he found her standing several feet back from a wall monitor, studying it. She didn't look directly at him. "Did the mighty doctors take care of it?"

He paused, unable to help himself as he glanced at her ass in the tight pants she wore. They left nothing to his imagination. Knowing she probably didn't understand the monitor as she wasn't a medical professional, he said, "There is nothing to be concerned over. It was an alarm test that should not have been scheduled when off-world dignitaries were on site."

She glanced at him and back at the wall. "Did my scan tell you anything?"

"Of course." He went to the medical scanner's controls and began scrolling through the information. A two-dimensional image of her naked outline appeared. Damn, he even found that sexy. Suddenly he was grateful for transport sleep. Otherwise it would be a very long, secluded drive to the facility to drop her off.

He paused, staring at her basic readings. They were off just a fraction, but enough to cause an anomaly. Curiously, he had never seen such a reading before, but it was the only thing he could find that might have such a side effect.

"Well?" she prompted when he didn't speak.

Sam blinked, realizing he was again staring at her naked outline in the charts. He typed in a quick prescription and then closed the file. "I can give you something that should help, but for a permanent solution I'll need to do more tests."

"Do you know what it is?"

"Yes, I understand your readings. I'll give you medicine that will help."

"What kind of readings? What kind of medicine?" she persisted.

"I understand you may be frightened, being in a new plane, but rest assured we know what we are doing." Sam went to the wall unit to retrieve the syringe he'd ordered, along with a medical chip necklace.

"I didn't ask if you knew what you were doing." Linnea sounded irritated with him and he wondered at it. "I asked what you were doing so I could know what you are going to do to my body."

"I'm giving you medicine. Something to help." He handed her the necklace. How could he explain complicated internal medicine to her in a way she'd understand? "Put this on."

"It's lovely, thank you." She did, albeit slowly. "So you think you can permanently fix me?"

He lifted the shot to her neck and stuck it in.

"Ow!" She jerked in surprise and quickly wrapped her fingers over the injection site. "What was that?"

"A shot to help alleviate your symptoms. This first one should take a few hours to work fully. After that, if you notice any electronic glitches, use the necklace to refill an injection by pressing to a monitor screen. The first shot should last you a long while."

"So you can't permanently fix me?"

"I might be able to, but I don't want to alter your genetics until I've had ample time to look over any side effects that might arise." He gave her a slight smile, trying to ease her fears "We wouldn't want you growing extra limbs."

Her eyes widened, clearly thinking he was serious. She took a small step back and he saw her arms stiffen as if she expected something to happen to them. "And the shot?"

"Temporary measure." Sam gave up any attempts at joking. He wasn't sure what had brought the inappropriate behavior on in the first place. "If you notice any side effects, report them to a local doctor."

"Not you?" She rubbed her neck as if he'd done her some great injury. "But you're the one who gave it to me."

"If I am around, yes, I will do. However any of the local doctors will be able to access your charts." The room felt small and the idea of seeing much more of her had a very uncomfortable effect on his body. He turned abruptly to the door. "We should go. They'll be expecting us at the biosphacility."

Chapter Six

Linnea followed the rude doctor out of the exam room and through the maze halls of the Central Hospital and Optimal Health Centre. Her neck was sore, and she didn't appreciate the surprise attack. A little warning would have been nice. A lot of explanation would have been better. Still, as she passed a wall monitor she noticed they didn't blink nearly as badly. Now, if she could manage not to grow any extra body parts, this could be a good thing for her. She fingered the necklace he'd given her. The purple stone matched her eyes. She thought that an interesting coincidence. At least it wasn't bright yellow or something obnoxious. The round stone looked like a rock, but apparently it held the code to her medicine inside.

If he could cure her, that meant she could get the chip. She could be tracked. A smile spread over her face. She could go to school. Her parents would stop making excuses about her. They'd invite her back to family functions. She'd be included.

Did she dare hope?

A bright light shone and she looked to see Dr. Swift walking through the front doors of the hospital. She momentarily forgot her medical condition as she looked at the new world. Linnea wasn't sure what she expected to see, but somehow this wasn't it. The planet, so far, appeared to be constructed of stone. The Central Hospital and Optimal Health Centre dominated the area. Thick columns and over-sized stone arches mimicked the smaller surrounding buildings. The outside architecture was nothing like the metal corridors within. The stone façade of the hospital joined the smooth stone of the empty streets, growing into a carved stone landscape. The streets, sidewalks and buildings seemed connected by one smooth formation of rock. Statues set on the ground and their stiff lines and symmetrical features were just as clean and orderly as the surrounding buildings. The only visible pieces of life, besides the two people walking toward the transport, were the small plants encased in large glass boxes.

"Where is it?" Sam said under his breath. He looked back and forth along the empty street.

"Perhaps your driver is running behind?" she offered.

He gave her a look that kind of made her feel like an idiot. She arched a brow at him and pretended not to care about his opinion. As a non-doctor, she wasn't going to be afforded much respect in this world. That was fine. She didn't get a lot of respect on her world either. She would simply keep her mouth shut, absorb as much information as she could, and hope for a cure that would change everything.

"I'm not an imbecile, you know." Linnea wasn't sure what prompted her to speak of it. She rubbed her neck. "You don't have to talk down to me or simplify things so I can understand them."

He didn't answer.

"Finally." Sam stepped toward the street as a large box hovered its way toward them. Linnea leaned over, looking under the vehicle. It didn't touch the ground. When she stood straight, her companion was staring at her.

"Interesting mechanics," she said, dismissively. Though, in truth, she wanted to ask him how it worked.

"If you like transporter mechanics." The doctor stepped inside the vehicle and disappeared within.

Linnea leaned in to look inside before stepping up the small steps that had appeared by the door. She found him seated in the near-empty space and slowly took a seat across from him. "How do you drive it?"

"Transporters drive themselves. The coordinates have already been programmed." Sam pressed a button and the door shut, sealing them in. Linnea leaned toward a window and looked out. There was no way to open the window for fresh air.

"What is your city called?" she asked, trying to make conversation. The vehicle was deafeningly silent, a strange contrast to the loud voices and equipment.

"Asclepius."

The vehicle began to move soundlessly, hovering over the earth as it self-navigated streets. It sped by quickly, making it impossible for her to focus on the passing building. She saw a few people, dressed like the doctor across from her, but they didn't pay any attention to the woman staring out at them.

"You might want to get comfortable," he said. "It's a long trip."

She took the hint and stopped gawking out of the window. Instead she looked at him. She opened her mouth to ask more questions, but a strange hissing sound came from the transport. She stiffened in her seat. Light smoke filtered in from the walls. Linnea covered her mouth, panicking. She stood, automatically reaching for the window. Unable to open it, she turned toward the door. It was over in moments. Her limbs became heavy, and as she turned she lost control of her body. She landed on her knees. Kneeling on the floor, she tried to stand but her body would not obey. Her eyes widened and she found her face falling toward Sam's lap.

Chapter Seven

S am fought the urge to awaken. His body was tired, his mind half-aware. The drugging effects of transport sleep did not concern him, but his brain should not be trying to wake his body.

The transport turned, swaying him. He felt pressure in his lap. That pressure felt like a dream. He gave a soft moan. The transport turned again. Something rocked against his cock like an erotic fantasy. Not fully aware, he reached to rub at his hard dick. His fingers instead met with soft hair. The contact caused her head to move on his lap. Who was he to deny the dream? He automatically tugged at his coat, lifting it out of her way. Oh, but his body needed this. He then fumbled for his waistband, tugging at it, freeing the head of his cock. He felt soft fingers and pulled them with his hand into his pants. They touched his arousal and he gave another moan before the drugged sleep overtook the growing pleasure.

Linnea's head bumped up and down in a steady rhythm. She inhaled deeply, caught in a haze of sleep. Her body ached, but it was a dull pain, far away and hardly noticeable. A new smell filled her as she breathed, erotically pleasant. It was an intimate smell, one she didn't readily know but one she wasn't too eager to escape. Her head bumped again, bouncing faster. She flexed her hand. Her fingers were moist and hot and trapped. Her elbow pointed out to the side. Smooth, firm skin pressed into her palm. Slowly, she became aware that her thumb and forefinger were gripping the base of a penis next to a man's balls.

Was she having sex? Had she drank too much and passed out on the guy? Her head bobbed again, the movement matching the man's press up into her hand. She blinked open her eyes, seeing blue material bunched by her face and little else. Her hand delved down the front of the guy's pants, her fingers wrapped around a very nice specimen of male virility. The intimate smell became stronger. She breathed deeper, opening her mouth. Her breath hit the shaft. Desire stung through her. Somehow, without her realizing it, her pussy had responded and was soaking her pants with a damp response. Automatically, without thought in her hazed state, she did what came naturally in such a situation and she stroked the thick cock. Damn, but it felt huge.

"Fuck," a man whispered at her bolder strokes. Hands grabbed her hair and pulled her head closer. Her lips hit the shaft and the man groaned in approval. "Fuck."

Before she could fully comprehend that she should even stop to think about what was happening, she had her mouth open and a thick cock being shoved inside. The man held her head and pressed his hips up, nearly choking her in his eagerness.

"Ah, fuck," he groaned. His legs stirred beneath her. She fell to the side, bumping her shoulder against the wall of the transport. Weakly, she braced herself with her hands as she became aware of the hard press of the transport floor against her knees. A dull pain slowly grew in intensity, radiating up her legs. She blinked again, fighting for consciousness.

"Don't stop...what the...?" A more alert tone entered the man's surprised voice.

Linnea glanced up, instantly becoming aware of where she was and who she was with. She pulled back and he let her head go. Her lips made a smacking noise as they left Dr. Swift's cock.

His glassy eyes blinked as if he fought to awaken fully. Conscious thought did not alleviate the aching in her sex. She tasted him on her tongue. Hands reached for her, tugging at her shirt to free her breasts. Time made little sense to her fogged brain. Linnea wasn't sure how, but she was suddenly naked and straddling Dr. Swift on the seat. His glassy eyes met hers and he blinked heavily. His cock bumped her pussy, missing entrance. It took several tries but they finally managed to correct the aim. He jerked her down on his lap and groaned loudly. Linnea gasped, the surprise of his large fit causing her to find a bit of reason. What was happening? Why was she straddling Dr. Swift? Why was he letting her? The last thing she remembered was his irritatingly superior look. Then smoke. Then...

He lifted her by her waist and jerked her down hard, going deeper. She inhaled sharply. The man was strong, able to control her with his hands. She braced herself on his shoulders. His eyes closed and he used her hips to make her fuck him. There was nothing sweet and tender about the way he lifted her up and then slammed her down onto his cock. Oh, but it was gratifying. She pressed her stomach forward to create a more pleasurable angle. Linnea let him fuck her.

"What are you doing?" he asked, confused, even as his hips thumped up into her. Sam made a loud animalistic noise and flipped her over onto the seat. His cock left her for the briefest of moments. Her back hit the slick material. Sam came over her, braced his arms, and began pumping his hips harder than before. The new position allowed him to go deeper. "Oh fuck, your pussy is..."

His incoherent mumblings were drowned out by the sound of her climax. She cried out as her orgasm hit her. Sam's release joined hers and he tensed over her.

For a long time she didn't move, only drifted between the haze of aftermath and the fog of drugged sleep. It would have been so easy to fall back into oblivion. The man above her shifted. She blinked heavily and pushed up from the seat.

Reason came back to her slowly, but when it finally dawned on her what she'd done, the truth hit hard. She'd fucked Dr. Swift.

Her knees ached as she pushed up. She looked at them, seeing they were bruised where she'd fallen on them. Feigning more innocence than she felt, she said, "What's happening? What was that smoke? Did you...?"

"How did you break out of transport sleep? I have a high tolerance and so my transport always emits a higher dose." He glanced over her naked body. His eyes stayed on her breasts a second longer than the rest of her. Feeling exposed, she tugged on her clothing. The shoulder was ripped and she was forced to tuck it in to hide the tear. It was much easier for him to right his clothing as he pulled his waistband up over his cock and pushed the facility uniform around his thighs. "I don't know how you are used to doing things on your plane, but normally there is a mutual understanding before sex."

"Mutual..." Her mouth dropped open. "Hey, *you* drugged *me*. On my plane we have forms to sign before sex can commence. I didn't consent to coitus *or* being drugged."

"I vaguely recall your head being in my lap."

"I didn't put it there," she defended. "I fell. That's not my fault. You drugged me." She rubbed her neck. "I asked you what you were giving me. You should have said it would have an arousal side effect."

"You didn't fall into my pants."

"You didn't fall into my pussy." She arched a brow, irritated beyond reason. The transport made another hissing noise. A mist entered. She lifted her hand. "Oh, no, you don't get to drug me again to try to get out of this."

"Relax. It's to help us wake up." He frowned at her. "We must be at the biosphacility."

Her head did begin to clear as the mist surrounded her. She swept her hands over her hair, smoothing it. As if by mutual agreement, they changed the subject. "Biosphacility?"

"It's short for Biosphere Facility. We call this location Biosphacility Three. This is the facility where Dr. Markos is assigned to work. It's one of the largest biosphacilities on the planet, and the most luxurious of our research bases. I am sure you will be comfortable, Sans Nel."

"Is there a medical library?" she asked.

"A computer will have access to any of the public records your boss requires." He frowned. "You forgot your parchments back at the hospital. I'll have someone scan them and notify you when it's complete. You should have access to it in a few days at most, probably sooner."

Linnea didn't respond to the veiled insult. What should have been a relaxing aftermath of great sex turned into a stiffly awkward conversation. Outside, fat trees opened up into a narrow ravine. Workers in full white containment suits kneeled around something on the forest floor. They were surrounded by green and purple plant life. "What's wrong with the air?"

He frowned, leaning forward to look at what she saw. "The air?"

Linnea pulled slightly away, not wanting to be too close to him now. "They wear suits. Has there been an outbreak of some kind?"

"It's protocol. There are pollens in the forest and any number of things that can create an allergic reaction." They watched one of the workers place a plant sample in a specimen jar. "They're testing the forest plants for genetic mutations."

The transport turned and Sam sat back in his seat. She continued to look out the window, very aware of where he was. She felt his eyes on her but she didn't meet his gaze. The biosphacility was a large dome, curving high off the ground. Tall gates encircled the stone encampment, keeping the forest separated from the inside. Covered walkways snaked out from the center facility like tentacles toward the gates, blocked by sealed doors to keep out the surrounding forest. The security gates were constructed of a ring of solid stone topped by several rows of thick metal bars. The closer they arrived, the taller the gates seemed until she could no longer see inside, her view blocked by the wall.

The transport stopped and made a series of fast beeps. The gate slid open just enough to let them slip through the wall. For a moment the transport became dark as they moved into the biosphacility.

"Won't the pollen get into the air supply anyway?" She glanced upward meaningfully, though she couldn't see the top of the security gate from where they were.

"The bars create a magnetic field that will keep out most pollens and any flying creatures. The thick wall keeps out other forest creatures that might otherwise cause allergic reactions in the staff. Sterilization protocols deals with any residual pollens and things we can't see." He paused in thought. "Once your boss learns our protocols, I'm sure she'll teach you whichever she deems necessary for your job. There is no reason for you to worry. The doctors have everything well in hand. You will be safe."

Linnea arched a brow. "Cecilia is not my boss. I am an inter-dimensional dignitary and merely here to assist." She was well aware she was making herself sound more qualified than she was. Well, she didn't have to tell him this was her first, and probably only, dignitary mission.

"My apologies." Though he said the words, he didn't sound apologetic.

"I might not have your doctor title, but I do have a brain." Linnea crossed her arms over her chest and sat back. She kept her eyes forward and didn't look out the window until the transport came to a full stop. Not for the first time she wondered what would happen to her. Would her plane abandon her here? Was this some elaborate plan to get rid of her, permanently?

She took a deep breath, refusing to give in to fear. If she kept her mind open, learned everything she could, more than Cecilia, her plane would have to take her back. She would know too much. If Sam couldn't cure her, then that was her next best bet—to be smarter and better than her traveling companion.

"Shouldn't be too hard," she mumbled.

"Excuse me?" He straightened his shoulders and quickly drew his hips back, clearly thinking she was talking about his arousal.

"Nothing." Linnea tried not to laugh as he adjusted himself on the seat. Dr. Arrogant might not like it, but it would seem he was still attracted to her and this time he couldn't blame it on being drugged.

The transport stopped and the door automatically slid open. Sam stepped out and held a hand out to help her down. Linnea gave him a knowing smile when she touched him, letting her fingers linger a little too long. He held his breath. Her smile widened. Good. Let him be uncomfortable.

Though, the way her body responded to him, this attempt at mischief might backfire.

The ground was covered with loose stones. Behind her, the transport door shut and the vehicle navigated itself to a parking spot in the biosphacility gate.

"I know you have a brain," Sam said, belatedly responding to her comment. "I saw your scans."

"Then do you think you can try talking to me like you do your doctor friends?" Linnea knew she should tread a little more gingerly with the Director of Central Hospital, but there was something about this frustrating man. She wanted him to know she was smart and not just some whore who pleasured men in power.

"Follow me, Sans Nel." Sam walked stiffly head of her.

"Yes, Dr. Swift." She mimicked his arrogantly cold tone. After a lifetime of defiance, she couldn't help herself.

The dome shone a little too brightly as the sunlight reflected off the shiny white plates of the exterior walls. Inside, he led her through a wide metal corridor lined with doors. She was beginning to sense an architectural theme on the planet.

"This is section one. This is where you will assist your boss, excuse me, Dr. Markos, in her work. The wall monitors, as well as the hand-held device we supply you with, will have access to the public records as well as your papers once they're scanned. A laboratory with standard samples has been provided for the doctor's work. Again, she will be able to tell you how to work anything she needs you to assist with."

Because I'm clearly an idiot who can't figure it out for myself, she thought resentfully.

He paused briefly as they passed a door. "This will be your assigned laboratory." He didn't bother to take her inside. "This way to your private quarters. Narrow halls are for private areas. Wider halls are for general use. I recommend staying out of private halls you don't belong in as a courtesy to others."

Did the man even realize how insulting he sounded? What? Was she going to go raid the doctors' belongings? Snoop in their rooms? Streak naked in an ancient act of chaos?

"Dr. Fauchet took care of the luggage. If it's not here, it will be soon." Sam went into a room and gave a sweeping gesture. "This is where you will stay. Press the green button on the monitor if you need help, or basic instructions on how to use anything."

The smooth walls of the chamber were bare and lacked personality of any kind. This was one of their most comfortable facilities? There was nothing special about it that would set it apart from any other room on dimensional plane 187. A thick mattress with silver covers had been placed on the platform in the middle of the room. A health monitor had turned on with the lights. There was a small area for personal needs, a row of drawers built into the wall, and every basic necessity she should need. Her black luggage was already on the bed.

"I will let Dr. Fauchet know you have arrived. Someone will be by to take care of your daily sustenance. I hope my explanations have satisfied your request that I interact with you as I would any visiting doctor."

Linnea opened her mouth to answer, but he was gone before she could even so much as get out a thank you. "Way to pick a charmer," she mumbled to herself as the door slid shut. Even now, she wanted seduce him. Pride kept her from even considering going after him. Instead, determined to get started learning, she opened drawers and poked around inside them. Only after she'd touched every strange, foreign object in the place did she turn to the monitor. "Okay, medical world, let's learn what you know."

Chapter Eight

Linnea was exhausted, but she wouldn't let that stop her. She needed every ounce of time to learn what she could from this medical plane. They made it very clear that all medical documents were not to leave the plane unless pre-negotiated between the Medical Supreme and her home world's politicians. Linnea doubted her governing politicians would care about negotiating documents for her reading enjoyment back home. They tended to prefer arresting her for trying to check out medical books from the library.

Actually, the information was quite fascinating. It had taken her a week to figure out their work methods, but after that it became easier to navigate their public records. Since she was used to learning on her own, she had an advantage over her traveling companion. Cecilia seemed to struggle with the work. Granted, it wasn't easy to learn what equated to a foreign medical language, but Linnea was doing it.

"It's like reading an ancient medical cipher," Cecilia mumbled at the other side of the laboratory. The lab was large and they were the only two working in it. There were work tables, dozens of items of medical testing equipment, sterile tubes lining one of the walls. Though different in design, it functioned much like the technology on their home plane did—only more advanced. In the corner there was a sleeping cot. For the first couple of weeks no one had used it, then Linnea began to notice body imprints in the material—right after Dr. Fauchet had returned from wherever he'd been. Cecilia tried to act as if nothing was going on, but Linnea wasn't naive.

Seeing Cecilia frown at an electronic clipboard and rub her temples, Linnea thought about offering to help. The woman looked up at her with the superior expression of disdain she often carried. Never mind, let the smart doctor figure out for herself that she was painstakingly reading the cure for Policompition Ten. On their plane they called it Firghelm Syndrome, a fancy name for itchy feet, and they'd cured it a lifetime ago.

Linnea chuckled to herself. She'd scanned over the same document their second week there. It was how she figured out that first translating the chemical formulas at the end of the document saved a lot of headache and time.

"Levels," Cecilia mumbled to herself. Linnea again considered helping the woman out with her translations, but realized the doctor would probably mock any attempt Linnea made.

The wall monitor dinged, indicating that Cecilia needed to take something to relax. It did that a lot. Apparently the woman was a giant ball of uptight.

"Can you shut that off?" Cecilia's tone was more of an order than a question.

Linnea looked up from her handheld, irritated to have her study interrupted yet again to do Dr. Markos's bidding. The other day the woman actually sent her to fetch food. Going to the wall monitor, she punched in a dismissal code to get the unit to stop beeping. If she wanted, she could have overridden the shot code. She'd discovered how to do so on accident in one of her readings. Instead, she left it. The monitors were set up to issue corrective shots whenever someone's emotional or physical levels strayed away from normal. It was designed for promoting an optimal work output. Cecilia was given a lot of shots. Linnea dismissed most of her personal ones, marking them as complete. The only shot she took was to correct her natural magnetism with the prescription Sam gave her.

"Our time here is nearly half over and all I've really learned is this plane is obsessed with immortality," Cecilia said.

Linnea knew from experience the woman wasn't really talking to her. There were numerous references in the public records relating to the pursuit of escaping death. Some tried to find the path to ascension, electrocuting themselves in the process, the rest of them just tried to cure everything and block out what they couldn't cure.

"Over half," Linnea corrected to get the woman to stop mumbling to herself.

"Half of what?" the doctor asked.

"You were mumbling out loud again," Linnea said, not glancing up from her work. "You said we were almost halfway done. In fact, we are over halfway done. As of yesterday, we are starting month two."

"It's this place. With no daylight it's impossible to keep track of the hours." Cecilia studied her.

"Go up to the top level. There's plenty of sunlight."

"The top level?"

"Haven't you wandered around at all?" Linnea asked, surprised. She'd explored most of the facility in the first week and talked with many of the staff.

"No. I've only gone where instructed, as should you. They showed us our quarters, the dining hall and our laboratory."

"Not surprising this," Linnea drawled. So much for friendly conversation. "You're one of those true believers in the anti-chaos, aren't you? One of the devout."

"No," the woman denied, obviously not liking the comparison to being a monk.

"Really?" Linnea was tired of being treated like some kind of imbecilic responsibility. She wasn't an idiot. She saw a lot more than Cecilia realized. "Then why all the shame about Dr. Fauchet?"

Cecilia stiffened. "I don't know what you mean."

"All right then." Linnea couldn't help herself. "It's about time for you to kick me out for your..." The woman paused, giving her a meaningful look. "Your nightly, serious, platonic, anti-chaos discussions with Dr. Fauchet."

Cecilia glared at her. "My professional medical conversations with

Dr. Fauchet, our inter-dimensional contact, are not of your concern. You haven't been to medical school so I understand that you have no idea the level of complicated maneuvering and paperwork involved in a mission such as ours."

Linnea set down her electronic clipboard and moved toward the door. If she didn't get away from the woman, she would do something she'd regret. Doing her best to look nonchalant, even though inside she churned with anger, she said, "A little hint, doctor." She ran her hand over the wall unit and smiled. "As you've pointed out on many occasions, I'm not a doctor, but in my experience, anti-chaos conversations work much better if you keep your clothes on."

Linnea left the woman gawking after her. Good. Let the superior doctor fret about just how much Linnea knew. It wasn't like she'd spread the gossip of it on their home plane, and no one on this plane cared about sexual affairs, but Cecilia didn't need to be told that. Let her worry about it. Maybe then the woman would treat her assistant with a bit more respect.

Thinking of sexual affairs caused her thoughts to naturally turn toward her own last encounter, Dr. Sam Swift. She hadn't seen him since he'd dropped her off, and she had no indication that she would ever see him again, but still she hoped. Her body ached for release, to be touched. She fingered the prescription necklace he'd given her. There were other opportunities at the facility, other doctors, some of them not bad to look at, yet she couldn't get Swift out of her mind. What she thought was a rude tour of the biosphacility turned out to be his way of treating other doctors. He might not always react when she spoke, but he had listened.

As she strode to the end of the corridor, she frowned, realizing she'd left her clipboard in the laboratory. There went her evening reading. She wasn't going to go back to retrieve it, not after the grandiose exit she'd just made. Deciding she didn't want to go to her quarters, she instead turned to go to the top of the dome. It was hard to tell time inside the base of the facility with its artificial lighting, but she estimated it to be evening by the subtle ways the lights dimmed in the narrow residential corridors.

"Dr. Lu will remain in Asclepius to oversee matters there."

Linnea stopped walking. The voice hit her like a shockwave. Sam was there, at the facility, and she hadn't known. Part of her was hurt that he would avoid her. The other part of her was all too willing to forgive him if he'd agree to fuck her again. She tried to push that primal part of herself down.

"I've commissioned Dr. Jonns to work on the problem like you asked, but I just gave him a piece of it and enacted Privacy Code Six. I don't trust him with secrets of this magnitude. He has been tasked with analyzing..." Dr. Gerard Fauchet's answer became muffled. Linnea couldn't be sure, but thought he mentioned some kind of virus. "...Sebastjan's new wife."

"Jonns is a capable doctor, but I agree," Sam said. "And our guests? Do they suspect anything?"

"No. Nothing. They spend all their time in the laboratory. Dr. Markos has had her assistant access several medical documents, more so than what shows up on her personal records, but I don't think she's trying to steal them. I think she might have trained Sans Nel to scan them for possible coding. If we weren't so busy, I'd have analyzed their scroll patterns."

"We'll order the dignitaries checked when the time comes for them to leave, *if* they leave. We don't need another Plane 33 incident on top of everything else," Sam said.

"I've integrated myself with Dr. Markos," Gerard said. "Do you want me to have one of the others speak to Sans Nel?"

There was a long pause. "No. I'll do it. We struck up a rapport in the transport. The less who know of what we are about, the better."

Linnea frowned. A rapport? Is that how he remembered it?

"I'm supposed to meet Dr. Markos in a half hour. I'll offer to extend their stay for learning purposes."

"Good idea. No one ever refuses that offer."

Linnea heard footsteps and hurried back away from the door. She barely made it around a corner as she saw the hint of a lab coat peek from behind the office doorframe. Only too late did she realize she'd ducked into a residential hall and there was nowhere to go. She pressed herself into a doorframe and waited. Unless someone looked directly at her, they might not notice her there. She watched, listening as footsteps drew nearer. Gerard passed by, heading toward their laboratory with a syringe in hand.

As much as she didn't like Cecilia, she couldn't abandon the woman in light of what she'd just heard. She made a move to go after him.

"Sans Nel."

Linnea stiffened. She hadn't heard Sam's footsteps behind Gerard's. She quickly turned. When she looked up at him she didn't want to believe him capable of deceit. Her mind froze and all reasonable thoughts left her. Desire instantly rose inside her, but she fought it, knowing she had to keep her wits about her. This plane had secrets and she needed to find out what those were. Her very future might depend upon it.

Chapter Nine

"What are you doing in my hall?" Sam asked the woman before him. He had not planned on seeking Linnea out so soon after his arrival, but that didn't mean he hadn't wanted to. In fact, he'd wanted to turn his transport around the second he stepped into it a month ago. Duty had called him away, but his body had begged him to stay. Duty won, as it always would, as it had to. Too much was at stake.

When Gerard mentioned someone else questioning her, he should have allowed it. They wouldn't be the first dignitaries who tried to sneak recordings of documents back with them. That was the least of his worries. What he didn't tell Gerard was that he had other orders. With Privacy Code Six, he only revealed that which Gerard needed to do his job. Sam's orders came from the Medical Supreme. Well, not directly, but they were clear. A strange outbreak had been discovered in the city that started the same time the two dignitaries arrived. There was no proof, but the coincidence couldn't be ignored. The alarm hadn't been a mistake. Not even the Medical Supreme could hide the virus report.

Linnea shot him a coy smile. Every thought slipped out of his head. Her tone lowered seductively, as she said, "I heard you were back."

"Oh?" That surprised him. "Did you require my assistance? How may I help you? Is it your prescription?"

She glanced down the hall both ways before again eyeing him. Her smile widened. "Transport ride."

At that he shook his head in denial. "I'm sorry. Now is not a good time to arrange trips."

Her smile didn't falter. She stepped closer and lowered her voice meaningfully. "Or perhaps just a ride?"

"Oh," Sam said, only getting her meaning seconds later. "Oh, you meant…"

"For a smart guy you're a little…" She chuckled to herself. "Never mind, Doc. You have a good night."

"Wait." Sam reached for her arm, not sure what to think about her offer or his sudden decision to take her up on it. "I apologize. It has been a very long month."

"I believe both of our months were the exact same length of time."

Sam wasn't sure if she was making a joke so he refrained from responding. Her smile dropped by small degrees. It was a subtle shift in her expression, but he caught it. In that moment, he had the feeling he couldn't fully trust her. And in that moment he wanted her even more.

"Are you upset with me?" Sam didn't let go of her arm, but instead began caressing the length of it.

Linnea trembled. "Why would I be upset with you?"

"For not contacting you after what happened in the transport." The second he said it, he saw her amusement and wished he could take it back.

"Well, according to my plane's customs, we are married now." She lifted her hand and stroked his cheek. "We did come together without consent forms. It is the law."

"Ah, I—" Marriage? A strange feeling began to unfurl inside him at her words.

Linnea burst into laughter. "Relax. We're not married. I'm teasing you. You're so serious."

"Of course." He dropped her arm. "I thought we were acting like doctors toward each other. I didn't expect the light comment."

"Forget I said anything about that. I was tired from the trip and I get grouchy when I first wake up." She dropped her hand from his face to his chest. "Show me this room of yours."

Sam didn't understand this woman. She teased him. She dismissed him. She had no regard for his high position of power. She wasn't afraid of him and she didn't seem to want anything from him personally.

Her hand slipped down to his hips.

Perhaps that last statement wasn't true. She did seem to want something very personal from him.

"My quarters." He gestured to his door.

"After you." She stepped aside to give him access to open the door. He waved his hand over the biometric scanner and led the way inside.

Linnea knew she could have walked away from Sam and he would not have followed her. She didn't trust him. She didn't trust his plane or his politicians. It was actually quite arousing, the mistrust, the suspicion. His very attitude brought out the rebel in her. His very nearness made her want to seduce him. Linnea smiled to herself. She always did have a problem with authority.

She had expected Sam's room to be bigger than hers, but in fact it was almost exactly the same. The only difference was the monitor on the wall. It was much bigger and appeared to have a lot more functions, including a small button in the corner marked "Privacy."

"Did you partake of your evening sustenance?" he asked.

Linnea reached for the hidden buttons fastening the uniform they'd given her to wear. She quickly undid them and let the material slide from her shoulders. His eyes instantly dropped to look at her body. The thin undershirt clung to her body, giving away the curves of her breasts and nipples. "No. You should probably feed me." She crossed to where he stood, took hold of his lab coat and pulled him toward the large bed in the center of the room.

MICHELLE M. PILLOW

He touched the prescription necklace he'd given her. "Has the treatment been working?"

Linnea nodded, the kindness in his voice causing her to falter a little. "Yes. Thank you. I've only needed two doses since that first."

"You've taken three?" He frowned. "The medicine should be lasting longer than that."

Linnea hid her emotions at the genuine concern in his eyes. She knew a cure was too good to be true, yet she'd dared to hope. Placing her hand over his, she urged his hand lower to cup her breast.

"Sam," she whispered, "I don't want to talk about my prescription. Either you'll find something to help me or you won't. Discussing it won't affect the outcome."

"You call me Sam," he said, as if surprised.

She pulled at his lab coat, tugging it open without unfastening the buttons. They gave under the force of strength. Leaning in to him, she kissed the center of his chest. "Doctor seems a little formal," she paused, kissing a few inches lower, "when," she kissed lower, "I'm about to..." Her words trailed off as she made her way to his waist. She tugged at his pants as she kissed his hip. He made a small moan of approval. His pants slid down his legs.

Linnea walked him around and then pushed his stomach so he sat on the bed. She explored his body, avoiding the towering arousal. His hips jerked whenever she rubbed her hands near his cock.

"Please," he begged, trembling at her touch. "Oh, *apolloa,* please."

Linnea smiled, liking that this powerful man succumbed so easily to her. She leaned over, letting her breath fall on the tip of his cock. His fingers threaded into her hair, but he didn't force her down, merely caressed her head. "I think it's about time I prescribed you something for this affliction."

"Yes, please, yes." He touched her breast, circling his thumb around her nipple.

She slipped a hand between his thighs, bracing her weight. The back of her wrist touched his balls. With her free hand she took hold of his cock, lightly gripping the smooth, firm shaft. "I think your temperature is elevated."

He groaned and stiffened.

"Let me see if I can bring this fever down." Linnea leaned over him and took the tip of his shaft into her mouth.

"I have never been with a woman like you, Linnea." The admission was more of a groan tinted with pleasure than actual words. "There is something special about you."

Linnea adjusted her positioning to take him deeper. She wrapped her hand around the base of his shaft, angling it to her mouth. He tensed, jerked, shivered, moaned for more. It didn't take long before he erupted between her lips. She pulled back and smiled at him. "I bet you say those sweet things to all your lovers."

"No," Sam breathed hard. He pushed up, maneuvering her body with his. "I don't keep other lovers."

The admission surprised her. "Surely a man in your position gets a lot of offers."

"I don't want to be used for my power." In one graceful motion he flipped her onto her back. Her body sank into the soft mattress.

Linnea let the playful mask slip from her face. She looked deep into his eyes, seeing the man he was within that gaze. "No one likes to be used or judged for what they are."

Sam kissed her, teasing her mouth with his. The light pressure sent little jolts of pleasure down her body. Her legs worked against him.

When he broke the kiss, he told her, "I have no reason to use you, and any judgment of you is favorable." Forcefully, he pushed apart her thighs. Gone was the submissive man from moments before.

She crawled up on the bed, moving away from him. He followed, again pushing apart her thighs. He looked up at her meaningfully as he lowered his mouth to her sex.

As his tongue tickled her clit with light, teasing flicks, he drew her knee over his shoulder. Her calf pressed over his back. He held her leg in place, anchoring her pussy to his mouth. She gasped, finding it hard to breathe.

Linnea wiggled beneath him. His tongue worked along her slit before a finger found its way inside her body. He licked harder. She pushed up on the bed. Warmth centered on her pussy. She tried to speak and only ended up gasping his name over and over, "Sam, Sam..."

Sam stroked her deep, pressing two fingers into her. He sucked her clit. Pleasure built. Her toes curled. Her legs stiffened. She climaxed against his lips. Before the tremors subsided, he dropped her leg and pushed up between her thighs.

Sam's cock slid easily in the moisture created with her release. He groaned in pleasure. Her muscles stretched to accept him. He thrust deep before pulling out and thrusting again. His hips moved in small circles as he fucked her.

Linnea moaned his name. Sam rubbed her nipple. He kissed her neck, her chest. The pleasure coursed through her, making her forget herself.

The pace quickened. Tension built before erupting through her. Linnea tensed, coming again. Sam's body responded instantly as he came inside her. He froze above her, holding stiff as the pleasure washed over them. Then, falling to her side, he lay next to her.

"You should stay tonight." He touched her face, drawing her lips to his in a lazy caress. The soft movements were tender and sweet.

Linnea didn't answer. How could she? His mouth was on hers and she couldn't form a word to save her life.

Chapter Ten

Linnea looked at the man sleeping next to her. Sam's hand rested on her thigh. He'd asked her to stay, but when the kiss ended he hadn't cuddled her next to his body. Instead he stared at her questioningly in those moments before his eyes closed for the night. She didn't know what he silently wanted to know.

Linnea concentrated on his breathing for a long time, making sure he would not wake back up. When she was convinced he wouldn't wake up, she slid her leg out from under his hand. The light was dim and she saw more the impression of his features than his actual face. For a moment, she hesitated. Yesterday, she would have said this man was an arrogant doctor who treated her like every other person of power she'd ever met. Earlier today, she would have said he was a devious doctor with possible evil tendencies who was up to something shady along with the others on his plane. When he'd kissed her, she would have said there was no possible way this man was evil. Now, as he slept, so sweet and trusting, she didn't think him devious or arrogant. Had she been wrong about him? Or were her emotions getting in the way of her judgment?

It was wiser to mistrust him. Safer too.

Crossing naked to the wall monitor, she hit the setting to dim the screen. As she suspected, the unit had higher security access than the one in her room. She mouthed as she typed, "Privacy Code Six."

The unit brought up information on the code. Basically, it meant no one could discuss anything with anyone. She frowned, not finding the definition very helpful.

Next, she typed, "Plane 33 incident."

A long report appeared. She scanned over it to get the basic idea of what had happened. When Plane 33 visited on a mission similar to Linnea's, the doctors tried to steal copies of all of 187's records. That was bad enough, but they didn't stop there. They tried to transport some virus samples through the portal. Unfortunately, the viruses weren't completely secured for transport and they were accidently released on the other side. Plane 33 was nearly wiped out when the virus mutated. The population's immune systems weren't capable of fighting off the disease. Report notes at the bottom of the file indicated Plane 33 blamed 187 for releasing the virus as punishment for taking the medical records. Divinity Corporation acquitted Plane 187 from all wrongdoing and Plane 33 was sealed off permanently.

Two questions from her eavesdropping answered. But what did a privacy code and an old incident have to do with keeping them trapped on this plane?

Linnea glanced over her shoulder. Sam hadn't moved. She swallowed nervously before snooping deeper.

After a month of learning their system, she found her way through his files with minimal trouble. Only, when she tried to open the documents, the computer requested a bio-scan. She frowned, resetting the device as if she'd never touched it.

"What are you doing?" Sam's voice was sleepy.

Linnea stiffened and touched the necklace. "I can't sleep sometimes. I wanted to see if my prescription was wearing off." She turned and pasted a smile on her lips. "I didn't mean to wake you."

He didn't answer.

Linnea wondered how much he'd seen, but knew better than to confess before she was caught. "I should go."

"Stay."

"I should find food, uh, sustenance." She leaned over to pick up her lab coat.

"No, you should stay." He lifted his arm and waved her back into the bed. "The morning sustenance will be served in a few hours for the doctors who head out into the forest before dawn. It will be better than anything you can find now."

Linnea wasn't sure why she obeyed, but she did. She lay next to him and kissed him. He moaned lightly into her mouth and dropped his arm over her hip.

"I want to taste you again." Sam broke the kiss. His hand lazily skimmed over her thigh and butt. His eyes closed and he sighed heavily. The hand on her ass didn't stop its caresses. He made slow circles on her skin, rubbing deeper with each pass.

Linnea pressed her leg forward, placing her knee between his thighs. His hands roamed her body in sleepy caresses. Sam made love to her slowly, taking his time exploring her. His mouth kissed every inch of her flesh before finally settling between her thighs. She writhed against his tongue as he licked her pussy. He pulled her clit into his mouth and released it. When she was breathlessly begging for completion, he came over her to end their torment. He entered her steady and sure, pumping his hips until they found sweet release.

Sam wanted to trust Linnea. When he looked deep into her beautiful purple eyes he sensed that he could. Holding her felt natural and right. Yet, when he closed his eyes, he was forced to remember his duty. Currently, the sick count was very low, but they didn't know how to cure the mystery virus. The idea frightened him. In his lifetime they had never seen a medical outbreak they didn't understand. There were diseases from other planes, but the similarities in biology combined with the collected knowledge from other realities only strengthened their medical confidence.

Linnea burrowed against his chest. He'd been hesitant to take this approach with her, but her teasing suggestions had been too much to resist. She wanted him and she boldly let him know as much. How could he refuse such an offer? After the thorough scan he'd given her on her arrival, he knew she wasn't a carrier of the new virus. He'd looked at her charts himself.

Nothing would be solved at this moment. His body was sated and relaxed for the first time in a month, actually much longer if he didn't count their brief encounter in the transport the day she arrived. He hadn't wanted his thoughts distracted by her, but he hadn't been able to stop thinking about her. Not even his former wife had made him feel this way.

Sam knew this moment wouldn't last. How could it? She would eventually go home. He would remain here. He was in charge of Central Hospital, a job that included overseeing countless projects.

"You can't sleep?" she asked, suppressing a yawn.

Sam realized he'd been stirring on the bed and must have awoken her. "I'm thinking about work. Go back to sleep."

She mumbled something incoherent and snuggled against him. He concentrated on her even breath before finally falling to sleep himself.

Chapter Eleven

"Dr. Markos?" Linnea's stomach knotted in fear. Cecilia was gone. She'd waited for the woman in the laboratory, but when she didn't show up for work, Linnea had gone looking for her in her quarters. Cecilia wasn't there. She tried locating the doctor on the wall monitor to no avail. A brisk, panicked walk of the facility proved fruitless. The woman was nowhere to be found.

Linnea went back to the lab and started pacing. Cecilia wasn't the type to skip out on her duties. The woman didn't even leave the portion of the biosphacility they'd specifically told her she could go to. Something must have happened to her traveling companion.

Linnea grabbed a laser scalpel off the supply wall and went back out into the hall to make her way toward the executive offices. She didn't really think about what she was doing. That seemed to be a problem she had lately. She'd slept with Sam and hadn't really thought out fully what she was doing. If Gerard had done something to Cecilia while she was busy sexing up the enemy, she would never forgive herself. She might not want to invite Cecilia over for drinks, but that didn't mean she wanted her harmed. She thought of the syringe Gerard had been carrying. At the time she assumed it was medicine. They were always injecting themselves with medicine to correct levels.

Luckily, when she woke up Sam had been gone and she didn't have to face him. Had she known he'd just leave her alone in his quarters, she would have waited until morning to search his wall monitor.

"Bedlam and anarchy, Cecilia, where are you?" she whispered.

She hid the scalpel behind her leg as she passed by a group of doctors. They were more interested in discussing the figures on their clipboards than looking at her. Still, she held her breath as she moved past them. What was she going to do? She was trapped here. The forest didn't look too scary. Maybe she could run away and they'd be too frightened of germs to come after her. But then what? She'd live in the forest eating twigs on an alternate plane of reality? How was that a good idea? And if she made it back to Central Hospital, then what? Even if she managed to find her way to the portal, she had no idea how to run it. She truly was at the mercy of plane 187.

Gerard's office was empty. Her hands shook and her heart pounded. She wasn't sure what was happening, but she didn't trust anyone on this plane.

"What am I going to do?" she whispered, staring a moment longer into Gerard's office. She continued to the next office, passing by when she saw Dr. Jonns on the inside. His back was to her as he transmitted a communication on the wall monitor. The image of another doctor shone back at him. Linnea couldn't hear what they were discussing from behind the thick glass wall separating the office from the hallway.

"Linnea?"

Linnea gripped the scalpel tighter and turned to Sam. His expression gave nothing away. The softness from the night before was gone, replaced by the serious expression he'd worn the day they met. He came closer.

"What are you doing here?" he asked.

Out of habit, she reacted to his authoritative tone and instantly gave a sarcastic answer, "What? Didn't you miss me, sweet one?"

He glanced around before taking her arm and ushering her inside an empty office. With a quick set of the wall controls, he dimmed the glass to give them privacy.

Before he could speak, she said, "Don't worry, Doctor, I'm not here for you. Dr. Markos is missing. You wouldn't happen to know anything about that, would you?"

"Missing?" His expression didn't change.

"Don't play innocent. I know something is going on here. I saw Dr. Fauchet going toward our lab last night with a syringe. What happened? Did she refuse your offer of an extended stay? She did, didn't she? Dr. Markos would never agree to an extension. Changes like that create chaos in the government schedule and Dr. Markos is all about maintaining order. So what? Did Dr. Fauchet do something to her because she didn't want to be here?"

"Do something to her?" he repeated before shaking his head. "Of course not. Dr. Fauchet arranged for her to leave the biosphacility."

"Without me?" She stiffened. Emotions welled inside her and she found it hard to hold them back. It had occurred to her at one point that her sister sent her to this new world to get rid of her. She'd never really believed they'd actually abandon her here. At least, she'd hoped not.

"Yes." The word was slow and confused.

What if he was lying? What if they'd done something to Cecilia? "I don't believe you. I know about Plane 33 and I know about the Privacy Code Six." She was probing, but he didn't have to know that.

"You know?" His blank expression filled with panic for the briefest of moments. "What did you do?"

She didn't know how to respond so she stayed quiet. Accusation was not the reaction she'd been expecting.

"Is this revenge for Plane 33?" He set his clipboard down a little too hard and took an aggressive step for her. "That wasn't our fault. They stole from us. I don't know what they told you but..."

Linnea stumbled back at his sudden moves and lifted the laser scalpel in warning. "Stay back. I know what's going on here. Your plan is to delay us. It won't work."

"Are they allies of yours? Is that why you infected the...?" He eyed her laser but didn't seem too concerned. He did, however, stay back. "Is this for revenge?"

"You're worried." Linnea lowered her arm. "There's a disease here that you don't know how to cure, isn't there? Someone important is sick and you're all scrambling around for an antidote. If you suspect us, it must be in your capital city and it must have started about the time we arrived. You started to say we infected *the*...so, who?" She frowned, studying him. "The Medical Supreme."

His tense expression and lack of denial was answer enough.

"I don't know what evidence you think you have, but we haven't done harm to anyone. We are what we say we are, dignitaries on a learning mission. That's it. If you're going to accuse us of being dangerous, you best have evidence."

He glanced at her weapon.

"This is for protection." She dropped her arm and hid the scalpel behind her leg. "You've been lying to us."

"Lying? No. We simply have no reason to tell you everything. Privacy Code Six has been enacted."

"Then you will let us go home?"

"I'm sorry." He shook his head in denial. "That is not possible at this time. All portal travel has been suspended. We will not risk an outbreak spreading to other planes. I'd hoped Dr. Markos would have agreed to stay longer for research."

"Without full disclosure of the risks?" Linnea arched a brow. "Why would we want to stay when you have some kind of outbreak?"

"It's contained for the moment. You would not be put into any undue danger. It is actually safer we keep you away from the capitol. If you were a doctor, I would explain it to you, but—"

Her hard look cut him off. She gripped the scalpel, resisting the urge to throw it at him. She was tired of being treated like an idiot. Through tight lips, she said, "Try."

"It's very complicated—"

"Then try hard."

"Sans Nel." He sounded exasperated. "Perhaps you have misinterpreted our intimacy to mean you should be afforded certain privileges. I take full responsibility for the lack of communication prior to seducing you. So to explain now, however belatedly, our intimacy does not equal full disclosure of my job. Some things I cannot discuss with you. It is not to insult you, but frankly it is very complicated and I don't have time to teach you how to be a doctor."

Linnea had never wanted to cut someone so badly in her life. "Oh? Did you drug me to make me have sex with you, powerful and great Dr. Swift?"

"Well, no, of course not." He looked insulted.

Good, he should be insulted, she thought, barely able to control her ire. "Then you're just an arrogant nit."

"I-I..."

"Make no mistake, Doctor, I seduced you. I'm not some helpless Sans who swoons at the very sight of your manly brain. And, to be honest, your records aren't all that hard to read. Our languages are similar enough, only your plane seems to like to name diseases after the doctors who discover them and mine likes to name them after dead politicians and anti-chaos heroes."

"So Dr. Markos taught you to read the medical documents?" he asked. "Dr. Fauchet mentioned she has had you access more of the records in the short time you've been here than most dignitaries do in most trips."

"Seriously?" Unable to help it, she gave a small laugh.

"What is so amusing?"

"Dr. Markos is a highly respected medical mind on our plane, but that doesn't automatically qualify her to understand everything you do here. Her traditional training may work against her in that regard. She's used to things being a certain way. I, however, am self-taught, so my method of learning tends to be less rigid than hers." Linnea felt as if she might be bragging, but she really wanted him to stop looking at her like she was some stupid Sans. "I accessed your documents for my own use. Dr. Markos has me logging notes and running errands."

"*You* read all those documents?" To his credit he didn't look totally shocked and insulting as he said it.

"I scanned most of them. Once I convert the charts over it's pretty easy to see if what I'm reading is comparable to what we know of on our plane. If it is, I move on. If it's not, I spend the time studying it."

She waited for his laughter. It didn't come. "I actually find it fascinating."

"If this is true, then why are you not a doctor?"

Linnea touched the purple stone at her neck. "Because of this. My anti-chaos chip doesn't work because my body rejects them. For this reason I was not allowed to continue my education beyond the basic required levels. This is the closest they'll let me get to medicine, assisting Dr. Markos."

"I won't pretend to understand the logic of refusing education to someone with a natural talent for it." Sam sighed. "My apologies for assuming you would not understand."

It was the first time someone actually, genuinely apologized to her since she was a child. She nodded, unable to speak as emotion choked her. Linnea set the scalpel on the desk.

"If you know of Privacy Code Six, can I take your word you will not discuss what I'm about to tell you?" He waited for her nod. "Good. This is not being made public. We would have a worldwide panic on our hands if people found out. This is no outbreak. The illness is contained for the time being. That alarm you heard when you arrived was the first indication of it. I have spent the last month ensuring a full sanitation of the hospital, transports, and the homes of anyone who could have come in contact with it. We've also isolated a way to detect the virus into the medical scans. We know you are not a carrier. We do not know why someone might be immune."

"How many?"

"At this time, one."

"Only one? So I was right? It's the Medical Supreme?"

"That cannot be known," Sam insisted. "Please, don't speak of it."

She nodded.

"I discussed the situation with Dr. Lu, whom you met when you arrived. We determined to authorize Dr. Markos, and this was before you told me of your knowledge, that if necessary we would allow her to work on the problem. Gerard vouched for her. Since you have clearly deduced the situation, I will allow you the same courtesy. We are not too proud as to refuse help. Our hope is that we can keep this incident contained. The Medical Supreme will not be pleased when he finds out about your involvement. If you agree, I cannot guarantee he might not institute consequences."

"Is that where you took Cecilia? To work on this?"

"No, Gerard took her out of the biosphacility. He thought she could use the break. Our logs show she's spent almost every hour between the laboratory and her quarters."

Linnea glanced toward the door. "So, you track where people go?"

He gave a small laugh. She quickly turned her attention back to him at the sound. "You like to wander."

"I call it exploring my environment."

Sam lifted his hand to touch her face. He looked as if he wanted to kiss her, but he held back. "I will have a private file sent to your clipboard. Use LinSanNel as an access code to open it."

Linnea stepped closer to him. With his easy acceptance of her intelligence, and his willingness to believe her without real proof, she found herself even more drawn to him. There had always been a connection between them, a strong physical pull, but this was different. She felt...well, honestly, she wasn't sure what she was feeling.

"Maybe you should send it to your room?" Her eyes dipped to his mouth, giving meaning to the words.

His breath caught. "I would like nothing more than to take you back to my quarters, but I have another conference scheduled with Dr. Lu."

"Perhaps later?" She arched a brow playfully.

Sam appeared torn. "I, ah, yes. We should...later."

Linnea pushed up on her toes and pressed her lips to his. Her hand went to his waist. "Or maybe we should now?"

It didn't take much convincing to get his pants around his ankles. There was one advantage to wearing multiple pieces of clothing compared to the one full suit common on her plane—better access. No doubt that is how the fashion of the single-piece jumpsuit evolved, to keep anything chaotic and fun from happening. She unfastened her pants before reaching for his cock. She stroked the hard shaft, which didn't need much provocation to find its full length. He backed her into the desk and lifted her ass so she sat on the edge. Coming between her thighs, he thrust in. He took her almost desperately, burying himself in her depths. The angle of their lovemaking forced her to fall back on her elbows. He held her thighs, rocking her body back and forth to keep rhythm with his hips. Her knees were enveloped by the length of his lab coat. Oh, but it was rough and hard and felt so good.

As the tension built, she stiffened. He kept moving as he watched her come. Tremors racked her with endless waves of pleasure. Only when they began to lessen did he allow himself to join her. He buried himself deep, jerking violently as he came. When he finally let her go, the sticky feel of his seed wet her thighs.

"I could keep you in here all day for that." His breath was labored as he righted his clothing.

"And miss your meeting?" She shook her head. "You just be sure to find me when you get a break later."

Chapter Twelve

D r. Lu's image flashed on Sam's monitor, indicating a call. The man was late for their meeting, but considering Sam needed a few minutes to right his clothing and smooth back his hair after his surprise encounter with Linnea, he was grateful for it. Just thinking of the woman caused him to take a deep breath before he could accept the call.

Dr. Lu wore a frown when the connection established. Without preamble, he said, "I just spoke with Dimensional Plane 303's politicians. Politician Shinclus emphatically explained on behalf of his people that they are not happy with the change in plans. He's threatened to inform Divinity Corporation if their dignitary is not returned on schedule. The Medical Supreme neglected to inform us of an Anti-Chaos treaty he signed with them. If we neglect to return their doctor, they are entitled to unlimited medical access."

"Why would the Medical Supreme agree to such a thing?" Sam shook his head in frustration. "That makes no sense. What do we get out of the deal? We're the hosts."

Dr. Lu didn't readily answer.

"It's a secure line. Speak." Sam leaned closer, even though no one could hear them.

351

"New Order Society made him a personal trade," Dr. Lu finally answered.

"Which is...?"

"Sans Nel. Apparently, she has something biological wrong with her that isn't dangerous, but that makes her incompatible with the technology on her plane. The New Order Society government of their plane gave her to the Medical Supreme as a ward. It is unclear if she knows about the arrangement." Lu averted his eyes. "I managed to read the copy Politician Shinclus was only too happy to supply. He already indicated that he expects a full list of all of our plane's technology and that is just to start."

"A ward?" Sam froze. He wasn't an idiot. He knew exactly what being a ward of Supreme Walter entailed.

"We have no choice. We have to send the doctor back in four weeks."

Sam shook his head. "We can't risk that this virus might mutate. The health risk later will be much greater than it is now."

"The Anti-Chaos treaty says nothing about sending her home early. Two weeks should be enough to confirm it's safe to use the portal if we follow all of the stringent protocols. I would bring them back here for the testing though, in case we need to send them home sooner." Lu shook his head. His eyes said more than his mouth ever would. He was not a fan of the Medical Supreme, though he had yet to vocalize an opinion on the man. Sam couldn't fault him for that. To speak out against the highest power on their planet was to commit career suicide. The Medical Supreme controlled everything. "I am handling Politician Shinclus for the time being, diplomatically. However, he continues to send demands."

"We should not have been put into this position," Sam grumbled under his breath.

"We have to show 303 we're in control," Lu insisted.

"I agree. Two weeks." Sam found the words hard to say. He didn't want to lose Linnea. The thought of her belonging to the Medical Supreme was intolerable. "But we're sending them both back. It will be a way to show them we do not need anything from them."

"Are you sure?" Lu's expression lightened some.

"Yes." Sam nodded. He knew the Medical Supreme wanted to trade for sexual wards. He'd already tested Sam's position on it. Sam couldn't do it. He had a feeling Linnea had not been told about New Society's plan for her. "And let's not mention the ward trade. I don't think Sans Nel is aware of the arrangement and we don't need an incident."

Lu seemed only too happy to agree. "I'll get the Medical Supreme to sign off on sending the dignitary back. I'll make the request vague and I'll get him to sign off on it."

"After medication might be the best time."

Lu nodded in agreement. "Consider it a supreme order."

"We'll leave in the morning." Sam pushed a button to end the communication.

Two weeks. It didn't seem fair. He wouldn't be ready to send her away in two weeks. However, it was for the best. He couldn't allow her to become a ward of the Medical Supreme. Nothing about that surprised him. Linnea was beautiful and spirited. Any man would be lucky to possess her. Sam was the lucky one she chose. The Medical Supreme's last ward, Sans Ariella, had just married his son. The timing was suspicious considering the wedding was planned right before Linnea arrived. Though, he couldn't see Sebastjan Walter marrying his father's lover.

Sam pressed his hands to his temples briefly before automatically going to the monitor to get an injection. The unit beeped as he was reaching for the syringe. The medicine might ease the headache, but it would do nothing for the stress that caused it.

Chapter Thirteen

Linnea toyed with the food on her plate. She found the things she missed about her home plane were few, but flavorful food was definitely one of them. Here, every meal tasted the same, unflavored and lacking in vibrant colors. Half the time, the food was in paste form and wanted for texture.

"Is the substance not to your liking?"

Linnea smiled before she met Sam's gaze.

"Your records indicated you have lost mass." He sat across from her with a plate.

"The substance is," she looked down at the pale green paste, "substance."

He chuckled. "I have been told though incredibly healthy, our food lacks the flavors of other planes." He took a bite. "It tastes normal to me."

"That's almost sad," Linnea said.

"We used to have culinary doctors, before the full enforcement of medical contraband laws. Most of the old spices were deemed unnecessary and unhealthy. Synthetic nutrients are much more optimal."

"I suppose it comes down to what you want most—a long life, or a flavorful one." She pushed the plate away. "I looked at the records. I'd like a couple days before I give any opinions."

"Of course." He ate, not really chewing before he swallowed. She wondered what he'd think of the food on her plane. "We leave in the morning for Asclepius. Will you tell Dr. Markos?"

Linnea nodded. "Of course."

"We'll have access to more tools at Central Hospital, and it is closer to the portal." Sam quickly finished his food and pushed it aside. Like most people, he considered the meals merely necessary breaks, like taking a shot when the monitor required it. There was no pleasure in the experience. "Do you miss your home?"

Linnea thought about his question. "Some things, yes. Like the food. Some things, no."

"It's been determined that you will be permitted to go home early."

"How early?" She wasn't ready to leave. There was so much she could still learn.

"Two weeks." He studied her face.

"I would rather stay the full term of my mission."

"It is for the best. We'll follow the most stringent of our protocols to ensure the safety of your plane, but then you should go." Sam kept his eyes steadily on her, as if taking in every nuance of her expression.

"I think Dr. Markos will be pleased. I'm not sure why she agreed to come on this mission." Linnea knew she shouldn't be talking about her companion, but there was something about Sam that drew her honesty. "That is not to say she is not very capable, but..."

"It is a big step for anyone to be one of the first to come through a portal. I will not think less of her for missing her home plane." His hand slid over the top of the table to rest near hers without touching her.

"Will two weeks be long enough for you to cure me?" Linnea's gaze traced the lines of his tapering fingers. She reached her pinkie toward his hand, barely touching him. Doctors ate around them, but none of them seemed to care about one of their highest medical officers talking to a lowly Sans. "I know it's selfish to ask. If it's not possible, I understand. The lives of many are worth more than my convenience."

"I could make sure you have the medicine you need. Whenever you had to be around computers, you could take it." His fingers inched closer to her hand. His little finger slipped over the top of hers.

"Thank you, but the injections are becoming more frequent as you warned they would. I'm not sure how much good they would do on my home plane. I need a cure. We have implants that don't work in my body for some reason. I can't be tracked. This makes me a threat to society. Without monitoring, I will still not be able to go to school or work in the medical field." She tried to hide her disappointment. "But the health of many takes precedence."

A small smile curled on his lips. "You have the doctor's spirit. Your plane is foolish for not seeing it in you."

Linnea drew her hand from his and stood. She trembled with emotion, but tried not to let it show. He was the first to see it in her. The knowledge was bittersweet. The one person who saw her potential didn't exist on her world and she was being sent away from his. In two weeks she would be exactly who she was before—an anti-chaos criminal who had to sneak into the library to read and who went home alone to a two-room apartment in the cheapest part of town.

"Thank you." She nodded. "I'll go inform Dr. Markos of the plan."

Sam looked like he'd stop her, but she turned and left before he could speak. Linnea wasn't sure why she walked so fast once she was out of his sight. She found it hard to breathe. She wasn't ready to go home. When it came down to it, she would do what was right, would put other people before her needs, but she really wanted a cure. If this plane did anything, it taught her how badly she wanted to study medicine and do research. It was what she was born to do. She'd had a taste of it here, with the documents Sam entrusted to her.

And then there was Sam. She stopped by the laboratory door before entering and took a deep breath. Sam.

"If you could come with me..." Cecilia's voice from inside broke into her thoughts.

Linnea blinked, realizing tears were in her eyes. She quickly brushed the moisture away to hide the emotion.

"That's not...no medical database is...with what I know, it would never be allowed," Gerard answered. Linnea leaned closer to better hear what they were saying. "We'll figure something out."

"It's not like we can send communications to each other or visit each other on work breaks," Cecilia said. "I told you from the beginning this couldn't go anywhere, that it couldn't mean anything. There will be this invisible wall between us, keeping us apart. We will spend our entire lives waiting on the whims of our politicians that I can someday come back."

"You would wait?" he asked.

"What do you think love is?" Cecilia responded, her voice rising. "You think I'll just go home through the portal and it will all go away?"

Linnea suddenly felt guilty. She shouldn't be listening to their private moment. Clearing her throat, she pushed open the door and stated, "Doctor."

Cecilia stiffened, startled by the intrusion. "What!"

Linnea stood in the doorway, uncomfortable. She averted her eyes. Gerard made no attempt to hide his emotions. The love he felt showed on his face.

"What is it?" Cecilia said, softer. The woman's expression was composed but she couldn't hide the truth of her feelings as they showed in her eyes.

Linnea slowly backed away. "Dr. Swift sent me to inform you we're leaving the facility in the morning."

"I didn't mean to yell at you." Cecilia looked helplessly at Gerard. "I'm overwhelmed at the moment."

"I understand." She nodded once. The second she was alone in the hall, she thought again of Sam. Would he ever look at her the way Gerard had been gazing at Cecilia?

Two weeks wasn't enough time.

Chapter Fourteen

Sam wasn't sure what he was expecting when he knocked for entrance into Linnea's quarters, but finding her sitting on the floor surrounded by electronic clipboards wasn't it. Her hair was twisted into strange knots at each side of her face, keeping the locks out of her eyes as she leaned over.

"I can't be sure, but..." She pointed at a clipboard to her left before looking up at him. "This thing looks like it's airborne, or at least mutated. Infected Subject One was infected, but no one seems to know how. A report just came in that two people on Infected Subject One's staff tested positive for the virus. I'm trying to determine the incubation period, but I can't find the earliest possible time the staff could have been exposed. I'm trying to access their work and travel records to see if they were with Infected Subject One prior to their staffing assignment."

"More are infected?" Sam hurried to look at what she was pointing at.

"The message just came in an hour ago," she said, looking almost guilty.

"How did you see this before me?" He picked up the clipboard and began scrolling through the file.

"I told you I have a knack for learning." Linnea stood. Her beautiful eyes searched his. "I read all the files and I wanted to make sure I had the most up-to-date information."

Sam wasn't sure if he was impressed or frightened by her talents. She'd broken some of their highest encryption keys.

When he didn't readily speak, she said, "It appears airborne. There was no direct contact, if the reports are to be believed. I've looked over your standard protocols and they're very detailed. Unless the Medical Supreme, I mean, unless Infected Subject One is intimate with his staff members, I doubt there is any other method of transmission."

"Not in quarantine. The computers would sense it if there were physical activities of that kind." Sam pushed a few of the clipboards over with his foot and sat next to where she had been on the floor. She rejoined him. "If these numbers are correct, the incubation period is short. That means it should be safe for you to go home. The Medical Supreme's staff was brought in for their specialties, so there was no prior exposure. If there were more infected, we would see more cases. Maybe it's contained?"

"I've been looking at something else. I don't have a formalized report, such as your plane seems to like, but..." She handed him one of the clipboards. "Does this look familiar to you?"

Sam eyed the virus. "Yes. It's the new—"

"No," Linnea interrupted. "It's not..." She pointed toward the far side of her layout. "Can you hand me that one?"

He obliged, but said, "Our databases were scanned. Nothing matched."

"I know I've seen something like this. When I first arrived I went through some of your older records. I stumbled my way into the archives." She handed him the clipboard with a sigh. "Can you bring up my viewing history? About a week after I arrived?"

Sam did, handing it back to her.

"I know I've seen this..." Linnea mumbled to herself as she worked, scrolling through documents. "Only it wasn't a virus. It was something..."

Sam watched her for a moment before picking up the new reports. This was not the evening he had planned, but he found he enjoyed sitting with her. She made adorable little noises when she read something she didn't like. His eyes strayed to her hair puffs. They revealed her delicate earlobes. He found himself leaning toward her neck, intent on kissing her.

"Here!" She gave a tiny jump and thrust the handheld to him. "It's a control substance of some sort. It seems to be a few mutations back, but do you see it?"

Sam took the document. She was right. The document was listed as a human control experiment, not as a disease, so it wouldn't have been logged and checked when the virus appeared. His stomach knotted. On principal he didn't like human control research. No person's will should be taken away. The thought reminded him of Linnea and how her plane traded her to the Medical Supreme. What was to stop them from trying to trade her through the portal again if he sent her back? He couldn't protect her if she wasn't with him. When he looked at her, he couldn't let her go. At least he had two weeks to convince her to stay.

"Sam?" Her tone was soft and questioning. "Why are you looking at me like that?"

"You're very..."

"Am I in trouble? Is it because I opened the document? I'm sorry. Sometimes when I'm working I get focused and I don't think of anything beyond the problem. And this is a big problem. It might be the only medical problem I'm ever allowed to work on, so I might have gotten a little too focused. I apologize. I never meant to—"

"Smart," he broke in. "You're very smart and beautiful and unique and special."

"Oh," she said in surprise. Her cheeks pinkened at his words.

"Human control was a fad science decades ago," he said. "I doubt anyone ever looks at these old documents."

"Maybe you just don't know that they do," she said carefully. At his arched brow, she added, "Look at the lead doctor on the document."

Sam gasped. "The Medical Supreme."

"He does seem to like control," Linnea offered. He could tell she was trying to be polite while still giving her opinion. "And he was the first one infected. Even with your protocols, laboratory accidents could happen."

Sam looked at the basic outline of information. It would require deeper reading. "If he was, that would explain why he didn't tell anyone what he was doing. He should have recognized his own work."

"This document is dated. It is possible he didn't remember," she tried diplomatically.

Sam shook his head, not believing it. "No. Men like the Medical Supreme *are* their work. He would have remembered."

"I didn't mean to cause trouble." She touched his arm and he felt a jolt through his nerves. "Sam, if you tell me, I'll forget I found this."

"Don't you dare! The pursuit of truth, no matter where it takes us, is paramount to a decent life." He put his hand over hers. "But, we do have to tread carefully. It is not wise to accuse the highest power on our plane without solid proof."

She nodded.

"It's late and we have a transport ride tomorrow." Sam stood, reaching to help her up. When she moved to pick up her mess he said, "Leave it."

Linnea let him pull her to her feet. She smiled up at him. He loved that smile. He loved the low, seductive sound of her voice even more. "I thought you liked transport sleep."

"After our last trip together? I'm thinking of disengaging the sleep aid." He caressed her cheek. He loved her soft skin. He loved her eyes. He loved her smell.

"Mm." The sound was a purr that made him shiver.

Sam was not one to lie to himself. He might have neglected to fully realize the truth until that moment, but now it stared up at him. He loved her. Not even the former wife had made him feel like this woman did. "I was married, previously."

Linnea blinked in surprise. "All right?"

"I thought you should know. It seems like something a person in a relationship would need to know." He placed his hand on her shoulder. "It did not work out and we parted ways. It was a convenient marriage for both of us. I don't have contact with her."

Linnea nodded but didn't speak.

Sam knew he was being ineloquent, but still he continued. "I don't have children. I have work."

"Are we in a relationship?" she asked.

"Yes." He nodded. Then, a little insecure, he added, "Aren't we?"

"I..." She hesitated. His stomach tightened and he found himself gripping her shoulder. He let go of her. "I think...yes."

He inhaled deeply. "Good."

"Good," she repeated. "I have never been married and I don't have children. I like children, but..."

"But?"

"On my plane, with my unique condition, I will never be permitted to have a child. My sister, Jinna, resents me a little because my condition will make her permit hard to obtain as well."

"You have a sister?"

"Yes, Politician Nel. She sent me here." Linnea gave a small, humorless laugh. "My family has written me off because I can't be monitored. I've always been an embarrassment to them."

"They are fools." Sam brushed his lips against hers. She accepted his kiss with a light moan of approval.

Her fingers skimmed over his chest to his neck. She pulled him closer. Her body pressed to his, molding perfectly against his muscles. He loved the feel of her. He loved everything about her. How could her family, her plane, not see how wonderful she was? One look at her clipboard notes and he could see she was highly intelligent. She found a very important key to their problem.

Their clothes seemed to melt away. Flesh glided against flesh. Sam lifted her and carried her to the bed. They made love slowly. Her delicate hands traced every inch of his body. He massaged her in return. Hard nipples beckoned his hands. Soft thighs called to his hips. Flicking tongues met and tangled in passion.

When he entered her, he felt complete. He was never one for

flowery thoughts, but he imagined this was what destiny felt like, the perfect fitting of two people. Her natural responses were timed to his. The tremors started deep inside her, calling forth his own release. When they came in unison, there was nothing else in all the planes he wanted.

Chapter Fifteen

Linnea stretched alongside Sam, suppressing a yawn. It was late, but her mind wouldn't shut off completely to let her rest. Sam's eyes opened at the movement. He didn't look as if he'd been sleeping much either.

"I should transmit our findings to the others," he said.

"The Medical Supreme won't like it." She rubbed her knee absently along his thigh, liking the texture of his naked skin.

"The document is in public records. I won't mention his name directly, but the others will see the truth for themselves. He won't be able to hide it." Sam pushed up from the bed. "You deserve the credit for your work. I'll call you Dignitary Nel, not Sans Nel, and I'll sign off as the doctor on your work. Please don't be insulted. If I call you Sans, they might not take the finding as seriously."

"I understand." She nodded, liking the sound of Dignitary more than Sans anyway.

"You realize this is your first official medical breakthrough." Sam gave her a quick smile as he picked up her clipboard and began organizing her findings into a preliminary report.

"Probably the only," she whispered. Linnea was keenly aware this would never happen again. In a way she was grateful for the opportunity to do what she always wanted to do. However, she had a feeling she would spend the rest of her life thinking back to this moment, to this wonderful man, and would languish over what once was.

"What?" he asked, glancing up at her.

"Thank you," she said louder. "I said thank you."

He smiled at her. There was an ease to him when he looked at her. Had it always been there? Had seeing the way Gerard looked at Cecilia opened her eyes to Sam?

She watched him compile his information, only speaking to offer suggestions a handful of times. He took her ideas graciously, adding them to his own. When he finished, he said, "I think that should do it for an update. We can write up a more formalized report for the records over the next few weeks."

A few weeks. Her smile fell at the reminder. A few weeks were not enough time.

"I'm sorry, I didn't mean to assume you needed my—"

"Yes, of course we'll do the report," she interrupted. "I'm just sleepy."

"You're right. It's late. We should sleep before the morning substance." He sent the update to his colleagues before turning off the clipboard. "Now the work is done there is nothing else to be done tonight."

"I wouldn't say nothing," she answered coyly, rolling to straddle his waist as he lay down. "I can think of one more thing we can do tonight."

"I am at your service, Dignitary Nel," he answered, opening his arms to accept her lovemaking.

Chapter Sixteen

Linnea hefted her luggage through the long halls toward the transport area. She hadn't expected to feel emotional about leaving, but her hands had trembled as she packed her belongings. It had been tempting to slide an electronic clipboard into her bags. She refrained. She wasn't a thief.

"Let me help you."

Linnea turned just as Sam reached to take her largest bag from her. She let him carry it as they fell into stride.

"Where were you this morning?" he asked.

"I needed to pack and I wanted to speak to Dr. Markos, but I couldn't find her." Linnea slowed as they passed her assigned laboratory.

"They are taking a transport ahead of us. You should see her at Central Hospital." Sam stared ahead, not meeting her gaze. She wondered at it but said nothing.

"Did you hear something about the report?" Linnea wondered aloud.

"I spoke with Dr. Lu."

Linnea waited for him to say more, but he didn't. When they walked outside, the transport box was waiting for them. She glanced around, half expecting someone from the biosphacility to take the time to see her off. The fact no one was outside to watch them go seemed a bit sad to her.

Sam put her luggage into a compartment below the seats of the transport before helping her inside. Once they were alone and on their way, she smiled at him. "Did you receive news from Dr. Lu?"

Sam reached into his lab coat and pulled out a small device. He fingered it gingerly, following the curved edge with his thumb. "He informed me that our report was received."

Her smile fell. The outside wall of the biosphacility passed by the window. "Did I cause problems?"

"No. We told the truth of what we found." He finally looked at her. "The report was automatically sent to the Medical Supreme. He wasn't pleased by the viral comparison to his old work."

"You didn't lose your job, did you?" The light smoke of the sleep aid began filtering into the transport. Linnea covered her mouth. "I thought you were turning the sleep aid off."

Sam took the small device and stuck it in his nose. "I'm sorry, Linnea."

"Sorry?" Panicked, she stood. Sam was there, holding his arms out to catch her as the drugs took effect.

"I love you, Linnea, I'm sorry."

It was the last thing she heard before sleep overtook her.

Chapter Seventeen

"Sorry?" Linnea croaked as she fought to wake up. Her blurred vision slid over the top of the transport. "Sam? Sorry?"

She pushed herself up too quickly and fell to the side, only to land on the floor. Crawling to the door, she managed to look out the window. Gerard ushered Cecilia inside the front door of Central Hospital. Sam stood behind them, waving that they should hurry. Linnea slapped her hand against the window. Sam glanced back at her, but didn't come to her.

"Sam?" Her voice became stronger. By sheer will she managed to stumble out of the transport toward the front of the hospital. What was happening? Why were they leaving her behind? Was she sick?

The hospital doors opened at her presence to let her inside. She heard footsteps and moved to follow them. Her shoulder hit the wall and she used the smooth metal to keep her body upright as she walked. The monitor screens fuzzed as she passed, reacting to her.

"I didn't get to say all I needed to."

Linnea followed Gerard's voice around a corner.

"You did what you had to," Sam said. "I'm under orders to lock down the portal. We should go."

Gerard's eyes met hers. "I thought you said Sans Nel missed the transport."

Linnea stopped walking.

Sam turned to her briefly. "I..."

She couldn't hear what they were saying so she forced herself forward.

"...you trapped Linnea?" Gerard suddenly struck out, pushing Sam in the chest. Sam fell back into the wall with a loud thud and didn't fight back.

"What is...?" Linnea's voice was weak.

"I love her!" Gerard yelled, interrupting her. "Look at me. We just sent the most vital part of who I am through that portal." He pointed at a nearby monitor to his readings. It dinged several times, demanding he take a shot to calm himself. "Look!"

Linnea stumbled closer. She felt dizzy. Her legs begged her to rest, to slide onto the floor and sleep.

"Then go. Take your chances. Go. Follow her. Just go. I'll say you were sent as a dignitary. I'll say it was to maintain peace." Sam reached for the wall and grabbed a clipboard. He handed it to Gerard along with a medical unit from his lab coat. "These will help ease your way with 303 politicians once you get there."

"I'll take Linnea," Gerard said, making a move to help the woman. Linnea began to shake her head in protest. What was happening?

Sam grabbed Gerard's arm to stop him. "No. That's the deal. She stays. She will be invaluable in helping stop this disease. Now go. They'll be watching to make sure this section is sealed. If I don't do it, they'll do it for me offsite."

"But..." Gerard frowned. He gave her a guilty look. "Thank you."

Linnea watched Gerard leave as she slid to the floor. Sam didn't look at her for a long moment. Instead, he stared at the monitor then the portal room door.

"Sam," she said, demanding he pay attention to her. When he looked at her, the guilt in his expression was palpable. She tried to make sense of what she'd seen. "What happened? Why did they leave me here?"

"This morning when Dr. Lu called, he informed me that the

Medical Supreme was not pleased with our report. He was going to send an order to us as soon as we arrived that the portal was to be sealed shut indefinitely. Both you and Gerard indicated that Dr. Markos would never be happy here so we sent her home."

"She left me?"

"She didn't want to," Sam said.

"That's a lie. My sister probably arranged to have me abandoned here." A tear slipped over her cheek. Her eyelids were heavy.

Sam kneeled beside her. "You know?"

Linnea hadn't expected him to admit it. "I saw you. You sent Cecilia away. You told Dr. Fauchet to leave me."

"I can explain. Gerard loves her. I had to let him go."

"You drugged me. You kept me here." She pulled her arm away from him when he tried to touch her.

"I needed more time to talk to you." He tried again to touch her and she slapped at his hand.

"We had time in the transport." Linnea managed to stand, forcing her trembling muscles to hold her weight.

Sam reached for her only to draw his hand away. He paced the width of the hall in agitation. "I couldn't risk you not listening to me. If you go home, I can't protect you."

"Protect me?" She frowned in confusion. "It's my home. There is nothing to protect me from."

"They traded you to be the Medical Supreme's personal ward, Linnea. Next time it might be to one of the gladiator planes, or the newly discovered Staria where the men are centuries behind our times and speak of nothing but war and weaponry. Who knows what those barbarians would do to you. I couldn't risk you telling me you wanted to go. If you said it, I couldn't keep you here."

"So you trapped me here instead without asking?" In a way his intentions were sweet, though terribly misguided. Then the full enormity of what he was saying struck her. "What do you mean they gave me to the Medical Supreme? Like a slave?"

"A ward," Sam corrected.

"What is a ward?"

"You belong to him and he..." Sam didn't need to explain. The truth of it was in his jealously possessive expression.

"Sex slave," Linnea concluded. "And you trapped me here? To that fate?" Then, tears falling harder now even as she tried to maintain her composure, she demanded, "And you can let the happen to me? I thought we...I thought you..."

"You can marry me," he blurted. "The Medical Supreme could not touch you."

"Marry?" Linnea's legs gave out and she slid down the wall in shock. The floor felt like it moved beneath her. "You?"

He hesitated but nodded. "Yes?"

Linnea moaned, passing out onto the floor.

Sam instantly caught Linnea in his arms and lifted her off the floor. He was surprised she'd managed to stay conscious as long as she had. He'd been even more surprised to see she'd managed to make it out of the transport and into the hospital on her own. The dose he'd given her had been strong.

"Well done, Sam," he grumbled sarcastically to himself. When Dr. Lu told him to send the women home, he'd panicked. He needed the transport time to think and plan. He needed to find the right words to tell her what her plane had done to her, what his plane had agreed to. That kind of thing wasn't easy to say. All of his medical training hadn't prepared him for it.

He carried her to a private room and laid her down on the examination table. The transport sleep aid was still in her system and he needed to deactivate it. Getting the right prescription from the wall unit, he spritzed her face a few times until she blinked and looked up at him.

"I didn't mean to trap you," Sam said before she could say anything. He was afraid she'd demand to leave before he had a chance to tell her what he needed to. "You were already planning on staying for four more weeks. I thought that would give us time. I thought if I..." Sam dropped his eyes. "No. These are all excuses. I cannot stand the idea of losing you. I love you, Linnea. You are smart and talented and you deserve to be a doctor. But I don't want those to be the reasons you stay with me. I want you to stay with me because you love me. If you don't, I won't force you. I will override the portal block and send you home. If you don't want to go home, I'll send you wherever you do want to go. If you want to stay here, I'll do everything I can to protect you from the Medical Supreme. It was selfish of me to not give you the option, but I panicked. I can run this hospital, coordinate doctors and researchers from around the known planes, but I don't really know how to do this. I love you. I don't want you to leave me. I don't want you to be a ward of the Medical Supreme. I don't want you to—"

"Sam," she said sternly.

"Don't leave," he insisted. Sam held his breath, waiting for her answer and afraid he'd been too ineloquent in his explanation.

"Sam—"

"If you don't want to marry me, that's fine. At least stay until this problem is resolved. The Medical Supreme is in quarantine. He can't have you."

"Sam—"

"Please, Linnea, I'll give you whatever you—"

"Anarchy and chaos, Sam, stop talking!" she yelled.

He snapped his mouth shut.

She pushed up from the examination table. That's when he realized he'd been leaning over her, pleading into her face, trapping her with his body. He stepped back, clearing his throat as he smoothed his lab coat nervously. His hands shook. His brain told him to speak, to fill the silence, to get on his knees and beg her. He'd never felt this before, not about work, nor his former wife, nor anything.

Linnea took a deep breath and looked around the room. Then, very calmly, she studied him. "I love you, too, Sam."

"No, you can't leave, please..." His words trailed off. He couldn't move. "Did you...?"

"Sam, I love you. You have shown me more respect than anyone I have ever met. I'm not pleased that you decided to let me deep transport sleep instead of telling me what was happening, and if you ever,

ever, do anything like that again, the Medical Supreme won't be the only man in quarantine." She gave a small smile to lighten the threat. "Is that clear?"

"I won't. I panicked. I—"

"Sam," she warned. He shut his mouth and nodded. "That's a good doctor. Now come over here and kiss me."

It was a command he'd easily follow. In fact, he was pretty sure he'd do anything she wanted. Happiness welled inside of him as their mouths met. Tongues merged and stroked with tender promise.

"Does this mean you'll marry me?" he asked against her lips?

"Only if you promise to keep kissing for the rest of our lives."

His answer came in the form of a deep moan as he pressed his future wife back onto the examination table to make love to her.

Chapter Eighteen
EPILOGUE

"So you're the little bird New Society sent for me." The Medical Supreme gave Linnea a long look, as if examining her body for flaws through the quarantine glass. The man was locked away, isolated in a private care center, and still he acted as if he controlled everything in his universe. "Now that my son has married my last ward, I have an opening in my home that I am eager to fill. Ariella was pretty, but she didn't do for me what you're going to do for me."

Linnea knew she was safe. Sam would never let anything happen to her, yet the lecherous way this man looked at her caused her skin to crawl and her stomach to tighten with nausea.

They were underneath a small square building at the edge of Asclepius. The place looked like an old medical storage warehouse with plain exterior walls, flat roof and nondescript stone walkway leading up to serviceable doors. Inside the warehouse were stacks of wooden crates marked as carrying old supplies that were no longer used by this plane—cloth masks, antique injectors, and empty medicine vials. Buried in this jungle of forgotten supplies was a single crate that hid the stairwell to the quarantine beneath. That was where she was now, hidden from the world above, in a place few people were permitted to know about. In the center of the large basement room the Medical Supreme sat on a bed surrounded by thick plastic walls. His ashen features were pulled tight, but his eyes were sharp and mean.

"Your government was right. They said I'd be very pleased if I agreed to let you stay as part of the arrangement." The Medical Supreme's words hurt. No, she didn't want to go home. She had everything she wanted on plane 187—a wonderful husband, a future as a doctor, a life. Her hand strayed to her stomach—and a family. He must have seen her irritated expression because the man laughed and explained, "They don't want you back, but don't worry. I don't mind if you can't use computers or imbedded chips. That's not what non-doctors like you are for, is it, Sans Nel? Women like you are made to be on your knees, subservient. Come on in here and be a good little bird. There are privileges to satisfying the most powerful man on the planet."

Linnea gagged a little at the offer. She studied him as she would a caged animal and said nothing.

"Wait until I'm free, little bird," he promised.

"I found out an interesting fact from Dr. Lu," Sam said to the Medical Supreme, joining her. "It appears you did know what caused this outbreak, because you designed it to trap Sans Ariella to this plane and force her to marry your son. Only, you didn't count on them falling in love, did you?"

"Love?" The Medical Supreme snorted. "Love is an illusion. My son needed to marry. How else are we to pass on the line of power?"

"Yours is not a hereditary title," Sam said.

"Tell that to my ancestors who have been passing it down," the Medical Supreme answered.

Linnea turned to see Ariella in the stairwell. They'd been waiting for the Medical Supreme's son and daughter-by-marriage to arrive.

"Feeling powerful in your gilded cage, Father?" Ariella asked.

"I told you, wife, it's called a quarantine laboratory," Sebastjan said.

Ariella chuckled. "A cage is a cage."

"Stop enjoying this so much," the Medical Supreme warned.

"You did it to yourself," Ariella countered. She looked at Linnea. "I heard what he said and am very glad that is not to be your fate."

"You have no say in her fate." The Medical Supreme glared at them.

"Neither do you," Sam said. "She decides her own fate." He placed his hand on her shoulder. "As my wife."

"Wife?" the Medical Supreme spat. "I did not give you permission to marry her."

"We didn't ask you," Sam said.

"They asked me," Sebastjan inserted.

"You?" the Medical Supreme frowned. "You have agreed to be my Medical Supreme Proxy?"

"I truly regret to inform you, Dr. Walter," Sebastjan said, though he hardly sounded upset, "that due to your incurable illness, it has been decided that you step down as Medical Supreme."

"You can't do that!" the now former Dr. Walter yelled. He hit his hand against the quarantine wall.

"It's been done. Your successor has been named," Ariella said, taking her husband's arm. "Just like you wanted."

"I knew you would take the title." Dr. Walter actually looked a little pleased with his son. "I knew you would grab the power when the time came."

"I have my duty to my people," Sebastjan said. "First, I informed the people of what you did to my wife and why it was necessary for you to step down from your position. Second, I approved Sam and Linnea's marriage. And last, I approved a new program to allow off-plane dignitaries to leave 187. Dr. Fauchet bravely volunteered to go to 303. Sam has already visited the plane and secured the position with Politician Shinclus. He was most pleased to deal with someone other than you. They were having a hard time coming up with the number of virginal women you had demanded in return for medical supplies."

"Suppressed hormones cause chaos," Linnea explained. "Virginity really isn't encouraged when people come of age."

"Last?" Dr. Walter asked his son, his hands pressing so hard to the transparent wall they turned white.

"Well, I supposed that was technically second to last. My last duty before resigning my post to Sam's very capable hands was to appoint Dr. Lu the new Director of Central Hospital." Sebastjan smiled.

"You can't do that!" Dr. Walter slammed his hands for emphasis. "That title of Medical Supreme belongs to our family!"

"I have told you before. I have no desire to be Medical Supreme," Sebastjan said. "The position requires fresh blood."

"It is your birthright," Dr. Walter interjected.

Linnea watched the scene play out with interest. She was proud to call Sebastjan and Ariella her new friends. Sebastjan was nothing like his father.

Sam's hand slipped around her waist and pulled her closer. "And my first duty was to appoint my new wife as the hospital coordinator. It was her hard work that discovered your virus's true origins as a human control agent. It turns out she has a real knack for organization."

"I gave them the mansion," Sebastjan said. "It does come with the job."

"That's mine!" Dr. Walter growled in frustration. "What are you going to do? Leave me here?"

"For a few months. Then you will be moved to a new quarantine facility being built in the country," Sam said. "There you will live the rest of your days with your two infected attendants. They've agreed to the arrangement, but do not mistake them for servants."

"It's your own fault." Ariella stepped to the wall and faced him. She placed her hands opposite his on the barrier. "You have learned nothing from your mistakes. You are a miserable person. The goddesses have seen fit to punish you for it. You will live as you had me live, as a prisoner within your new home."

"Enough of your goddesses." The confined man snorted.

Sebastjan took his wife's arm and led her toward the stairs.

"Wait!" Dr. Walter yelled, almost desperate. Sebastjan looked at him. "You will come to visit me?"

Linnea almost felt sorry for the man. She did not know the former Medical Supreme as these people did, but he seemed almost broken in that moment. Sebastjan took pity on his father and nodded once before disappearing.

When the couple was gone, the man turned to Sam and Linnea. "What will become of me?"

"You will be allowed to work on curing this virus you created," Sam said, "but your laboratory will be closely monitored. Your need for control could have killed this entire plane and several others. Ariella's lucky she did not carry the mutated strain and your original safeguard worked in reversing her illness. We'll monitor your sickness the best we can and make sure you're comfortable. As long as you are given regular doses of the medication you required Ariella to take, your illness should be manageable."

Linnea let Sam lead her from the room. Dr. Walter looked as if he would beg them to stay, but refrained. As the door closed behind them, she wrapped her arm around her husband's waist as they walked next to the dimly lit crates.

"I can't believe how things have worked out," Linnea said, smiling at her husband. "Though I do feel a little sorry for him, I suppose the punishment is just."

"You have a kind heart, wife." Sam touched her face and then her stomach. His eyes drifted down to her neck where she wore the purple prescription necklace. "I am sorry I haven't been able to cure you."

"And risk our child?" Linnea shook her head. So much had seemed impossible that was now a reality. She was able to have a baby, a husband, a life and a career. "No. Some things are not worth the risk. I can wait. Besides, here, my genetic abnormality doesn't matter."

"There is nothing genetically abnormal about you." He chuckled, trying to kiss her neck. She swatted his arm and forced him to walk out of the old warehouse. He continued, "I am truly a blessed man."

"You are a loved man," she corrected. "I love you, Sam."

"And I you." He stopped just outside the front door as the light streamed onto them and kissed her deeply. Only when she was breathless did he pull his mouth away. "Come, let me take you to our new home. I understand they have a bed."

"A bed?" She laughed. "Just a bed?"

"What else do we need?" With that he swept her up into his arms and whisked her away.

The End

About Michelle

Michelle M. Pillow
New York Times & USA TODAY
Bestselling Author

Michelle loves to travel and try new things, whether it's a paranormal investigation of an old Vaudeville Theatre or climbing Mayan temples in Belize. She believes life is an adventure fueled by copious amounts of coffee.

Newly relocated to the American South, Michelle is involved in various film and documentary projects with her talented director husband. She is mom to a fantastic artist. And she's managed by a dog and cat who make sure she's meeting her deadlines.

For the most part she can be found wearing pajama pants and working in her office. There may or may not be dancing. It's all part of the creative process.

Michelle loves talking with readers on social media!

www.MichellePillow.com

facebook.com/AuthorMichellePillow

twitter.com/michellepillow

instagram.com/michellempillow

bookbub.com/authors/michelle-m-pillow

goodreads.com/Michelle_Pillow

amazon.com/author/michellepillow

youtube.com/michellepillow

pinterest.com/michellepillow

Please Leave a Review

THANK YOU FOR READING!